Praise for

DEBORAH RANEY
and her novels

"Raney has fashioned a startlingly honest portrayal of love, commitment, and redemption in the midst of tragedy that will appeal strongly to fans of Janette Oke and Neva Coyle."
—*Library Journal* on *A Vow to Cherish*

"Raney immediately draws the reader into the story. Well-defined, empathetic characters have true-to-life motivations, and the strife-filled country of Haiti is depicted so that readers will feel compassion rather than despair."
—*Romantic Times BOOKreviews* on
Over the Waters

"[Her characters] slipped from the pages of [*Beneath a Southern Sky*] and into my heart. I experienced all their heart-wrenching emotions and rejoiced as they triumphed by God's grace. Bravo, Ms. Raney!"
—Robin Lee Hatcher, bestselling author of
Diamond Place

"Readers will lose their hearts to the characters in this jewel of a story. Polished and excellently plotted...engrossing from start to finish. 4.5 stars, Top Pick."
—*Romantic Times BOOKreviews* on
A Nest of Sparrows

"Deborah Raney is a skillful novelist who weaves a powerful story that stays with you...authentic and credible, with characters you care about, who live and breathe inside you.... Her books are a delight to read."
—Randy Alcorn, author of *Heaven,* on
A Nest of Sparrows

"Deborah Raney's writing is always full of warmth and hope."
—James Scott Bell, Christy Award-winning author of *Sins of the Fathers,* on *A Nest of Sparrows*

A *Vow* TO CHERISH

DEBORAH RANEY

Newly revised and expanded by author.

Steeple
Hill®

Published by Steeple Hill Books™

STEEPLE HILL BOOKS

Steeple
Hill®

ISBN-13: 978-0-373-78592-6
ISBN-10:   0-373-78592-5

A VOW TO CHERISH

Steeple Hill Books/October 2007

First published by Bethany House

www.SteepleHill.com

Printed in U.S.A.

To Daddy

and

To my husband, Ken

Two men whose integrity inspired
the character of John Brighton.

January 1996

This novel would never have become a reality without the love, support and encouragement of the following people:

Thank you, "Mothe," for reading to me when I was little, for instilling in me the love for libraries and literature that was the seed of this novel. Thank you to "Mothe" and Daddy and to my sisters for reading my manuscript in its earliest form and for encouraging me to keep writing.

Special thanks to Ellen Voth, Michelle DeHoogh-Kliewer, Doris DeHoogh, Tanya Keim, Kerry Grosch, Patrick Briar and Claudia Luthi. Your suggestions and insights were invaluable to a beginning writer.

To my special friends, Marcy, Sharon, Terry, Lynn and Mary—thank you for believing that I had a story to tell and for reminding me that I had a life apart from the computer! I love you guys.

Thank you, editors Sharon Madison and Ann Parrish, for your enthusiasm and encouragement. Your phone calls and letters kept me going.

To Sharon Asmus, my very first editor, thank you for walking me through the process of writing this book, for making it such a hands-on experience. I learned so much from you, and I'm sure you were more patient than I'll ever know.

Most of all, thank you, Ken—for your support, your enthusiasm, your constant encouragement. Thank you for buying no-iron pants, ordering carry-out pizza and taking Tavia to the park so I could keep writing. Thank you for being a man of God. I really, really couldn't have done it without you, honey.

And thank you, Lord, for the most priceless blessing of my life—my family: "Mothe" and Daddy, my grandparents, my brother, Brad, my sisters, Vicky and Beverly, and their families; Mom and Dad, Grandma and Grandpa, and all the rest of Ken's wonderful family; and for the most precious gifts of all—my husband, Ken, and our children, Tarl, Tobi, Trey and Tavia. I have a rich heritage of love, and I am so very grateful.

January 2006

Ten years have come and gone (at lightning speed, I might add) and the Lord has taken my simple story about family and faith to places I never dreamed. Who would have *ever* guessed that this Kansas farm girl would get to see her words come to life on the silver screen at a Hollywood movie premiere? But more importantly, through World Wide Pictures' film, inspired by *A Vow to Cherish,* and available in seven languages, God has touched the lives of thousands of people all over the world, and many have come to a saving knowledge of Jesus Christ.

Now I'm delighted to have had the opportunity to rewrite my very first novel for a new generation. Besides getting the chance to apply some of what I've learned about the craft of writing since I first hammered out the original manuscript on my little Macintosh Classic computer, I also discovered that my story needed some updates! Much has changed in the medical world since I first wrote this story about a family dealing with Alzheimer's disease. The news is encouraging, with promising discoveries being made daily on the medical frontier of Alzheimer's. It is my prayer that by the time you read this, this horrible disease will be well on its way to being ancient history.

A rather humorous discovery during the rewrite process necessitated changes I hadn't expected. Not until I found myself shouting at my characters—"Call her on your cell phone, silly!" and "Duh! Why don't you look it up on the Internet?"—did I realize how many technological advances the past ten years have brought. I was grateful for a chance to move my characters into the twenty-first century.

Reading over my original acknowledgments made me smile, as I thought about how many of those precious relationships I still treasure. But it also brought a few tears as I realized how many of the people who shaped my life and my writing are now gone or living far from home. My father-in-law and all four of my grandparents reside in heaven now. Three of our children have graduated college and now live out of state and many dear friends have moved away or lost touch.

But I was blessed to also realize that God has brought many new people into my life in the years since *A Vow to Cherish* was first released—a wonderful son-in-law and our first precious grandbaby, new grandnephews and -nieces and my wonderful Debbies Gang. I've also made many new and dear friends in the writing world—my pals in ChiLibris and ACFW; my "critical" friends, Tammy, Meredith and Jill.

I am so grateful to my wonderful editors at Steeple Hill Books, Joan Marlow Golan and Krista Stroever, whose incredible talent and skill helped me resurrect an old story for a new audience. I can truthfully say, as I did in 1996, "This novel would never have become a reality without you."

More than anything, I am touched and blessed that my dedication can remain unchanged from a decade ago: my father and my husband continue to faithfully keep the covenants of their marriages—fifty-one and thirty-one years, respectively—and to live lives of godly integrity.

Thank you, all of you, from the bottom of my heart. I have been blessed indeed.

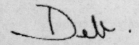

Prologue

John rolled over in bed and propped one elbow on the pillow. He rubbed his eyes, disoriented, then groped in the dark to find the other side of the bed empty. Holding his breath, he listened. The shower in the bathroom off the master bedroom droned. He threw back the covers. Why had Ellen allowed him to oversleep? She knew he had an important meeting this morning.

Easing his long legs over the side of the bed, he tried to focus on the digital clock on his bedside table. The red numbers blurred and faded, but it looked like one-fifteen.

Not yet fully awake, he plodded into the bathroom. Through the steam of the shower he saw that Ellen's carriage clock on the counter also read one-fifteen.

"Ellen? What's wrong? Are you sick?"

"Well, sleepyhead," she called cheerfully through the shower curtain, "you're finally up. No, I'm not sick. What makes you ask?"

"It's one o'clock, El. You just went to bed two hours ago."

The spray stopped abruptly. "One o'clock? In the morning? It can't be."

"Well, it is." He yawned and stretched. "Come back to bed, you silly girl."

Wrapped in a thick white towel, she stepped from the shower. Her pale auburn hair clung in ringlets to her forehead and the nape of her neck. John planted a soft kiss behind her left ear.

But she brushed him off and leaned to inspect the clock, her forehead furrowed. She picked up the clock and held it to her ear, bemused laughter rising in her throat. "That's strange…I could have sworn it was morning."

She looked so bewildered that John thought for a minute she might truly be ill. But she dried off, retrieved her nightshirt from the floor and followed him back to bed.

Later, at breakfast, John teased her about her nocturnal wandering, and they laughed together.

Six months later he would look back to that incident as the beginning of their nightmare.

John & Ellen

Chapter One

The auditorium was crowded and stifling on an unseasonably warm May evening. The band tuned their instruments in hushed dissonance, and soon the strains of Pomp and Circumstance filled the air. Accompanied by the squeaking and grating of chairs, the audience rose to their feet and turned to watch the capped-and-gowned students file to the stage and mount the steps.

Kyle Brighton's family took up nearly one whole row of seats in the old Calypso High School auditorium. His grandparents, Howard and MaryEllen Randolph, sat in the center of this contingent. They were flanked by Kyle's sister, Jana, and her husband on one side, and his brother, Brant, on the other.

John and Ellen Brighton were at the end of the row on the aisle, where Ellen had insisted they sit, so they could snap a quick picture of their son as he entered.

The music rose and the first graduates filed sober-faced through the doors, their gowns swaying in time with the tassels on their caps as they did an awkward hesitation step down the carpeted aisle.

Ellen spotted Kyle first and tugged on her husband's sleeve. "John…John, what did you do with the camera?"

He looked on the seat behind him, then turned to Ellen with a shrug, shaking his head.

She knew the camera had been there just moments before. She swept aside his jacket and her purse, searching. "Hurry up, honey," she whispered, elbowing him. "We've got to find it. You'll miss him!"

John's gaze moved to her hand. His eyes widened and his shoulders shook with silent laughter as he pointed to the camera—in Ellen's hand.

She looked down and gave a little gasp. Rolling her eyes in self-deprecation, she shoved the camera at him. He took it from her and quickly knelt in the aisle, waiting for Kyle to reach them. Kyle spotted his father and hammed a goofy grin just as the flash went off.

That kid! Ellen shot him an exaggerated scowl, and his smile turned genuine.

As the last crescendo peaked and receded, and the graduates took their seats on the dais, John reached for Ellen's hand. She squeezed his fingers and turned to give him a wobbly smile. Kyle was their "baby," so they'd been through this twice already. Ellen thought she was immune to the sentiment of the ceremony, but the music set off a rush of memories. She gulped back tears. She *couldn't* cry. Kyle would be mortified if he looked out over the crowd and caught his mom blubbering like a baby.

In truth, she wasn't being maudlin. She always cried on happy occasions, and she was truly delighted that they had reached this milestone in their lives. Their last child had made his way safely through the labyrinth of adolescence, and this was undeniably a celebration of that fact. But she'd always felt bittersweet about any transition in her life, and this one would certainly be significant.

In two weeks, Kyle would pack his bags and head to New Mexico for a hard-won summer job at a resort. He'd come home in August, just in time to pack and leave for Urbana where he would start classes at the University of Illinois.

Ellen gave a little sigh. By the middle of June, 245 West Oaklawn would officially be an empty nest. While some of her friends had found the empty-nest stage a difficult passage, she looked forward to it.

Perhaps some of her optimism was due to the fact that her family still surrounded her. Jana and her husband lived nearby in Chicago and visited often. Brant was only two hours away, also at the university in Urbana. He wasn't quite as faithful about getting home—especially now that they were hearing more and more about someone named Cynthia—but they talked with him on the phone nearly every weekend.

It would be a comfort to her and John to have the boys at school together. Kyle would be staying in the dorm for the first year at least, but Brant lived near the campus, and she knew he would keep an eye out for his little brother.

The commencement speaker stepped to the podium, and a hush descended over the auditorium. Her hand warm in John's, Ellen allowed her thoughts to drift. Soon, the local dignitary's voice faded into a pleasant murmur. Time rolled back as the lifetime of events that had brought them to this moment paraded through her mind.

Ellen Randolph's childhood had been idyllic. Howard and MaryEllen Randolph worked their farm six days a week from sunup to sundown, and by the time their four daughters left home, the Randolphs owned their five hundred acres free and clear.

Having four daughters in succession had not disappointed Howard Randolph in the least, but neither had he made any concessions to their femininity. His girls could drive any tractor or truck on the place, and the miles of fence that surrounded their land had been mended by the Randolph sisters—Ellen, Kathy, Carol and Diana. The Four Musketeers was what their dad had called them—still called them.

The pleasures of Ellen's childhood on the Illinois farm came mostly from simple things—working side by side with her father in the fields, or gardening and then canning in the steamy kitchen with her mother. Money was scarce, and though there had been occasional vacations—camping in the mountains or visiting relatives in California—these were not the substance of Ellen's memories. The delight lay in the everyday things: Sunday-night popcorn, catching fireflies behind the barn, snowball fights and sledding till midnight on the frozen pond in the pasture.

Her memories were full of grandmothers and grandfathers, aunts and uncles and cousins who seemed almost a part of her immediate family. She had a rich heritage of love and a legacy of faith that she had made her own at an early age.

Ellen graduated from college in her small hometown, packed her bags six weeks later and moved to Chicago, where she had accepted a position teaching kindergarten in North Lawndale, a rough inner-city neighborhood.

Ellen was a true farmer's daughter whose sole experience in the city up to that time had consisted of a field trip with her high school civics class. There, from the window of the chartered bus, she and a friend had witnessed a mugging in a dark alley of the Loop. They had shouted for the bus driver's attention and pleaded with him to stop and help, but no one else had actually seen it happen, and the driver dismissed it, saying, "Get used to it, honey. These things happen every day in the city."

That incident made a deep impression on Ellen, and it defined Chicago for her the day her parents kissed her goodbye and left her alone in the city. Though she tried to act sophisticated and worldly-wise as she watched her parents' car disappear from sight, in truth she was trembling like the leaves on the elm trees that lined the Windy City's streets.

Ellen had rented a small apartment, and though it was only eight blocks from the school, she took the bus to and from work. North Lawndale was not a safe place for a young woman to walk alone, even in the daytime. In those first weeks, she often longed for the refuge of the farm, but she soon settled into her teaching job, and it, at least, was a comfortable fit.

And then John Brighton came along.

From the time Ellen was a little girl wanting to grow up and marry a farmer like her daddy, she'd had a romanticized picture of marriage. Her parents had always been openly affectionate, and the Randolph girls had a rosy model of marriage to follow. But in her wildest dreams, Ellen couldn't have imagined how truly lovely being married would be.

In the semidarkness of the auditorium, Ellen turned and looked up at her husband's strong profile. He seemed absorbed in the speaker's message, unmindful of her gaze. At fifty, his hair was graying at the temples, his eyes crinkled with lines, but he was still handsome, and Ellen didn't miss the appreciative lingering glances he often got from other women. She wasn't jealous, but proud she could lay claim to this fascinating man. If anything riled her about John's good looks, it was the fact that men in general seemed to become more dignified looking as they aged, while women—herself included—had to fight the lines, the bulges and the gray every inch of the way.

At forty-six, Ellen had managed to keep her trim figure, and people were always surprised to hear she had grown children. Oh, she found a thread of gray in her auburn curls from time to time, and the brightly lit mirror on her dressing table was ruthless in pointing out the lines that had begun to crease the corners of her eyes and her mouth. But Ellen had never been vain, and she was thankful John was diplomatic in overlooking these presages of middle age. He often borrowed the line from an ancient television commercial: "You're not getting older, you're getting better."

Their marriage wasn't perfect. She and John had their share of disagreements and misunderstandings. John could be incredibly stubborn, and he had an irritating tendency toward perfectionism. But after twenty-four years, their conversations still sparkled, and her heart still did a little flutter when he walked in the back door each evening after work. She could think of no one she would rather be marooned on a desert island with than this man who sat beside her now, waiting to watch their youngest son take his diploma in hand. Ellen squeezed John's hand—her husband, her friend, her lover…

He turned and gave her a knowing smile.

John recognized the faraway look in Ellen's eyes and knew that she was walking through the corridors of their shared history. He looked down the row at his family, now grown and writing their own histories.

He'd had such a different childhood than his own children, growing up in the city, an only child. His father had been a lawyer who lived for his thriving firm on the city's West Side. More accurately, Robert Brighton had lived *at* the firm. He'd kept a foldaway cot in a closet of his large office, and to the young John it seemed the man slept there more nights than he slept at home. Not until John was older did he discover that his father's long nights at the office were not always spent alone.

His parents divorced when he was twelve and John didn't hear of his father again until his mother mailed the obituary to him his first year at university. Robert Brighton had suffered a heart attack in the early morning hours on the cot in his office. Alone. He was forty-eight years old.

After that, John had rarely seen his mother smile. He knew that she'd lived all those years hoping for reconciliation. He vowed that whatever he chose to do with his life, he would never allow it to become an obsession. Above all, if he were lucky enough to have a family, he would be a devoted husband and a loving father. He'd spoken his intentions aloud in the privacy of his cramped college dorm room, before crumpling his father's obituary into a ball and throwing it ceremoniously into the trash.

It had taken years, but the closeness he and Ellen shared with each other and with their children had finally banished his fears that he might be incapable of being a better man than his father had been.

John shifted in his seat and looked over at Ellen. A quiet smile softened her pretty face, reminding him that the years since had been happier than he could have imagined—full of joy and great hope for the future.

How quickly that future had melded into the past. And now their nest was all but empty. But oh, how they'd treasured their little family through the years! It was not so long ago that he had come home each evening to the happy sounds of laughter filling their home. He would watch Ellen playing with the children when she was unaware of his gaze. It had filled him with deep contentment to see his wife's smile—a demonstration of her happiness. Her days as a young mother at home were full and busy, and she declared her own contentment often to John.

When Kyle started first grade, Ellen had gone back to work, teaching second grade. Teaching had allowed her to be home with her own children, and John knew that it, too, brought her deep fulfillment. Even after a dozen years, she remained enthusiastic about her role as a teacher.

John served as principal of Calypso Elementary for almost ten years, working his way through graduate school, taking night classes and summer school. It was a challenge, trying to juggle a demanding career, grad classes and a young family, but when he'd been promoted to the position of high school principal, and seven years later was offered the position of superintendent of schools, it all seemed worthwhile.

Yes, their life had been full of blessings. And as he sat at this crossroad in his life, John Brighton took stock, numbering the gifts the Lord had bestowed on him.

Their children were all happy and healthy and finding their places in life. Kyle already knew that he wanted to teach—a decision that thrilled John and Ellen. And Brant was content at the university.

Jana had married her college sweetheart, Mark McFarlane, and they both had good jobs in the city.

Ellen's parents still lived on the family farmstead, and though their age was beginning to slow them down a bit, they remained healthy and active.

John's mother had died suddenly last summer, but Margaret Brighton's last decade had been almost a redemption of the years John's father had taken from her. She had doted on her three grandchildren, and when she was with them, John had often caught a glimpse of the lighthearted woman he'd almost forgotten existed.

It seemed strange that he and Ellen were quickly becoming the older generation; neither of them was quite comfortable in the role yet. Time had flown so quickly. How was it possible that their last tiny baby was all grown up and nearly on his own? Today's commencement marked a new beginning—not just for Kyle, but for him and Ellen, as well.

The bright lights of the auditorium came up and he squinted against their sudden glare. The swell of the recessional signaled the end of the ceremony, and John brought Ellen's hand to his mouth, pressed his lips against the back of her hand before he released her.

Kyle winked at them as he came up the aisle with a bounce in his step.

And with that, the last little bird was pushed from the nest.

Chapter Two

Ellen kicked off her shoes with a weary but satisfied sigh and slouched into a plump, overstuffed chair in the living room. From her perch, she could see through to the brightly lit kitchen. The sink overflowed with dirty dishes, the countertops were littered with half-empty glasses and crumpled napkins, and the floor was a collage of sticky spills and crumbs.

The last of the guests had just left Kyle's graduation party, and the rest of the family had retreated to the deck in the backyard, leaving Ellen in the quiet but messy house. It had been a wonderful party, and Ellen didn't begrudge the work she had ahead of her. But she was exhausted.

The back door swung open and Jana appeared in the doorway. Boisterous male voices drifted in on the night air. The men of the family were in a heated discussion about the predicted outcome of a postseason tournament.

Jana caught her mother's eye and rolled her own eyes toward the ceiling. "There's way too much testosterone out there," she declared. A burst of raucous laughter from the deck was cut off abruptly as she closed the door behind her.

Ellen laughed. "Well, you'd better decide which is worse. Testosterone out there, or a sink full of dirty dishes in here."

Jana looked the kitchen over. "Ugh! Tough choice." But she pushed up her sleeves and came over to where Ellen sat. "Okay…" She took her mother by both hands and playfully hauled her out of the chair. "Let's get this over with." They walked into the kitchen arm in arm.

Together they cleared off the counters; then Ellen rinsed the dishes while Jana loaded the dishwasher.

"I'm glad you and Mark decided to stay overnight," Ellen said, handing Jana an oval platter that had held sandwiches an hour earlier.

"Oh sure," Jana teased. "You're just happy to have help with the dishes."

Ellen smiled. "Well, that, too. But seriously, I know it means a lot to Kyle to have you and Mark here tonight."

"I'm glad we stayed, too, Mom. It's been a fun evening. We would have been too tired to drive back tonight anyway."

The two worked in comfortable silence for a while. Then Jana turned to Ellen. "Didn't Kyle look cute up there tonight? I just can't believe my baby brother has graduated!"

"I know. I can't believe my baby boy is headed to college."

Just then Kyle popped in through the back door.

Ellen winked at Jana. "And speaking of my baby, here he is, just in time to help with the dishes."

Kyle did an abrupt about-face and tried to escape through the still-open door. But his sister grabbed him by the arm and dragged him, kicking and howling, back into the house. Ellen watched their lighthearted exchange wistfully. It was so good to have everyone home together—just like old times.

The rest of the men straggled in from outdoors. John came up behind Ellen at the sink and rubbed her aching shoulders.

Her hands still in dishwater, she closed her eyes, relishing the massage. "Mmm… Don't stop…that feels great. But you guys picked a bad time to come in." She lifted a hand from the warm water and tossed a damp dishrag over her shoulder in Brant's direction. "Here… Wipe that counter off, will you?"

Brant wadded the rag into a wet ball and threw it at Kyle, who, in turn, lobbed it across the room to Mark. Even John got in on the game of "hot potato" until things got so rowdy that Ellen—only half kidding—scolded them. "Hey, you guys! Cut it out!"

John took charge. "Come on, guys. Let's help your mother out. It's been a long day." He motioned to the dining room. "Brant, will you get those leaves out of the table? And, Kyle, you can carry these folding chairs out to the garage."

They cooperated, though not without some good-natured protests. Twenty minutes later, the kitchen was spotless, and Brant and Kyle were raiding the refrigerator for a midnight snack.

Kyle held up a leftover corner of his thickly frosted graduation cake, covered with foil. "Anybody care if I finish this off?"

Ellen huffed out a short breath of air. "As long as you wash your dishes when you're through."

Kyle rummaged in a drawer for a fork, then came over to where Ellen was standing. He leaned his elbow heavily on her shoulder, using her for a table while he polished off the cake in four man-sized bites. He was a head taller than his mother and outweighed her by at least seventy pounds. This was her baby! It didn't seem possible!

"Good party, Mom…thanks," he mumbled through a mouthful of frosting.

"It was fun, wasn't it?"

"Did you get some good pictures at graduation, Dad?"

Ellen intercepted the question. "Yeah, very funny, Kyle. So help me, if you're grinning like Howdy Doody in all your pictures, I'll wring your neck!" She demonstrated just how she would do it. Kyle grinned and ducked out of her grasp and ran up the stairs two at a time.

"Good night, everybody," he hollered down behind him. "Thanks for all the loot…"

"You're welcome…. Good night, Kyle," Mark and Jana said in unison.

"Good night, honey…love you," Ellen said, a lump thickening her throat.

Oh, how she would miss that boy!

John and Ellen stood in the driveway watching Kyle's little Toyota round the curve and disappear out of sight.

John sighed. New Mexico was too far away, but in just a few weeks Kyle would be closer to home in Urbana. He found himself smiling in spite of the poignancy of the moment. It had been a tearful, but joyful, goodbye. Kyle's excitement was contagious, and John couldn't begrudge him his eagerness to be on the road.

The morning was chilly for June, but the birds were singing and the sky was clear. He put an arm around Ellen and drew her to him as they strolled back up to the house. "Well, Mrs. Brighton. Looks like it's just you and me."

She glanced up at him beneath tendrils of auburn hair. "Are you trying to make me cry again?"

"No, ma'am. Actually, I kind of like the sound of it…just the two of us. No phone ringing off the hook, no doors slamming, actual food in the refrigerator." He chuckled. "Why, we might even be able to finish a conversation in one sitting."

She leaned her head on his shoulder and sighed contentedly. "Won't *that* be nice?"

They stopped and stood in the driveway looking up at the big house.

John sighed. "I wish Oscar and Hattie could see how the kids have turned out. They'd be pleased with all the happiness this old house has held for us."

"Yes, they would," Ellen agreed in a thin voice that told John her thoughts were far away. "I miss them."

Oscar and Hattie Miles had become surrogate parents to John in his college years and had been like grandparents to the Brighton children. The elderly couple had been gone for several years now, but John saw their faces before him now, indelibly etched in a cherished niche of his memory.

Oscar Miles had immigrated to the States from London when he was just fourteen, and though he'd cherished his American citizenship, he'd never lost the trace of London that lingered in his deep voice. His wife was a plump and cheerful angel with a halo of white hair. If he closed his eyes, John could almost taste the sweet, flaky tarts and cobblers and English scones Hattie had seemed determined to stuff him with.

It was at her table that John had found true meaning in his life. For Hattie had shown him God. God had been as real and as personal to her as Oscar was, and her relationship with her God was not much different than her friendship with her husband.

One night, after Oscar shared his own experiences of faith—faith in a living God through His Son Jesus Christ—John could no longer find a reason not to believe.

That night John had found healing for the pain of an absent father and a distant mother. He'd found meaning for his work with the children at school and a reason to hope for their future, as well as his own.

Then John had introduced Ellen to Oscar and Hattie, and they had grown to love her as their own. They were ecstatic when John announced their engagement. And when he told them that he and Ellen wanted to keep his apartment after their marriage, Oscar proceeded to paint the kitchen and have new carpeting put in the living room. Hattie all but banished John from the place while she scrubbed floors and washed windows and swept away cobwebs.

With Ellen's collection of furniture from the farm, and John's mishmash acquired at garage sales and flea markets, the apartment soon became a quaint and cozy haven. They had spent many a leisurely afternoon browsing flea markets and dusty antique shops, finding just the right touches to make the rooms of the apartment their own. John taught Ellen the fine art of bargaining, and soon she was wheedling the stingiest of proprietors into incredible deals. Ellen reveled in making curtains and pillows for the tiny bedroom and drove John crazy arranging and rearranging the furniture.

He grinned to himself. She still did that sometimes. But he'd learned to put up with it, even enjoy it as one of the quirks that made her his Ellen. He reached to caress the back of her neck.

She leaned into him and let out a murmur of pleasure. After a minute she turned back to meet his eye. "What are you thinking about?"

"Same things you are. Life. How fast it's going by."

"You've got that right. It's scary."

"Scary, yes. But good. Life *is* good."

And it was. He breathed in the morning air and looked up toward the wing of the house where they'd begun their marriage. The house sat on an oak-canopied avenue not far from Calypso's Main Street, but the expansive yard and surrounding woods gave it the feel of an old country home.

Oscar and Hattie had eventually moved into a retirement home, and John and Ellen moved into the big house, paying a ridiculously low sum in rent each month.

When Hattie died, just months after they buried Oscar, John and Ellen learned that the couple had left them more than a legacy of faith and love. The precious couple had willed the beautiful house to John. For the growing Brighton family, the gift of the house was almost too good to be true. Oscar and Hattie were sorely missed, and of course the house hardly made up for the loss of the couple's friendship and wise counsel. But they had bequeathed a legacy of happy memories that would always be a part of John and Ellen's life together.

Over the years, they had spent countless hours refinishing woodwork, painting and wallpapering. One memorable year, they completely remodeled the kitchen and turned the summer porch behind it into a modest conservatory. They'd done all the exhausting work themselves. It tested their mettle and their marriage, but when John and Ellen stepped over the threshold the day the last piece of furniture was in place, they felt they had come full circle. There was now a bedroom for each of the children on the second floor, and John and Ellen had appropriated the attic—their first home—as a master suite, complete with bathroom, sitting room and kitchenette. It was hard to believe they had once lived solely in this tiny space. But it made a wonderful hideaway from the stresses of teaching children all day and coming home to three of their own.

Today, having ushered the last of their children out of this house, they stood at the entrance to the back door—the entrance to a new future together—perhaps a little apprehensive about facing the uncertainty. John reached to turn the doorknob but suddenly changed his mind.

"Want to go for a walk? This morning is too pretty to waste."

Ellen tipped her head, as if his suggestion surprised her. But she nodded. "Sure. But let me change my shoes and get a jacket."

A few minutes later, they set out along West Oaklawn at a brisk pace. They usually took their walks together in the evenings, and the street looked different in the early-morning light. The leaves still wore the yellow-green of spring, and in the dawning sunlight the flower gardens glimmered with dew. It was easy to feel optimistic in this pristine world.

Ellen sighed. "Kyle seems so happy. I hope his job goes as well as he thinks it will. He's not exactly realistic about life sometimes."

"He is kind of a Pollyanna," John conceded, "but I think I'd rather have him that way than have him as serious as Brant was about everything. Remember what a lost soul he was before he left for college?"

She gave a knowing snort. "I'd almost forgotten about that. He's so different now."

Brant had been the most rebellious of their three, but now he was finding his place in life. He'd found his niche in computer science at the university, and had a job he loved in the computer lab on campus.

And Brant was in love. He'd brought Cynthia Riley home to meet the family the weekend after Kyle's graduation. John sensed there was something special between the two.

Ellen was quiet for a moment, seeming deep in thought. "Cynthia has been good for Brant," she said finally. "I hope he doesn't let her get away. He's grown up so much in the past year, I can't help feeling I've lost my little boy." A faraway look came to her eyes. "Both my little boys. But I guess you're right. Kyle will find his way, too."

They walked in silence for a while.

"We did a good job, didn't we, El?" John asked, feeling suddenly a little melancholy.

She looked at him, questioning in her eyes. "With the kids? Oh, I'm so proud of them I could just pop sometimes. We did have some help though, John," she teased. "I think the Lord should probably get a little credit."

He responded to her teasing rebuke with a frown. "You're right, of course." He shook his head. "Every year I look at the families enrolling their kids in kindergarten, and I don't envy them a bit. In some ways, they have some of the best years of their lives ahead, but I have to say, I'm thankful we've done our job and can heave a sigh of relief."

"John!" Ellen stopped dead in the street, her hands-on-hip stance matching the exasperation in her tone. "I don't think I'll ever feel like I can quit worrying. I still fret over Jana, even though she has her wonderful Mark, a job she loves, a nice apartment. But there's still just so much that can happen." Her eyes sparked. "And about the time we think we can quit worrying about Mark and Jana, we'll have grandchildren to lose sleep over! I'm not holding my breath for that, though. I'm afraid those two are both far too wrapped up in their careers and—"

"Hey… You worry too much, Mama." John tousled her hair playfully, loving the soft feel of her curls between his fingers. "There's plenty of time for that."

She leaned into his shoulder. "I know. And I know Mark

and Jana are happy together. I have to let them live their own lives. Kyle, too. I'm sure he'll be better off if we let him make a few mistakes. I just feel like worrying is part of my job description."

"Well, don't look now, but our job description just changed rather drastically."

She sighed. "I can handle that, I guess. But it's going to feel strange. It might take some getting used to."

He started back up the street, picking up the pace. She followed, lengthening her stride to keep up with him, and breathing hard. They circled the neighborhood and ended up back in their driveway.

"Hey." He put a hand on Ellen's shoulder. "Let's celebrate our freedom. How does breakfast at Perkins sound?"

"Mmm. Sounds great." She shot him a mischievous grin and took off running. "Beat you to the shower!"

John easily overtook her, and they pushed and shoved their way up to their attic room, Ellen squealing like a schoolgirl.

They ended up sharing the shower, laughing, suddenly carefree and young again.

Half an hour later they climbed into the car and headed toward the restaurant. John felt Ellen's eyes on him as he navigated the heavy morning traffic.

He glanced over to find her gazing at him with misted eyes. "What's wrong?"

She shook her head and cleared her throat. "I'm just thinking…how much I'm looking forward to the rest of my life with you."

Concentrating on the busy street, he reached for her hand and squeezed it.

Suddenly, the empty nest felt wonderfully full.

Chapter Three

Exactly six weeks later Ellen wound up in the shower at one o'clock in the morning. She and John had laughed about it at the time, and had gone back to bed and slept soundly. She didn't give it much thought beyond that morning.

Until it happened again a few weeks later.

Only that time, she was dressed for work and almost out the door before John stopped her and sent her back to bed. And now it had happened again last night. Alarm bells went off in her head. She couldn't put her finger on it, but something wasn't right.

She'd felt tired and run-down for a couple of months, but she'd never had trouble sleeping before. "I don't know why I don't check the clock before I get out of bed," she told John.

She didn't know why, except that her usual morning routine involved slamming the alarm off, heading blindly for the shower and not opening her eyes until the hot spray hit her face.

She was a few months overdue for her annual physical exam, so she scheduled an appointment. She intended to mention the incidents to Dr. Morton, but by the time she sat on the edge of the examining table, vulnerable and covered only by the flimsy white gown, it seemed like a silly thing to bother such a busy man with.

To her surprise, he brought up the subject. "Let's see, Ellen…" He leafed through her chart. "How old are you now?"

"This is strictly confidential, right?" she teased. Jerry Morton had been their family physician for almost twenty years, and Ellen was comfortable joking with him. "I'll be forty-seven next month."

"Are you still getting your periods regularly?"

"Like clockwork."

"Any problems with hot flashes or night sweats?"

She shook her head. What was he suggesting?

"Moodiness? Sleeplessness?"

She seized the opening. "Well, actually, I have felt kind of run-down lately, but I've been…having a little trouble sleeping, so I just attributed it to that. It's no big deal, except that I've always slept like a log." She didn't tell him about her confusion, getting dressed for work in the wee hours of morning. It seemed silly now and inconsequential.

"Unfortunately, waking up in the middle of the night is common in menopause."

Dr. Morton's statement jarred her.

Her face must have reflected her surprise because he put up a hand and smiled. "Don't worry. With your regular periods, you're not there yet, but it's quite possible you are in what we call perimenopause—the early stages. It's not at all unusual for the transition between regular periods and full-blown menopause to begin as early as forty, or even before."

She hadn't given that possibility a thought. She wasn't even forty-seven yet. Surely she had a few years before she had to worry about that.

Dr. Morton seemed not to notice her dismay. He gave her a handful of pamphlets and explained some of the symptoms she might expect to experience over the next months. She left his office in a haze, but with a clean bill of health.

Two weeks later, on a stifling August day, Ellen walked through the front doors of Calypso Elementary on the first day

of school. She'd had the same classroom in this building for
ten years, and she had spent most of the past two weeks decorating bulletin boards and arranging the desks and other furniture in her room.

She'd arrived almost twenty minutes later than she
planned. Now she stood in the middle of a hallway bustling
with parents dropping off children, and she felt completely
disoriented. She didn't know which way to turn. She could
picture her classroom, where just yesterday she'd taped cute
little frog-shaped name tags to the front of each desk. But suddenly, she hadn't a clue where to find that room. She looked
to the left and saw nothing familiar. Calypso Elementary
wasn't that big. She turned right. Same thing.

She stumbled down the hallway in a daze, peering into
each classroom she passed. She had no idea how she'd gotten into this strange place. Had she somehow gone to the
wrong building? But there was only this one building on the
grounds. Wasn't there? At the end of the hallway, she turned
and started back in the other direction.

"Ellen! Did you lose somebody already?" A friendly voice
greeted her.

She looked up and recognized Ginger Barkley, a fourth-
grade teacher. "As a matter of fact, *I'm* lost." Maybe Ginger
knew what was going on.

The teacher gave her a funny look. "What do you mean?"

"I…I think they switched rooms on me."

Ginger pointed to the other hallway, looking more puzzled than Ellen felt. "What do you mean? You're in the east
hall, right?"

She looked down the corridor Ginger indicated. As quickly
as the confusion had come over her, everything suddenly
came back into focus. She *was* in the wrong hall. *What is
wrong with me? Ginger must think I'm crazy.* She feigned a
laugh, trying to cover up her confusion. "Oh, I'm just getting
my exercise."

Ginger laughed nervously and Ellen hurried away, certain

the teacher was staring after her. Ellen walked straight to her room, everything suddenly set right.

The rest of the day went fine, but the incident left her unsettled. She was too embarrassed to mention it to John that evening.

She had a larger class than usual this year, and the next days were full, trying to establish classroom rules and a routine for twenty-seven excitable second graders.

The weekend came and Ellen found herself exhausted. "Boy, I must be getting old," she told John as she dumped spaghetti in a pot for Friday night's supper. "I am beat."

"Well, it happens to the best of us." John was preoccupied, searching the kitchen for something. He sifted through a stack of magazines on the telephone desk. "Ellen, didn't you bring the mail in?"

"Yes. I thought I laid it on the desk. It's right there, isn't it?"

"No. It isn't. I looked there and everywhere else in the house."

"Well, I know I brought it in." She turned down the burner on the stove and joined the search. Ellen even went back out to the mailbox to see if maybe she'd only imagined bringing it into the house. When ten minutes of hunting hadn't produced anything, they gave up.

John's tight-lipped silence told her how irritated he was with her. He was Mr. Organization and they often squabbled over her haphazard ways.

Ellen shrugged off his attitude and went to the kitchen to try to decide what to fix for dinner. She opened the refrigerator and reached for the crisper drawer. She couldn't remember if she had salad makings or not. But as she bent to pull out the drawer, she gave a little gasp. There, on the shelf in front of her, limp with moisture, was the stack of bills and letters. They sat accusing her.

"Good grief!" She rolled her eyes, knowing immediately that she was the culprit.

John appeared in the doorway between the kitchen and dining room, a question in his eyes.

She stood in front of the open refrigerator door holding the droopy envelopes. "Well…I found the mail."

"It was in the fridge?" He tipped his head. "Are you losing it, Ellen?"

She laughed, embarrassed. "I guess I'm more tired than I thought."

He shrugged with that half-disgusted air she knew too well, and took the mail from her hands. After raising a skeptical eyebrow in her direction, he headed down the hall toward the den.

That night, when they were getting ready for bed, she tried to soothe his testiness. "I just thought all those bills needed to be put on ice for a while," she said, forcing a laugh.

No response.

"It's a joke, John."

But he apparently didn't see the humor. The corners of his mouth turned down as he studied her intently. "Are you okay, El? You've been so preoccupied lately. It's not like you to be so…so flighty."

She shrugged. "I guess I'm just tired. Work is kind of wearing on me this year for some reason. I've got a bigger class than I'm used to and—"

"Well, get some sleep." He cut her off, sounding unconvinced. "You need it." He turned out the light and rolled over.

Ten minutes later, she heard the soft snuffling that told her John was asleep. But she lay awake a long time, mulling things over. She finally entered a fitful, restless sleep, punctuated by a bizarre dream.

In her dream, she was lost in a long dark hallway. She shouted for help again and again, but no one came to rescue her. She walked on and on down the ever-narrowing passage, never finding a doorway, meeting only strangers who were as lost as she.

The next weeks were too much like the nightmare. Ellen started to seriously fear she was having a nervous breakdown. Many days she felt her old self, perfectly in control. But just when she started to put the disturbing incidents out of her mind, that disoriented, on-edge feeling would steal upon her, as it had that first frightening day of school. On those days she couldn't find any orderliness to her teaching. She would start a math lesson and ten minutes later, it was as though she were waking from a deep sleep, and she would realize that she was repeating the same material over again.

Her students, bless their hearts, took it all as a joke. "Mrs. Brighton, you're teasing us! We already did that page." They accused her of pulling another of her famous April Fool's tricks. Except April was a long ways off.

As the days passed, she distanced herself from her students more and more, assigning group work and reading time, and showing films to fill in for what she seemed to have forgotten to prepare for.

She began avoiding her coworkers, purposefully arriving at school late and leaving early. She couldn't trust her own actions and reactions to others, and she never knew when she might say or do something stupid. As many times as she realized her gaffe after the fact, it made her tremble to wonder how many times she'd blundered without knowing it. She feared the other teachers might not be as forgiving as the children.

And so, Ellen faked her way through a month of school days.

Chapter Four

John was having a busy and frustrating year with a controversial school-bond election coming before the voters. There were meetings with the school board and public forums to preside over.

Ellen had drawn into a shell, avoiding him. He knew something was eating at her, something wasn't right. But frankly, he didn't have time to make an issue of it.

Whenever he found his thoughts hovering on the subject of Ellen's erratic behavior, he pulled them swiftly away. Instead, he often found himself reliving their early days together, drawing comfort from memories of their past.

He would never forget the first time he'd gotten up the courage to speak to the pretty new teacher, Miss Randolph. Well, it hadn't been like that exactly. He smiled to himself. He'd been trying to get up his courage all right. But Ellen had beat him to the punch.

He'd been in his fourth year of teaching, and his life was full and busy with classroom projects, grading papers and staff meetings. John had fallen in love with his students. He was captivated by his second graders' enthusiasm for the simplest pleasures. He was drawn to their innocent trust in life's goodness.

One of his responsibilities was supervising an early-morning detention hall for kids who, for one reason or another, couldn't serve their time after school. The same group of delinquents seemed to make their way to his classroom every few weeks. These were the kids who especially stole his heart. He ached for them. At seven and eight they seemed so innocent, so full of hope and promise. Some of them were truly bright. In fact, it was their very keenness that sometimes got them into trouble. Their detentions were, for the most part, the result of pranks, tardiness or occasional cheating. But by the time they were ten or eleven, these same kids would be pulled into the sordid world of drugs and gangs that seemed to be the inevitable destination for boys (and more than a few girls) of the projects.

He saw some of them—his former students—on the sidewalks after school making their deals. They acknowledged him with glazed eyes, revealing a glimmer of guilt, but gone were the warmth and candor that had existed between Mr. Brighton and his young charges in those morning hours just a few years earlier. When he saw hardened eyes in faces still soft and whiskerless, and heard youthful lips utter ugly curses, he couldn't help feeling as though he had somehow failed them.

It was this he'd been contemplating the afternoon Ellen Randolph came into his classroom the second week of the school year. He stood in his room gazing out the window at a group of boys clustered in front of the old building.

So deep in thought was he that she was standing right behind him before he realized anyone had entered the room. She cleared her throat loudly, and he spun around, his heart pounding. And not because of her fresh-faced beauty. Though there was certainly that.

Ellen burst out laughing. "I'm sorry." She muffled another giggle with the back of her hand. "I didn't mean to scare you like that."

"My fault." His mouth turned up in a sheepish smile. "I was a million miles away." He regained his composure and stuck out a hand. "I'm John Brighton. You're the new kindergarten teacher, right?" All innocence, as if he hadn't already gleaned every tidbit of information he could find out about her.

She nodded. "Right. Ellen Randolph. I remember seeing you at the first staff meeting. But you haven't been to one since…"

"No. No, I get the honor of monitoring detention hall that time of morning. You'd think we could at least wait till school has been in session for a couple weeks before we start handing out detentions. I guess they want it known in no uncertain terms that 'violators will be punished.'" He curled his fingers into quote marks and chalked them in the air to emphasize the legalese. "Actually, that's what I was pondering so intently when you walked in here and scared the daylights out of me."

She smiled. "I'm really sorry about that."

There was something powerfully endearing about the glint of humor her eyes held—as if she wanted to burst out laughing at him, but was much too nice to do so.

Now her expression turned serious. "Rough bunch of kids, huh?"

"Oh no, it's not that. Actually, they're some of my favorites. They've got spirit, you know?"

She nodded her agreement, her auburn curls bouncing against her cheeks.

"They're not bad kids," he said. "Not yet anyway. That's what bothers me. I look out there—" he gestured toward the window "—and I see what they have waiting for them a few years down the road. I just wish I could do something to keep them away from all that."

Her gaze followed his to the unruly group gathered outside. "I know what you mean," she said. "I grew up on a farm, and I guess I was a little naive. I came here thinking I could make a difference in these kids' lives. But how can I really do anything for them when they're surrounded by bad influences day in and day out? Sometimes I just want to load all my little kindergartners on a bus and take them to the farm and let my mom and dad have them for a few years."

Her smile held a hint of sadness, and immediately John was drawn to her compassion for these kids he'd come to love so much.

"Well, if you're an example of what your mom and dad can do with a kid," he told her, "I'm all for that idea!"

Ellen's face colored, and she quickly changed the subject. "I guess I'd better get moving if I'm going to finish all my papers and still catch a bus before dark." She was halfway out the door when she stopped abruptly and put her hand to her mouth, flustered. "Oh! I almost forgot why I came down here in the first place."

He waited, enjoyed watching her cheeks grow pinker.

"I was wondering if you have a state map I could borrow for tomorrow morning. I've been up and down the hall and nobody else seems to have one."

"Well, this is your lucky day. I have one—it's kind of ancient, like everything else around here, but you're welcome to use it. It's heavy, though…it's on a roller. Here, I'll show you." He rolled down two or three maps that were mounted like window shades at the back of the room. "Here we are—Illinois. How about if I bring it down to your classroom first thing in the morning?"

"Oh, that'd be great. Thanks." She turned to go. "See you around, Mr. Brighton."

I hope so, John had thought as he watched Ellen walk down the hallway.

And the next morning as soon as his detention class had been dismissed, he took the map to her classroom. She was standing on a chair tacking some of the children's artwork high on a bulletin board. He purposely sneaked up behind her and then cleared his throat loudly. She gasped and lost her balance. Her arms flailed in the air as she involuntarily and ungracefully leaped from the chair to keep from falling.

When she righted herself and saw that it was John, she burst out laughing at her own exaggerated antics. "Well, I guess I had that coming!" she conceded blushing.

He put a steadying hand on her shoulder. "Yes, you did, but I really didn't mean to knock you off the chair. I'm sorry. Are you okay?"

"I'm fine. It served me right." She shook a finger playfully in his face. "But you do it again, and I'll send you straight to detention, young man!"

He laughed. "I'll bet you've got a reputation around here already. Mean ole Miss Randolph."

"Well, I'm working on it. It's 'kids' like you who turn perfectly nice teachers like me into old crabs, you know."

John was taken with her lighthearted teasing and those smiling blue-gray eyes.

"Hey! Do you like Chinese food?" he asked impulsively.

"Well, to tell you the truth I've never tasted it, unless you count the chow mein in a can that my mom used to make when there was nothing else in the cupboards."

John shook his head. "That doesn't count. Listen, there's a place in Calypso, where I live, that makes the greatest Chinese this side of the globe. Would you like to go there with me Friday night?"

She flashed a smile. "Friday? I'd like that. What time?"

"Would you mind leaving from here after school? It takes almost an hour on the bus. I don't have a car yet." He shrugged an apology.

"I don't mind the bus, really. I'm just not too crazy about taking it back into the city late at night."

"Oh, don't worry. I'll ride back with you. My mom lives on the West Side, and I can stay with her if it's too late."

"It's a date, then. I'll wait here for you after school."

John started to leave the room, then he laughed and turned to hold up the unwieldy rolled-up map. "I'm getting to be almost as forgetful as you are."

The memory startled John, seeming almost to have been

a prediction of what they were going through now, more than twenty-five years later.

But he let his thoughts continue to ramble, unwilling to leave the comforting reminiscences of the past.

Friday nights in Calypso had become a standing date for John and Ellen. Back then the Friday-night special at the China Garden was egg foo yong, and it was so exquisite they rarely ventured another choice. John had never felt so comfortable with a girl before. Not that Ellen was just "comfortable." He was incredibly attracted to her. But there came a time when he was afraid if he brought romance into the picture he might lose the best friend he'd ever had.

He found he could talk to Ellen about anything. She listened to his ideas, and understood his feelings like no one he had ever known. With no qualms or hesitation, he shared parts of himself that he had never let anyone else get close to. His feelings about his father, his fears that he might turn out to be too much like Robert Brighton. She listened without judgment and asked questions that helped him understand himself better. He trusted Ellen. It was a new experience for John, who had grown up in such a silent home.

And while Ellen tended to be quiet and reserved in social situations, with him she was vocal and exuberant. Their time together was punctuated with jokes and teasing. He'd never known there could be so much to laugh at in the world.

The hour on the bus from the city each week was spent in rapt conversation. Over the months, John poured out his whole life story to Ellen. Somehow, her compassion soothed the pain of his past.

She in turn opened up her life to him. Together they mulled over problems they encountered with their students; they analyzed the world and everything in it; and one day, somewhere along Eden's Expressway, John knew he was in love with her.

They got married on a hot August evening. Illinois was parched and dusty in the midst of a drought that had brought creases of worry to Howard Randolph's forehead. But John saw the worry change to pride as the older man brought his daughter to meet John at the altar of the little country church.

It was a brief ceremony, beautiful in its simplicity. Ellen looked trustingly into John's eyes as he spoke to her the vows that a myriad of couples down through the centuries had spoken.

"I, John, take thee, Ellen, to be my lawful wedded wife. To have and to hold from this day forward, for better or for worse, for richer, for poorer, in sickness and in health, to love and to cherish, and to thee only will I cleave, as long as we both shall live."

And Ellen, lovely in her grandmother's gown, ivory with age, echoed the troth in a voice strong and full of confidence.

Ellen's parents gave the newlyweds money for a motel in Springfield and loaned them their car for the trip. They drove away from the church, replete with promise for the life they would live together. Over and over they exclaimed to each other, "Can you believe it? We're really married!" They manufactured excuses to say "my husband" and "my wife."

It was after midnight when they finally found the motel. It was on the edge of town and had seen better days. The paint was peeling inside and out, and the curtains and bedspread were straight out of the thirties. "The dirty thirties," John had joked.

But the yearning and passion and pure love that burned in their hearts that night as they became one in body and spirit belied the humble room they shared.

John raked his hands through his hair and forced his thoughts back to the present. Would he and Ellen ever share that sweet, simple love again? Just months ago, they'd been eagerly looking toward this golden time in their lives. A time when they finally had the house to themselves, and time to enjoy some of the things they'd put off while they raised their family.

How had life suddenly become so complicated and confusing—and frightening?

Chapter Five

John sat in his office on a Monday morning reviewing a budget proposal. School was out for spring break, so no one else was in the office, but he was swamped with paperwork and had decided to play catch-up. Ellen had gone shopping and wouldn't be home till after lunch.

The telephone broke the silence in the empty office. He wasn't accustomed to answering his own phone, and it rang four or five times before he remembered that his secretary wasn't there to field his calls.

He picked up the receiver. "This is John Brighton."

"John…" It was Ellen and she was crying.

"Ellen. What's wrong? Where are you?"

"I'm at the mall." Her voice quavered. "I think my car's been stolen."

"What?"

"I've looked all over the parking lot, and it's not there."

"Where were you parked?"

"I—I'm not sure. I think I was in front of Nordstrom, but the car's not…" She was sobbing now. "John, could you just come and help me find it?"

How could she not remember where she had parked?

"Where are you now, Ellen?" He was trying to be patient and not upset her any more than she already was.

"I…I think I'm on the south side of the mall. You know—where the parking garage is. Isn't that south?"

"Yes, that's south. Are you inside?"

"Uh-huh. By the pay phones."

"Okay. Stay right where you are, and I'll be there as soon as I can. But it'll take me at least twenty minutes to get there if I leave right now. Okay?"

Silence.

"El? Are you there?"

"I'm here."

"Are you okay?"

"Yes. Just…please hurry."

"Okay. It'll be all right. Just stay there, Ellen, okay? I love you."

She started to cry again. "I love you, too," she sobbed.

John locked up the office and hurried to his car. Something was terribly wrong. It wasn't like Ellen to fall apart in a situation like this. And how could she be sure the car had been stolen if she couldn't even remember where she'd parked? Her memory had been terrible lately, but good grief, people didn't just completely forget where they were parked at the mall!

He broke every speed limit, and fifteen minutes later parked illegally near the south entrance. He ran inside and stopped short just inside the door. Ellen sat on the tiled floor beside a pay phone, her hair disheveled, mascara streaking her cheeks, a couple of shopping bags crumpled beside her. She looked like a derelict. It was a wonder someone hadn't reported her. He was almost embarrassed to claim her. Shame washed over him for feeling that way about the woman he loved.

He went to her and reached out his hand.

Her eyes widened as if she'd just recognized him. "Oh! John. You're here."

"What happened?" He helped her to her feet.

She collapsed against him with relief, and he was surprised at how fragile she felt. She'd always been thin, but he wondered now if she'd lost weight and he hadn't noticed.

He ushered her out to his car.

As soon as they were both sitting inside, Ellen poured out her story. "I…I shopped all morning and then decided to get some lunch. But when I came out to the parking lot, the car was just…gone." She glanced up at him, then quickly turned her eyes back to her lap. "At first I thought maybe I'd gone out the wrong entrance, so I went back in and went around to the other side, but it wasn't there either. I…I don't know what happened to it. I can't remember for sure where I parked. I…I'm sorry." She started to cry again, silently this time, her shoulders shaking.

"Well, don't cry," he said, putting a hand briefly on her shoulder. He didn't know what to think. This was so unlike Ellen. "We'll find the car. Let's drive around and see if we can see it. Now, where do you think you parked?"

"Right in front of Nordstrom…I thought. But I'm so upset now, I don't know if that's right."

John cruised slowly up and down the rows of parked vehicles in front of the Nordstrom store. As he maneuvered a corner, he did a double take. In the third row, in plain sight of the entrance, sat Ellen's car.

"Ellen. There it is."

"Where?"

"Right there," he pointed.

"Where? I don't see it."

He drove over to the car and stopped directly behind it.

"What are you doing?"

"What do you mean? There's the car, right in front of you. Don't you see it?" His voice rose, and he bit his lip to keep from shouting at her. Again, he felt guilty for feeling so frustrated with her. But she was acting like a child. "I'll follow you home if you want me to. Are you done shopping?"

"I want to go home." She didn't make a move to get out of the car. "Please…just take me home. I'm so mixed up."

"Ellen? What is the matter with you? You're going to have to drive the car home."

"I don't know where it is," she wailed.

Now alarm rose in him. She was totally disoriented. This couldn't have upset her so much. Something else was wrong.

He reached for her across the car's console and held her until her sobs subsided. His thoughts were as jumbled as hers seemed when he finally let go. He reached down beside the seat for her seat belt, buckled her in as he would a child, then turned the car toward home. They could come back for her car tonight.

Ellen was silent all the way home. She walked into the house and collapsed on the couch.

John went to her and sat beside her for a long time, stroking her forehead. "Honey, what is wrong? I've never seen you this upset over such a little thing."

"John, I'm so mixed up. I don't understand it. One minute I'm happily shopping away, and the next minute I can't even find my own car."

"Well, I'm worried about you. I think you ought to call Jerry and make an appointment. This kind of stuff has been happening too much lately. I don't like it."

"John, I just had a checkup five or six months ago. I'm in perfect health. Jerry will think I'm crazy."

"Well, I'm beginning to wonder…." He grinned at her, trying to lighten the moment, but he was only half teasing.

And Ellen was not having any of it.

He was afraid to leave her alone. He worked at his desk in the den the rest of the afternoon. She puttered around the house, doing laundry, straightening her desk. By evening she seemed to be feeling better. She was cheerful, though obviously a little embarrassed over what had happened.

After supper they went back for the car, and she followed him home without incident.

That night Ellen slept soundly, curled against John in their big bed. But he woke several times during the night, a sick feeling in his gut. His mind took him to dark places as he finally admitted that he hadn't wanted to explore the reasons why his wife could no longer balance the checkbook without his help; why she asked him the same question three times in one evening; or why Ellen, usually so decisive, now sometimes struggled to make the simplest of decisions.

When he'd dared to contemplate these questions for more than a fleeting minute, it had been easy to rationalize: Maybe this empty-nest business was having more of an effect on her than either of them had bargained for. Maybe Jerry was right, and the hormonal changes of menopause were to blame. Maybe Ellen just had a lot on her mind. The way he did.

But he couldn't rationalize her behavior away any longer. He had to do something.

After a fitful sleep, John crept silently from bed early the next morning, taking care not to wake Ellen. He went into the den and dialed Jerry Morton.

"Jerry? John Brighton here. Sorry to bother you at home."

"John, what can I do for you?"

"Well, I'm not sure. I know Ellen was in to see you a few months ago, and she said everything was fine, but something happened yesterday that has me worried." He told Dr. Morton the whole story, remembering the mail in the refrigerator and the 1:00 a.m. showers as he spoke. Jerry listened intently, and John wasn't comforted by their friend's response. Jerry sounded genuinely concerned.

"I think you'd better get her in here as soon as possible, John. It sounds like there's definitely something going on. I've got a pretty heavy schedule this morning, but bring her in around ten and I'll work her in. I think this is important. If for no other reason than to ease her mind—and yours."

"Thanks, Jerry. I'm really sorry to have bothered you like this, but frankly, I'm worried."

"Don't think a thing of it. You did the right thing to call me. I'll see you at ten."

Later, when John woke Ellen to get ready for the appointment, her clenched jaw and quiet compliance told him she was angry he'd called Jerry without consulting her. But she showered and dressed for the appointment without arguing.

John was surprised when Dr. Morton led them to his private office rather than to an examination room. After reviewing Ellen's charts, Jerry asked each of them a barrage of questions, and the answers brought to light just how erratic Ellen's actions had been over the past months.

"Ellen, I'm just a family practice doctor, so I don't feel qualified to make anything more than an educated guess here, but I definitely think there are some things going on here that need to be looked into. I want to refer you to a specialist I know in Chicago—a neurologist. We'll get his evaluation, and then we can go from there. If you'd like me to, I can call him and set up an appointment for you. His name is Dr. Patrick Muñoz."

Before John and Ellen left Jerry's office that morning, they had an appointment to see Dr. Muñoz the following Wednesday morning.

They spent the next days in a stupor—going through the motions at work and walking on eggshells at home. Ellen was sensitive and emotional. John felt irritable and impatient with her, then angry with himself for not being the shoulder Ellen needed to lean on.

On Wednesday morning they got up at six o'clock, drove into the city, and ordered breakfast at a café near the medical center. They sat across from each other in a large booth, the distance widened further by their silence. They picked at their eggs and let their coffee grow cold. Finally John went to the counter to pay their bill, and they walked out to the parking lot and got in the car.

They arrived at Dr. Muñoz's office almost thirty minutes

early and sat nervously in the waiting room, leafing blindly through ancient magazines.

Dr. Muñoz looked carefully over the charts Jerry had sent, asked a few terse questions of his own, and before they knew what had hit them, Ellen was checked into Northwestern Memorial for what would stretch into three days of testing.

They had not come prepared to stay, so John helped Ellen get settled before driving back to Calypso to pack a few of her things. He'd expected Ellen to be upset about the unplanned hospitalization, but she took the news well. In fact, he thought she seemed relieved to finally be on the brink of some answers.

John stayed at a hotel near the hospital on Wednesday night. He looked in on Ellen at seven o'clock the following morning, then drove back to Calypso to be at work by nine.

He came home from the office exhausted. With two important appointments scheduled at the schools the next morning, he wasn't crazy about making the drive back into the city.

When he called Ellen, he found her in good spirits. They chatted about their separate days for several minutes.

He launched into a story about a meeting at work, then stopped abruptly. "Well, I'll tell you about it when I see you later. Can I bring you anything?"

"Listen, honey, you don't need to make the trip back to the hospital tonight."

"Are you sure?"

"Of course. There's no reason for you to come. I'm fine. Besides, with any luck, you can come Saturday and take me home."

John didn't argue with her.

But the evening dragged endlessly. He fixed a turkey sandwich and ate alone at the kitchen table. By nine o'clock, he was bored and restless, and wandered aimlessly through the big house. He watched the first twenty minutes of the local news and decided to turn in early.

Their big bed, usually so welcoming and warm, was cold

and empty without Ellen. The darkness brought out fears he hadn't yet let himself examine, and he lay awake into the early hours of the morning making deals with God.

Chapter Six

Ellen came home from the hospital with more questions than answers. The tests had shown "nothing conclusive" and the hospital had scheduled an appointment the following week with a Dr. Gallia in Chicago, warning her to expect further testing. Jerry claimed the man was the best neurologist in the country, and told them most people had to wait months to get an appointment. Ellen did not find that information comforting.

As she counted down the days until the appointment, her mind insisted on carrying her to the past, to the earliest days of her marriage. It was a mixed blessing that her thoughts compelled her also to the greatest sorrow of their lives, for in this crease of her brain, at least, her thinking was utterly lucid.

When they'd come back from their honeymoon to the teaching jobs awaiting them in North Lawndale, she and John had made lofty plans. Starry-eyed and ignorant, they lay awake under the rafters of their cozy apartment dreaming and scheming late into the nights, timing the events of their young lives to perfection.

But Providence paid no attention to their plans. Just after Christmas, completely contrary to the schedule they'd made, Ellen began to suspect she might be pregnant. She was only a few days late, but her body had taken on a new fullness, and the queasiness in her stomach on the bus each morning became more and more difficult to ignore. She and John had talked often about the children they would have someday, but both had agreed that they wanted to have more than the tiny apartment and teachers' salaries to offer their babies. They hadn't even felt they could afford a car yet, though Oscar was generous in lending them his.

Ellen was afraid to tell John her suspicions. He was so careful with their money and had such a precise plan set out: teach another year, buy a car then go back to school for his master's degree so he could find a job that would allow Ellen to quit teaching and have their babies. It was a good plan— a reasonable plan. But as the signs became ever more evident that Ellen was indeed pregnant, her joy grew proportionately. She thought of nothing else. She decorated nurseries in her dreams and even bought a book of baby names, which she hid under her side of the bed. She looked at it furtively—and guiltily—while John was in the shower or out playing tennis. She started to feel dishonest keeping this momentous news from the one who had helped make it so but, after all, it had not yet been confirmed by a doctor.

Three weeks passed and still her period had not come, and the morning nausea was getting worse. She would have to tell John sooner or later. Would he blame her—or worse, would he grow to resent the baby for making such a drastic revision to their well-planned blueprint?

Ellen made an appointment at the county health clinic to have a pregnancy test. As she sat in the reception room waiting for the results, she realized that even greater than her fear of what John would say if she was pregnant, was the fear that the test would show she *wasn't* pregnant. She desperately wanted the little life she was certain grew inside her.

After twenty minutes of nervous waiting, Ellen heard her name. She looked up to see the nurse standing in the doorway, an enigmatic expression on her face. The woman motioned to Ellen and led the way to a small room at the end of the hall.

"Well, Mrs. Brighton, you are indeed pregnant. I hope that's good news." She glanced suspiciously at Ellen's plain gold wedding band. "Of course you'll need to make an appointment with your doctor to determine an accurate due date and make sure everything is progressing as it should."

She handed Ellen a small stack of pamphlets. Ellen muttered a thank-you, gathered her coat and purse, and made her way down the corridor that led to the street. She had walked the mile and a half from the apartment, and now, in spite of the biting cold, she welcomed the time it would take her to get home.

As the confirmation of her suspicions sank in, Ellen was filled not with apprehension, but with the purest joy she had ever known. She was carrying the child of the man she loved more than anyone or anything in the world. She wanted to turn cartwheels and shout at the top of her lungs. She felt invincible. They would find a way around any obstacles to have this child. Their humble plans suddenly seemed insignificant in the face of this new life they had created.

But as each step took her closer to the apartment—and John—her confidence dwindled. By the time she pushed open their front door, the joy had been displaced by uncertainty.

The house still smelled like this morning's bacon and eggs. John was sitting at the small table in the kitchen, reading the newspaper. They couldn't afford a subscription to the *Tribune,* but Oscar and Hattie shared their paper with them each day. John looked up. "Hey, where have you—"

Ellen burst into tears. "Oh, John, I'm pregnant!"

His face registered shock, but no words came from his gaping mouth. He pushed the newspaper to the floor and stood up hesitantly. Then he gathered Ellen in his arms and held her as great sobs racked her thin frame. They stood that way for long minutes until finally he croaked, "Ellen, are you sure?"

"Yes, I'm sure." She gulped back her sobs. "I just had a

test at the clinic. Oh, John, I'm sorry. I thought I was so careful."

He held her at arm's length. "Ellen, is it that terrible? I mean, are you okay? Everything's all right, isn't it?" There was worry in his voice now.

"Everything's okay with the baby, but look what I've done, John. How will you ever go back to school now? How will we buy a car?" She pointed to the newspaper that lay tented on the floor. "We can't even afford to buy a newspaper," she wailed. "And where will we put the baby?" She dissolved into tears again, collapsing against his chest.

He gave a quiet laugh that startled her and made her draw back and look into his eyes.

"Um…excuse me, Mrs. Brighton, but if I remember my biology correctly, I get just a *little* credit for this, too!"

Ellen smiled through her tears. "Oh, John… A baby! I've worried so much that you'd be upset…but…oh, honey, I'm so happy. I can't help it. I want this baby—more than you can imagine."

John was thoughtful for a moment. "You've been acting really strange the last couple weeks. I couldn't figure out what I'd done to upset you. Now it all makes sense."

She laughed. "Was I that obvious?"

He nodded. "How long have you known?"

"I started to get suspicious right after Christmas, but I didn't know for sure until the test today. I know the timing is terrible, but I've been so happy thinking about this baby, I would have been crushed if the test had been negative. Is that awful of me?"

"Honey, it's…it's wonderful! So we'll have to change our plans a little. Will it really make any difference twenty years from now that we got a little behind on our big financial schedule? I'm just relieved that this is what has been eating you. I've felt like you were a million miles away lately, and I couldn't figure out what I'd done." His tone turned stern. "You should have told me. Don't ever keep anything this important from me, El." Softening, he took her face tenderly in his hands and touched his nose to hers. "I love you, Ellen Brighton." He crushed her fiercely to himself. "Our baby will have the most beautiful mother in the world. This is a blessing." He spoke the words like a decree.

Catherine MaryEllen Brighton was born August 17 at five o'clock in the afternoon. After twelve hours of labor Ellen had given birth with relative ease, but as soon as the doctor announced it was a girl, the nurses whisked the baby out of the room with grim faces. John stood over her at the head of the delivery table, stroking hair away from her face while the doctor stitched her up.

"What's wrong?" Ellen asked. "Is my baby okay?"

The doctor evaded her question. "The nurse will be in with a sedative."

"But my baby? Our baby...is she okay?"

The doctor scooted his stool away from the foot of the bed and murmured something to the remaining nurse.

Something was terribly wrong.

Things went fuzzy then. Ellen gripped John's hand, drifting in and out. She awoke to John's gentle nudging and Dr. Jensen's low voice.

"I'm so sorry." The doctor shuffled his feet and looked at the floor before meeting Ellen's eyes. "Your baby died a few minutes ago. She was born with a severe heart defect. We did everything we could for her, but there was really never any hope. It was nothing you did...nothing you could have known or done anything about. Please don't blame yourselves. This is a very rare occurrence, and there's no reason you cannot have another healthy baby when Mrs. Brighton has recovered sufficiently."

Though Ellen was lying flat in the bed, the room started to spin. An oddly hushed buzzing pounded in her head. In the hour since the baby's birth, she had tried to prepare herself for the possibility of this news, and had prayerfully, agonizingly given the child into God's hands. But now the uncertain fear had become a cruel reality. The baby they had dreamed about, planned for and waited nine endless months for was gone before they could hold her in their arms. They had loved this baby before they had even felt her move within Ellen's belly. Ellen felt the emptiness like a deep abyss. It was too much to bear. How could the doctor even speak about another baby? How could anyone be expected to survive such grief?

John sat in a straight chair beside Ellen's hospital bed. He had barely moved from this place for almost fourteen hours. Through a haze of grief Ellen watched him sitting there, his head buried in his hands, but she was too numb to reach out to him.

Then suddenly summoning strength, she spoke, her voice fierce. "I want to see my baby."

"Mrs. Brighton…" The doctor seemed to grasp for words. "Do you…do you understand that your baby is gone?"

"I understand. I just want to hold her one time." Her voice broke. "Please don't deny me that."

Dr. Jensen hesitated. "All right. It will be some time before they can bring her up to your room, but I'll let them know your wishes." The doctor scribbled a note on Ellen's chart and left the room.

At twilight a nurse brought the baby to Ellen's room. The young woman—no older than Ellen—was teary-eyed and unable to speak, but she put the bundle gently in Ellen's arms and left the young couple alone.

Someone had dressed the baby in a tiny undershirt and booties and wrapped her in a soft pink blanket. Her face was translucent as fine porcelain, with blue veins tracing a pale web. She was perfect. She had fine auburn hair that curled around her neck and forehead. "Like yours, Ellen," John said. His words were a gift.

For half an hour they held their baby and marveled at her beauty. They counted her fingers and toes. They called her by her name and told her they loved her. And they said goodbye. It was almost more than they could bear when the nurse came and took the baby from Ellen's arms and carried her forever from their lives. But John and Ellen never regretted having spent that sacred time with their firstborn. They often spoke of it as a blessing, and they were to look back on those moments as the beginning of their healing.

They buried Catherine in a tiny white coffin under an ancient oak tree in the Randolph family plot. The cemetery was a peaceful, secluded place in the country. It sat on a hill behind Ellen's childhood church, surrounded protectively by a wrought-iron fence. As children, Ellen and her sisters had scaled the fence and played hide-and-seek there while their parents visited after Sunday services. It comforted Ellen to think of their baby in a setting from her own childhood.

John and Ellen stayed with the Randolphs until the weekend. Ellen was feeling strong physically, though the fullness of her breasts and the dwindling flow of blood were constant reminders of how recently her baby had been cradled warm and safe in her womb. But it was heartening to be pampered by her mother and her sisters, and it was a bittersweet pleasure to share the farm with John. They walked in the fields and along the country roads for hours, praying together, talking out their feelings and planning how they would go on with their lives after this bitter disappointment. And somehow in spite of the sorrow, they knew there was a blessing hidden somewhere in the pain. They had a child in heaven. No one could take away the love that had grown in their hearts for this child, or the bond that had melded them together through the joy and the sorrow and the hope.

When they got back to Calypso, Oscar and Hattie were there to offer their sympathy. They enveloped John and Ellen in warm hugs.

"The good Lord has a reason for everything, child," Hattie told Ellen. "Just give Him time and He'll take care of the hurt. I speak from experience, you know. Time and God are mighty healers…you'll see."

There were the nursery things tucked in the corner of the bedroom to deal with. On the first night they were back, John carried the cradle down to Oscar's garage and then came up and sat on the bed as Ellen folded the blankets and packed the tiny sleepers and gowns into a cardboard box.

Ellen warmed a can of tomato soup and set a package of stale saltines on the table, but they ate little. They prepared for bed wordlessly and fell asleep, exhausted, in each other's arms.

She awoke several hours later to find John's side of the bed empty. Seeing the bathroom light was off, she padded silently into the living room and found him hunched over the desk, his head on his arms. At first she thought he had fallen asleep, but as she moved toward him she saw his shoulders heave and fall. And then she heard him. She stood there in agony, frozen, unable to move, while her husband sobbed like a child. Not knowing how to comfort him, she crept back to bed and lay quietly, sick at heart, until she finally heard him wash his face and come to bed. He pulled her to himself, not realizing she was fully awake. They lay together, her body curved to his, like nesting spoons, until at last she felt his even breaths on the back of her neck and knew he slept. She lay awake till dawn, aching more for her husband than for the child they had lost.

Yes, there had been sorrowful times early in their marriage. And though it was a tired cliché, time and God really had healed their wounds. Of course, wounds left scars that would always be there, a testament to the pain they'd endured. Catherine's death would forever be a tender spot in their memories. But John and Ellen had found comfort in the psalmist's words, "Joy comes in the morning."

Now, as Ellen thrashed to the surface of reality, she wondered: Would there be a morning of joy to this dark night? Had their luck run out? The young wife and mother from those memories hadn't believed in luck. But sometimes, when her thoughts blurred and the future turned murky, luck seemed easier to grasp than faith.

Chapter Seven

The receptionist pointed John and Ellen toward a small alcove near the elevators, and they took seats and waited there.

Clinic waiting rooms were becoming far too familiar. Two more days of testing at Northwestern Memorial had still produced nothing definite. They'd waited an endless ten days for the last test results, and finally, they'd been called in for this consultation with Dr. William Gallia.

Ellen sat erect and motionless on a gray metal chair, while John fidgeted in the seat beside her. He jumped up and paced to the window and back, picked up a magazine from the stack on a low table and leafed aimlessly through it, then tossed it back on the pile and resumed his pacing. It struck him that anyone watching them would have thought *he* was the patient.

Finally a nurse appeared in the doorway. "Ellen Brighton?"

Ellen looked up, obviously recognizing her name, but she didn't move from her seat. John nodded to the nurse and took Ellen's arm and led her, following the nurse down the unadorned hallway.

Dr. Gallia's office was cold and austere, like the man who inhabited it. The pungent odor of alcohol and disinfectant assaulted John's nostrils. Once he would have perceived the odor as clean, even wholesome. Now it repulsed him, conjuring images of death and decay.

The nurse motioned for Ellen to take a seat on the side of the examining table. John felt awkward and irrelevant, towering as he did over both women. He perched on the rolling stool at the foot of the table and then realized this was the doctor's seat. Finally, he settled on a folding chair that had been hidden behind the open door.

Ellen had not spoken since they got off the elevator. John wondered what she was thinking. The thoughts she'd given voice to lately were so inscrutable that some days he despaired of ever understanding her mind again.

He'd tried to talk to her about the problems she was having. He knew she must be worried, too. They had always been able to talk things out with each other. But whenever he questioned her now—and he was always gentle about it— she'd pretend she hadn't heard him, or she changed the subject. Or she would give him a quasi reply that had little to do with what he'd asked.

The nurse took Ellen's blood pressure, pulse and temperature, recording them on the chart in silence. Then without explanation or instruction, she left the room. John was becoming frustrated with the sterility—not only of the premises, but the personnel, as well. How out of place a warm smile would have been in this frigid clinic—but how welcome.

Finally, after twenty minutes, Dr. Gallia tapped on the door and entered before either of them could respond. He was short of stature, with a fringe of white hair emphasizing the shiny baldness of his head. He wore wire-framed glasses low on his nose and looked over these as he addressed Ellen.

"Hello, Mrs. Brighton. How are you feeling today?"

Ellen spoke slowly, suspicion tingeing her voice. "I'm fine, I guess. I wish you people would figure out what's wrong with me so I can get on with my life."

She didn't sound like herself, and John wanted to apologize for her. Compared to her usual friendly manner, she seemed almost rude. But this man didn't know Ellen, so John kept silent.

Ellen seemed to have retreated to that place deep inside her mind where she fled so often recently.

The doctor looked at the chart in his hands, appearing to avoid her eyes as he spoke. "Well, for starters, I'm going to have you answer a few questions." He spent five or ten minutes going over the same questions Ellen had been asked by nearly every specialist they'd seen. He put her through a battery of simple questions about the day's date and identifying simple objects like his watch and a pencil. As before, she answered the questions easily until the doctor asked her to spell a word backward, and count backward from one hundred.

It was all John could do not to prompt her. The task seemed simple to him. He couldn't imagine why Ellen was making it so difficult.

Like the others, Dr. Gallia asked about Ellen's daily routine and inquired about her health history. Didn't they have these things on file? Why couldn't these doctors get their information together and save themselves—and Ellen—the annoyance of going through the same routine all over again.

Some of the questions were deflected to John. He answered as briefly and honestly as he could.

Finally, the doctor closed the folder that held Ellen's chart and abruptly left the room without explanation.

John thought it rude, but Ellen seemed not to notice.

Dr. Gallia had a reputation for being one of Chicago's finest neurologists, but John decided the man's talents must lie in an area other than patient-physician rapport.

After another ten minutes, a nurse—a different one than before—stuck her head in the door. "Would you come with me, please."

She led them down the hall to a small but handsomely appointed office. "The doctor will be with you in a few minutes."

They sat facing the desk, backs to the door, not speaking, like defendants waiting for a judge to sentence them—or acquit them.

Dr. Gallia entered the room and situated himself at the desk. "Mrs. Brighton, Mr. Brighton, as you know, we have all the results back now from the tests that were completed at the medical center?" He spoke it like a question but didn't pause for a response. "I'm very sorry to have to be the bearer of bad news, but all the test results are consistent with my original suspicion of Alzheimer's disease. I assume you are familiar with the term?"

Stunned, John nodded mechanically. He reached for Ellen's hand and squeezed it.

"Do you understand what I'm saying, Mrs. Brighton?"

Ellen turned her head toward John, but her eyes glazed over and her gaze traveled beyond him. He knew she had not understood at all.

Dr. Gallia apparently realized it, too, for he directed his next comments at John, speaking as though Ellen wasn't in the room. And in many ways, she wasn't.

"It is rather unusual, though not unheard of, to see Alzheimer's in someone as young as your wife," the doctor said, shifting in his seat. "Unfortunately, we are beginning to see it more and more in people in their forties and fifties. You must understand that there isn't a definitive test for Alzheimer's, except with an autopsy."

Though John heard the doctor's words clearly, they came as through a long tunnel, muffled and echoing harshly back at him.

"With this disease we rely a great deal on the process of elimination. The tests your wife went through rule out the other disorders we might suspect with her symptoms—" he counted them off on his fingers "—Parkinson's, multi-infarct dementia, Pick's disease…"

John had been doing his own research on the Internet late at night after Ellen had gone to bed. These names were all too familiar. It had seemed that for each new disease he'd read about, he found a paragraph that seemed to describe Ellen's symptoms perfectly. Before, he'd skimmed over words like *senility* and *dementia*. Ellen was too young for those words. But now he had a name—a label to put on all this craziness. *Alzheimer's.*

Dr. Gallia continued. "We can't detect any evidence of a stroke or hormone imbalance. Of course, as I said, though we've made great strides, Alzheimer's still cannot be confirmed definitively except by autopsy. But your wife's test results pretty much exclude any other possibilities. I think we're looking at a solid case of Alzheimer's here, with the only variable being the early onset."

John watched the doctor in a state of shock, detached from the scene…everything seemed to be in slow motion. Dr. Gallia took off his glasses, rubbed the bridge of his nose and sat with his head bent for so long that John began to wonder if he was fighting his emotions…or if he'd gone to sleep. But when the doctor looked up, his expression was matter-of-fact. He picked up a prescription pad, writing as he spoke.

"I'm going to refer you to the Alzheimer's Association. It is an excellent national organization that was started right here in Chicago. They can recommend some books and other literature that will be helpful. They also have a number of support groups in this area. At some point I think you will find it very helpful to speak with others who are going through the same things you will be."

John was numb. He felt his heart begin to beat erratically in his chest, and the color drained from his face. He stroked Ellen's hand and managed to blurt out a few rudimentary questions while she sat seemingly oblivious.

"Where…where do we go from here? Isn't there some sort of medicine, some drug you can give her?"

The doctor nodded, pulled a prescription pad from the pocket of his lab coat and began scribbling. "Yes. I'm going to give you a couple of prescriptions she can start." He rattled off the names of the drugs and some instructions that may as well have been in a foreign language for all John understood.

"The clinical trials on some of these newer drugs are promising." Dr. Gallia leaned toward him, warming to the subject. "A lot of progress has been made even in the last five or ten years, and researchers are much more optimistic, but the outcomes vary widely from individual to individual. We'll just have to see how she responds. Don't expect a miracle."

John was incredulous. "But…there has to be some therapy or—*something* else we can do…"

Dr. Gallia sighed deeply, the first sign of empathy John had seen him exhibit. He pushed a button on his telephone and within a few seconds the nurse who'd ushered them in to the office appeared. "Mrs. Brighton, could you go with Carol to the waiting room, please?"

Panic crawled up the back of his throat. He stood, and Ellen echoed his movements.

"Follow me, Mrs. Brighton," the nurse said cheerfully.

Ellen did so, as if she were a robot taking an order.

When the door closed behind them, John slumped back into the chair.

Dr. Gallia placed his hands together and steepled his fingers under his chin. "Mr. Brighton, what you can do is take your wife home and enjoy the next days and weeks and months as much as possible. Try to keep life as normal and routine as you can. Above all, don't fall into the trap of treating her like an invalid. There will be plenty of time for that later. See to it that she does everything she can possibly do for herself for as long as she can. It may be helpful to seek counseling for both your wife and yourself. This is a very difficult disease to deal with. Certainly if you want to try some physical therapy or speech therapy when the time comes, you have every right to do that, but my personal opinion is that those things are basically a waste of valuable time."

He paused to let his words sink in. "I won't lie to you, Mr.

Brighton. This is not a pretty disease. You must accept the fact that over the next few years your wife is going to change drastically. Of course, we can't predict how quickly the disease will progress. It varies greatly from one person to the next."

The truth slowly began to register. John stumbled to his feet and stood behind his chair, clutching its back for support. "But surely there must be something you can do!"

John started to pace back and forth in the tiny space in front of the doctor's desk. Panic rose in his throat. His hands grasped at the empty air as though he could pull an answer from its nothingness.

He was met with Dr. Gallia's calm, clinical reply. "At some point we will probably prescribe tranquilizers or possibly an antidepressant, depending on the direction the disease takes with your wife. There are always new experimental drugs in the works, but as far as a wonder drug, I'm sorry, there just isn't anything yet."

John abruptly stopped pacing. "What…what caused this? Why Ellen?"

"We don't know. Some studies seem to indicate…"

But John wasn't listening. His mind raced, and he interrupted as a new thought pounded into his brain. "Is this…is it terminal?"

"Alzheimer's causes actual disintegration of the tissues of the brain, so yes, in that sense it is terminal. And there is no cure. Of course, every case is different."

"How…how much time does she have?" He couldn't believe he was asking this question. Couldn't believe he was getting this news.

"Each case is different," the doctor said again. "I don't ever put a time frame on it, but generally we see patients surviving anywhere from five to fifteen years, possibly a bit longer, though frankly, that is no blessing. Quite honestly, when early onset is a factor, the survival time is sometimes shorter. In any case, it's often infections—pneumonia and such—that cause death in these patients, especially after they have become bedridden."

"I know I've given you a great deal to think about, Mr. Brighton." Dr. Gallia stood, tacitly dismissing John. "Please get in touch with the Alzheimer's Association. They will be very helpful in answering your questions…and it's understandable that you will have many questions."

"When…when do you want to see her again?" John was grasping at straws. He wasn't ready to be dismissed. He couldn't deal with this yet. How could he face Ellen with such devastating news?

"I don't see any reason why your own physician—" he leafed through the chart "—Dr. Morton, isn't it?"

John nodded.

"He can monitor your wife's prescriptions and answer any questions you have about that. Unless she gets sick, there's really no reason for her to see a doctor more often than her regular checkups. Of course, if she begins to decline rapidly, or if you feel she would benefit from antidepressant medication or sedatives, then you may want to have her reevaluated."

John slammed his fist into the palm of his other hand, wishing it were a wall. *Gets sick?* Good grief! What was wrong with this man? Couldn't he see that she *was* sick? How could he calmly sit here and tell him that his Ellen—his sweet, beautiful Ellen—was going to die a slow, horrible death…was going to mentally rot away? And there wasn't a blessed thing he could do about it.

His anger threatened to explode in physical violence. He clasped his hands in front of him and willed himself to calm down. He had to face Ellen on the other side of this door, and he couldn't do it in anger.

He took a deep breath to compose himself. He gave the doctor a curt nod and left the room, closing the door behind him.

Chapter Eight

Ellen was waiting for him in an alcove of the waiting room. She stood and walked to meet him by the elevator. They rode to the lobby in silence. *So much silence between them now.* It nearly killed him.

He drove home while she dozed in the front seat beside him. Watching her, he remembered a long-ago day when he'd felt equally desolate—the day he'd brought Ellen home from the hospital after they'd lost little Catherine. Ellen had slept on that trip, too, as if slumber could shut out the tragedy of what had happened.

But that was different. After Catherine's death, joy had returned to John and Ellen threefold in the precious lives of their other children. The hum of the tires on the highway hypnotized him as his thoughts returned to that tenuous time. It hadn't been an easy road back to happiness.

She had seemed so strong in the first days after Catherine's death. But when they returned to their classrooms, and life resumed its routine, a gloom had enveloped her. For months she seemed immersed in a dark depression that threatened to drown John, too, as he struggled to pull her out of its murky waters. She went through her days at school like an automaton. She'd made an obvious effort to be cheerful for

John's sake, but her laughter rang false, and he would often find her staring into nothingness, oblivious to his words and his comfort.

Sometimes when she didn't know he was near, he heard her cry out to God, begging to know why he had taken their innocent child.

The doctor had said they could try for another baby after three months, but when that time came and John broached the subject with Ellen, she tersely said she wasn't ready yet, and closed the topic by leaving the room.

As the days passed, he'd begun to fear she would never recover. More and more, her behavior reminded him of his mother's in the days after his father had left them. The same vacant stare, the same self-absorbed manner. Ellen seemed indifferent to his personal grief as had his mother to his adolescent misery. But he could not find it in himself to be angry with Ellen. He knew that, though he felt the loss of their child deeply, his heartache was more akin to disappointment—the death of a dream. He had not carried their child under his heart for nine months; he had not felt her tiny arms and legs fluttering inside him. He had not suffered the travail of giving birth, only to have the reward of such pain snatched away so cruelly. How could he deny Ellen license to rail against whatever had willed her this cross? So he kept silent. And the silence was a brash echo in their little apartment under the eaves.

But a year after they had buried Catherine, Ellen was pregnant again. Once more, the pregnancy had not been planned, but John hoped beyond hope that this baby would bring back the glow to Ellen's face.

For the first few months Ellen's eyes were filled with fear, but suddenly as if a dam had broken, instead of holding her feelings inside, she lay awake late into the nights talking and talking with John. As Ellen confided her darkest fears to her husband, he watched them evaporate like dew in the sun, to be replaced with tiny buds of hope.

That such profound sorrow could be replaced by such great joy was a mystery he would never truly comprehend. But perhaps one could not feel happiness with such depth if one had not first known the fathoms of anguish.

The night Jana Beth's first lusty cries filled the delivery room, and the doctor placed the baby, whole and perfect, on Ellen's belly, John watched the last remnant of her grief vanish. It was as though Ellen herself was the one newly born—hope giving full bloom to joy. Though she confided to John that she would never truly understand why Catherine had been taken from them, Ellen acknowledged that Jana's birth had restored her faith in the God to whom she had entrusted her life. And now she ran confidently back into His arms.

Shortly after Jana's birth, John had applied for a position as Calypso's elementary school principal. It was a coveted position, and he had little hope of even being considered for the job. To their amazement, he was offered the job with only one stipulation—that he take a few courses at the university to comply with the qualifications. Ellen and John were elated. Not only would he have a job in the suburbs, but he would also have financial assistance in working toward the degree he had planned to get anyway. And the new salary would boost the meager bank account they had struggled with since Ellen quit teaching to be home with Jana.

They'd borrowed three thousand dollars from Howard and MaryEllen to put a down payment on a little house three blocks from Oscar and Hattie's. The house needed painting inside and out, and the yard was a tangle of weeds, but it was structurally sound and, more importantly, it was theirs. They spent their weekends raking and seeding the lawn, and by the time school started, the grass was green and lush and the backyard had been enclosed with a rough board fence. The inside of the house could wait until winter.

Now as their precious little girl toddled across their hearts, another little life waited to make entrance into their world.

Brant Allen Brighton was born in January, and much to their surprise, Kyle Andrew had followed along only fourteen months later.

Now, as John turned onto Oaklawn and their house came into view, his mind churned with thoughts of what the future might hold for them. He tried to will the awful visions away, but it was a physical battle. He touched the cloth of his shirt, shocked to realize that he was drenched in sweat. His breath came in short gasps. What would they do? What would he do without Ellen?

He turned to watch her. She was still asleep, slack-mouthed beside him. He was unable to fathom that inside the beautiful head that lay on his shoulder each night—the head he cradled so tenderly—a vile thing was eating away at her brain. It was incomprehensible. It had to be a bad dream. Surely he would wake up, and they would laugh together about it as they had often laughed about each other's silly dreams.

As he pulled into their driveway, Ellen instinctively woke up. Without speaking, they carried the paraphernalia of the day's trip into the kitchen. Ellen puttered around the house, hanging up jackets and putting receipts in the desk drawer. She went to the sink and began washing the few dishes left there from breakfast. John watched her perform these mundane chores with new eyes. How long would she be able to do these simple, homely things?

Like a tidal wave, an overwhelming love and tenderness welled within him for this woman—his wife. He went to her as she stood at the sink and wrapped his arms around her, resting his chin on the top of her head. Her hair was disheveled from sleeping in the car, and her skin was damp from the steam of the dishwater. She turned to him, put her arms around his waist, and laid her head on his chest, uttering two simple words: "Tell me."

John fought to control his emotions. "It…it's Alzheimer's, Ellen. At least it's not any of the other things they tested you for, so they think that's what it has to be."

Calmly, as though it were a relief to finally have a name for this intruder, she sighed. "I thought that's what you were going to tell me."

In her moments of clarity, Ellen had been researching, too. John knew she had tried not to look very far into her future, but words like *dementia* and, yes, even *Alzheimer's,* must have danced disturbingly through her mind in the past weeks and months as she'd leafed through health magazines and searched the Internet.

"John?" Her voice sounded strangely serene. "How long do I have?"

"They don't know, Ellen. There's no way of knowing. And there are promising new drugs that might help. We'll get the prescription filled tonight that Dr. Gallia gave us and get you started on it right away and—"

She put her hands on either side of his face. "I want the truth, John."

Oddly, she'd never seemed so sane, so much herself. He sighed. He wouldn't play games with her. She deserved the truth. "Things will probably get…they will get progressively worse. We can't know how quickly that will happen, or…how long you have." He couldn't bring himself to tell her what the doctor had said: five years, ten years, possibly fifteen. But those extra years would be no blessing.

Ellen began to cry. With tears streaming down her face, her voice quivering, she wailed, "Oh, John! I'm so sorry. I didn't want it to happen this way. I always pictured us growing old together…enjoying our grandchildren…and even great-grandchildren." She gave a little gasp. "Oh, the kids…how will we tell the kids, John?"

He opened his mouth to answer, but she spoke first. "I guess they already know something's wrong with me, as crazy as I've been acting lately." She breathed out a harsh chuckle. "It's funny, but it's kind of nice to know I'm not losing my marbles…well, I am, but at least I have an excuse."

She was more lucid than John had seen her in weeks. He

felt an urgent need to tell her all the things he loved about her. But how did you tell someone that they are life itself to you? How did you say goodbye when there is no leave-taking? Yet they might not have another time to say goodbye. There might not be another day when she would understand his words of love. And so he ventured to speak what was beyond words.

He led her to the darkened living room and laid a fire in the fireplace while she watched in silence. She sat down on the sofa, but John sat on the floor in front of the hearth and pulled her onto his lap.

"Ellen…" His voice faltered. He stroked her temple and traced the lines that so many years of smiles had etched on her face. "Ellen, I love you with all my heart. I never knew a man could be so happy and so utterly content until I met you. Do you know how happy you make me, El? You mean everything to me…*everything*."

He stopped, not trusting his voice. But the need to spill everything that was in his heart persisted, and he went on. "I don't know what this is we're facing now, but if it means losing you I'm not sure how I'll go on. Whatever happens, El, I don't want you to be afraid of anything. No matter how awful it might get, I'll be here for you. We'll…"

He started to say, "We'll beat this thing," but he knew better, and he knew that she knew better. He wanted to keep things honest between them. They had never kept secrets from each other. "We'll get through this," he said finally. "Somehow, we'll get through it."

She reached up to press her palm to his cheek. "Oh, John, if I died tomorrow, I'd have no regrets." Her voice was beautiful in his ear—low and husky and familiar.

A glint of fear came to her eyes and the corners of her mouth turned down. "But…I'm afraid of living beyond tomorrow…. Oh, John. I'm going to be such a burden to you and the kids. I…I love you, John. I love you so much…so very much. And I know with all my heart that you love me, but I'm terrified our love won't survive this…this monster!" Her voice rose a tremulous octave and she grabbed tufts of hair at the side of her head and yanked. "I feel…possessed! I've never felt so out of control like this before. It terrifies me! Oh, John, I'm so scared."

"Shh, shh…" He held her, stroking her hair until she calmed down. And they held each other that way, praying together, drawing strength and comfort from the physical embrace and from the presence of the God they knew and trusted, even though they didn't understand.

As the fire in the hearth waned, their embrace turned to passion. They drank each other in, making love unhurriedly, but with fervid insistence…with sweet familiarity.

Afterward, John brought a quilt and pillows from their bed. He stoked the fire, and they slept on the floor in front of the hearth until the harsh light of morning flooded their pallet, and the embers grew as cold as the reality they woke to face.

Chapter Nine

John stood at the fireplace gazing into the fading embers of the first fire of autumn. One by one, the sparks grew faint and died. It seemed rife with symbolism.

Dr. Gallia's words the previous spring had proven prophetic. As the months passed, John had watched Ellen fade before his eyes. Her memory losses became more frequent and more glaring with every week that passed.

Ellen had always loved to cook, but now, most days she could no longer remember even the simple recipes she'd made from scratch since she was a young girl growing up on the farm.

She would try to tell John about a phone call and come up completely blank. She could tell him someone had called, and that it was important, but she couldn't remember what the message was about, or whether it was a man or a woman she'd spoken to. She tried writing down phone messages, but too often the jumbled scribblings on the notepad failed to give John—or Ellen—a clue about the call. Sometimes he wondered if she was remembering a call from last week—or worse, if the calls were all in her imagination.

After missing half a dozen important calls, John finally bought an answering machine. But he couldn't make Ellen understand that she should wait to see who was calling and then decide whether to answer the call. The first time John called, Ellen answered on the second ring.

"Ellen." He tried to keep the impatience from his voice. "I thought you were going to wait and let the machine pick up."

"But it's you, John. Why did you call if you didn't want to talk to me?"

"But what if it hadn't been me? That's the whole point," he explained patiently, "so you can let the machine take the call after you find out if it's me or not."

"But…but it is you," she stuttered.

He laughed in spite of his frustration, and tried to explain it to her again.

"But what if one of the kids tries to call, John?"

"You can pick up if you recognize their voice, Ellen."

"But…I won't know it's them unless I pick up."

"Yes, you will, Ellen. Don't you understand how an answering machine works?" He felt his blood pressure rising. "It's like your voice mail at work."

"What do you want for dinner?"

He sighed. She'd taken to changing the subject whenever she got frustrated. It was a challenge not to let his exasperation match hers. An answering machine was apparently too confusing and complicated for her. He let it drop.

"We could eat out," he said. "Maybe you'd like to call someone to go out with us?"

"Oh! I hadn't thought of that. We could have those people…you know…those people from church…"

"What people?"

"You know. The ones we like so well."

"Rob and Cathy?" Lately the names of even her closest friends seemed to escape her, and though she could usually conjure them up eventually, increasingly her conversations had become erratic and bizarre.

"Is that their names? Rob and Cathy?"

"Yes, honey. You know that. Rob and Cathy McLaughlin. We've known them since the kids were babies." He bit his lower lip. He wasn't sure he was up for socializing, especially if Ellen was in one of her less lucid states.

"I'll get my coat." The phone went silent and he guessed that she was already headed for the hall closet. He wondered if she would remember what she was looking for by the time she got there.

Almost comically, John started finding things in the strangest places. A pencil in the toothbrush holder, a slice of toast in the desk drawer by the telephone and a stick of butter—thankfully still in its wrapper—in his sock drawer. He had to laugh at that one. Even Ellen had seen the humor in it, though she was angry when she heard him laugh with Brant about it on the phone.

They hadn't yet told the kids about the diagnosis. "I don't want them worrying," Ellen had told John the last time he broached the subject. John had to respect her wishes, but he knew that the children were worried and puzzled by the changes they saw in their mother. They had caught her in some of her silly mistakes.

"Maybe they got a little carried away with those highlights in your hair, Mom," Kyle had said when Ellen had put ketchup on the table with the pancakes one morning when he was home for the weekend.

"Huh? What are you talking about, Kyle?"

"A little too much blond in the mix, maybe? Get it?" he joked, wiggling his eyebrows Groucho Marx style.

"Oh, Kyle, stop." Ellen smiled, but John sensed the tears were threatening.

John pulled Kyle aside later. "Hey, bud, go easy on Mom, okay? She…she's got a lot on her mind right now."

"Hey, I was only kidding."

"I know, but…just take it easy. She's a little emotional right now."

"Yeah, okay. Sorry." Kyle shrugged and looked at John as though he was the one losing it.

He tried to prepare Brant and Jana for the news, too, dropping little hints about Ellen not feeling well, and having a lot on her plate. But they were busy with their own lives, and he wasn't sure they caught the concern in his voice.

There were brief intermissions—sometimes lasting for days or even weeks—when Ellen seemed to be her old self. During those times, John found himself hoping it had all been a terrible mistake. Maybe the doctors were wrong. Maybe this was something else. Maybe it was all a terrible mix-up and she was getting well after all.

It amazed him that he could be so devastated when the symptoms returned. It was like finding out about the Alzheimer's all over again. He almost wished those little remissions wouldn't occur, because the telltale warnings always came back, and when they did, they seemed worse than before, usually bringing some new loss of memory or function.

Sometimes she just lost words. She would be talking along making perfect sense, when suddenly she would stop mid-sentence, unable to think of the next word she wanted to say. Often, John could supply it for her. They'd always finished each other's sentences. But more and more she lost words that he couldn't find for her. And she would become agitated when he reeled off a multiple-choice list.

Unfortunately, the answer was often "none of the above." Occasionally, if he was patient and allowed her to concentrate, she could dredge up the word. But most times she would wave him away, leaving the thought unfinished and both of them feeling frustrated.

More disturbing, John noticed that she had begun to use completely nonsensical words. Sometimes she was aware that what she said hadn't made a whit of sense, and she could backtrack and find the right word, the right phrase. But most of the time she seemed unaware that she had spoken amiss. If it hadn't been so tragic, it might have been comical.

One October evening, while she and John were watching TV in the den, she turned to him, eyebrows arched, fire in her eyes. "I don't see why these donney on the brackers!"

"What?" John asked, looking at her askance.

She sighed and slowly articulated, as though speaking to a half-wit, "I don't see why these donney on the brackers!"

"Ellen, I don't have the faintest idea what you are talking about." A sinister warning bell clanged in his subconscious.

But she laughed and wagged her head like a dog shaking dry after a bath. "Well, I don't either, John." She started giggling. It was a contagious, bubbling laughter, and John had to laugh with her. They laughed till they were holding their bellies and wiping away tears. Then abruptly Ellen's face contorted, and her guffaws became sobs—maniacal, bellowing sobs. Within seconds, she was hysterical and inconsolable. Alarmed, John tried to put his arms around her, but she shoved him away with a strength that surprised him.

When she finally quit thrashing, she hunched on the sofa hugging her knees to her chin, rocking back and forth, weeping uncontrollably.

John felt like a spineless coward, but he could not stay in the room with her another minute. He backed away, grabbed his jacket off the hook in the front hall and fled into the chilly night.

The street was dark and a light mist dampened the pavement so the streetlights were multiplied in the reflection. He jogged briskly for a few minutes. Then, out of breath, he slowed to a walk.

The streets were deserted, but he was painfully aware of the lights that burned in the windows of the stately two-story homes lining either side of the street. Here and there he could hear music floating from an open door. And through curtains, not yet closed to the evening darkness, he saw life going on as usual for those within. Businessmen read newspapers in their easy chairs; children argued over games; mothers rocked their babies. Their world—his and Ellen's—was falling in upon them, yet all around them life went on.

Despair crept over him like a vine. What would become of them? Communication had always been the foundation of their marriage. He and Ellen had taken immense joy in discussing people, politics, philosophy, psychology. And if an exchange turned into a debate or even an argument, so much the better. They had never been happier than when they wrangled over some controversial topic. It had become a high for them, an energizer. With their words, they played an exhilarating game of catch—tossing ideas and waiting with anticipation for them to be thrown back. Now he threw words against a hard wall, and if they came back to him at all, they came back senseless and unpredictable.

There were so many things he and Ellen could have gone without—their wealth, their sight, their arms or legs. *Why?* John railed. Why did it have to be their words? And it was *their* words, for Ellen's silences left him as impotent of speech as if he physically shared her disease.

The rage simmering in him boiled over. He shook his fist at the heavens, and through clenched teeth he shouted into the darkness, not caring who heard. "Why, God? Tell me *why!*" But the heavens were like a canyon. His voice echoed back to him through the empty street—the only answer the gentle sound of rain on the pavement.

He sat down on the curb, utterly exhausted. The rain soaked into his jeans, leaving him shivering and damp. Hopelessness seeped into every fiber of his being, and for the first time since little Catherine had died, he put his head in his hands and sobbed.

He wept till there were no tears left. Finally, he picked himself up leadenly and walked slowly back to the house. The lights were off downstairs, but the lamp in their attic bedroom still burned.

When John came up the stairs, he saw Ellen through the bedroom door. She was sitting up in bed reading—or pretending to read. John wasn't sure she could even make sense of the printed page anymore. He came quietly into the room. He looked at her and shrugged, having no idea what he could say to her that would make things right.

She started to cry. "Oh, John. Please. Please don't look at me that way. I don't want to be this way…can't you see? I want what we had before. I want my…my life back. I want…I want…oh, I don't even know what to say…how to say it. I don't even know…" She gave him a look of sorrowful apology. "I'm losing my mind, John. I feel like I'm losing my mind." She grabbed her head and started rocking.

The resignation in her voice, in her posture, broke his heart. He went to her and sat down beside her on the bed. He wrapped his arms around her and pulled her into his embrace, leaning back against the headboard, cradling her in his arms.

They lay that way for a long while, until gently, wordlessly, John got up from the bed. He kissed her cheek and pulled the covers around her, tucking her in like a small child.

Then he went into the bathroom to perform his nightly ritual of brushing his teeth and washing his face.

Chapter Ten

"No, John! Please. I'm begging you. I don't want them to worry about me!" Ellen's voice rose an octave and she kneaded the linen placemat underneath her dinner plate.

"They're already worried, Ellen. I'm sorry. But I don't think we should put this off one more day. It's time the kids were told what's going on." John had agreed to hold off as long as they could, but in the months since Ellen had been diagnosed, her children had become all too aware that something was wrong, and had been for a long time.

She looked up at John, her eyes pleading. "I don't want to spend the time I have left with them watching me…waiting for me to do something stupid—just waiting for me to go crazy."

"You think it's better for them to wonder why you're…behaving the way you are? I'm sorry, but that's not fair. Not to them or to you."

"Or to *you,* you mean." Now anger tinged her voice.

He wasn't sure how to field that one. Yes, he wanted to get things out in the open and get it over with. And maybe it was for his own sake. It had been agony trying to keep up appearances for the kids, being careful not to slip up and say something that would give away Ellen's secret—*their* secret.

"Please, John, just let me wait until they're all home for Christmas. We…we can tell them then—after the holidays are over. But let me have one last *normal* Thanksgiving and Christmas. Please…"

He'd finally relented, but Thanksgiving was anything but normal. Ellen had been withdrawn and irritable from the moment the kids stepped through the front door. After a subdued dinner, Mark and Jana left early in the evening and the boys had decided to drive back to school Saturday morning, claiming they had papers to write before Monday morning. Worst of all, Ellen seemed not to mind—or realize—that she'd chased everyone off.

The following week, Dr. Morton started Ellen on a new medication, and by mid-December John thought maybe it was doing some good. But then the boys came home for Christmas and Ellen sank into a depression, taking to her bed most of the time, and she was distant and short-tempered with everyone when she was awake.

John made a wide berth for her, keeping Brant and Kyle occupied decorating for Christmas. It was a Brighton tradition, since they'd moved into the big Miles house, to outline the roof, doors and windows with white lights. He'd waited until the boys were home to help him; he certainly didn't want Ellen on the roof. Now, perched precariously on the roof with his sons feeding him strings of lights, John was grateful for the warmer-than-usual December weather and the absence of ice or snow.

It was late in the season to be putting up lights, but he couldn't bear to not put them up at all. When the lights were all in place, the Brighton men put the tree up in the living room and hung five stockings on the mantel. Ellen was up, though still in her bathrobe. She shouted suggestions from the kitchen but left the decorating to them.

The rest of the days leading to Christmas were spent playing basketball at the high school gym and watching football on TV.

Jana and Mark came from Chicago two days before Christmas. They hadn't been there an hour before Jana cornered John in the kitchen.

She looked around at the empty countertops. "Dad? Mom hasn't done any baking yet? I was going to help, but I checked the cupboards and there's not even enough flour or sugar to make cookies, let alone all the other stuff for Christmas dinner."

He looked at the floor. "Your mom has…she's been a little under the weather lately." It was true, but he felt like a liar. "We'll go shopping this afternoon."

She eyed him suspiciously. "Okay. Well, let me know what I can do."

"Thanks, honey."

He escaped to the den to try to make a grocery list. He wrote down flour and sugar, then realized that he hadn't a clue what else they would need for the dinner. He prayed Ellen would be coherent enough to fill in the blanks while they were at the store.

She came along with him agreeably and was actually pleasant company, though not very helpful. He bought cranberries for his favorite sauce…a dish Ellen had made for him every year of their married life. He doubted now that she could remember how to make it. Oh, well. Howard and MaryEllen were arriving on Christmas Eve. Maybe MaryEllen could be persuaded to prepare the sauce. It didn't matter anymore, really.

They finished their shopping, and drove home. John carried the groceries into the kitchen, setting the heavy bags on the countertop. Ellen made no move to put things away, so John enlisted Mark and Jana to do the job while he hunted for the recipes and assembled the ingredients for the dishes that needed to be started early.

Jana tried to catch his eye several times, but he avoided her and pretended not to see her questioning glances. It was so out of character for him to be supervising the kitchen. He knew Jana must be terribly confused and worried.

"Are you feeling okay, Mom?" Jana put a hand on her mother's arm.

"I'm fine."

"Are you sure? You look tired."

"I'm just fine."

It was obvious that Ellen's terse reply only served to worry Jana more.

For the rest of the afternoon Ellen hovered in the kitchen, but she seemed content to let Jana and John do most of the cooking and cleaning. She was cranky and short with both of them. John could see that Jana's feelings were hurt.

His daughter disappeared, and twenty minutes later, he discovered her in tears in the downstairs bedroom that had been hers as a teenager. Looking at Jana's tearstained face, John decided they couldn't wait another minute to get things out in the open.

He put an arm around Jana's shoulders. "We need to talk. I'm going to go talk to your mom. Get Mark and your brothers and meet us in the living room in a few minutes."

She looked up at him, confusion deepening the furrows in her forehead, but she slid off the bed and left the room.

John went to find Ellen. She was in the kitchen, standing in front of the open cupboard doors with a blank look on her face. "We need to talk to the kids, Ellen. Now."

She whirled to face him. "No! No, John. You promised. Not until after. I don't want to ruin everybody's Christmas," she snarled between clenched teeth.

"El, everybody's Christmas is already being ruined by the way you are acting. You're just putting off the inevitable. Either you tell them or I will." He knew it was cruel, but it was the truth, and she needed to hear it.

Uncharacteristically she sulked. But finally she acquiesced, and John led her out to the living room where they were waiting.

Ellen sat beside him on the sofa, silent and sheepish.

John took her hand and drew a deep breath. "I know you

kids are aware that something has been going on here for a while that we haven't let you in on. I'm sorry for the worry it has caused you, but we…Mom…didn't want to worry you any sooner than we had to. We're not ready to tell this to anyone else, but…well, it's time you know the truth. We'll tell Grandma and Grandpa tomorrow."

The stark fear on their faces made him wish he had never opened his mouth. He despised having to tell his precious children this news! At this moment he suddenly understood more clearly the reservations Ellen had about revealing her illness. He paused and sighed heavily, gathering his courage. "We found out a few months ago that the doctors think Mom has Alzheimer's disease. You've heard of that?"

Kyle was hesitant. "Alzheimer's? I thought…I thought that was like being senile…like old people get. I think that's what Travis Manderlee's grandma has. But she's wacko." He circled a finger beside his ear, the universal sign for crazy.

"Well, Alzheimer's is sort of like senility, Kyle. Except you don't necessarily have to be old to get it."

"Mom's not crazy!"

"No, of course not." John went on to explain everything they'd learned over the past months. It was a tearful meeting, and John knew from his own experience that it would take a while for the import of what he'd told the kids to soak in. He and Ellen were just beginning to accept what was happening to them, and they'd had months to get used to the idea.

It turned out to be a week of special closeness for the family. John and Ellen together told her parents the next day, and while Howard and MaryEllen were stunned, they had known something was wrong. They put up a strong front for Ellen's sake, and she seemed comforted by their presence and relieved to have the burden of secrecy lifted.

The kids were refreshingly open and candid about everything. Jana went straight to the library and checked out a stack of books on Alzheimer's. She brought them home and plopped them ceremoniously in the middle of the dining room table. All evening long, she and the boys pored over them, reading paragraphs aloud and grilling their parents about the symptoms Ellen had experienced so far. Brant searched the Internet and found more up-to-date information.

The three of them were like detectives hot on the trail of solving a mystery. Somehow, they were even able to find humor in the sorrow.

"Maybe you should just dye your hair blond, Mom," Brant teased. "Then you'd have a built-in excuse to act ditzy."

"Hey, buddy, you might just be on to something there." Ellen affected a goofy grin.

They all laughed, and the laughter was a profound comfort, but John knew they each had their moments of private anguish.

Kyle, especially, seemed to be somewhat in denial. He would read about a particular symptom and say, "You've never done that, Mom. Maybe the doctors are wrong. All these books say they really can't know for sure if it's Alzheimer's. Maybe they're wrong about you!"

"Honey, I think I *have* done that. Ask Dad."

John would confirm it, and Kyle would go to the books again, looking for nonexistent proof that this was all a horrible mistake.

John wished he could muster the hope and optimism his son seemed to have. And he wanted to weep for the inevitable day when Kyle's hope would be destroyed.

Chapter Eleven

Ellen sat at the kitchen table across from Kyle and saw the pain that darkened her youngest son's eyes. She longed to see a glimpse of the carefree, mischievous boy who had brightened this house only a few months ago. But the boy was becoming a man. Ellen's heart ached for him. *Oh, this boy…this boy of mine. He's trying so hard. Why do I have to hurt him like this? Why? My little boy. Sometimes I can't even remember his name. But I know he's mine… and he's trying so hard…so hard.* The thoughts roiled disjointedly in her mind, as all her thoughts seemed to do now.

As if no time had passed, suddenly the Christmas vacation was almost over. Ellen tried to replay the holiday events in her mind and found her memories void.

The day before the boys were to go back to school, Ellen looked out the living room window onto the wide driveway. Kyle was on the concrete, wearing only shorts and a sweatshirt in spite of the cold. He stood under the basketball hoop that John had erected when the boys were just learning to play. He was smashing the ball into the net, hooking the rebound and smashing it up again with all his strength. From his reddened face and clenched jaw, Ellen knew he was furious. She started out the door and then thought better of it. Best to let him get it out of his system. Maybe this was his way of working out his anger.

And sure enough, Kyle came in an hour later with a new peacefulness about him. He was so sweet with Ellen that it made her heart ache. But it was also a healing balm for her spirit.

When the boys pulled out of the driveway in Brant's car on Sunday night, she lifted a hand in farewell. They all knew now. And they still loved her. They were still a family. She could quit hiding this terrible secret.

She realized and accepted that nothing had really changed: she was no less forgetful, her thoughts no less chaotic, her actions no less awkward. But her children's love had transformed her. Tranquility laved over her and a renewed sense of self-worth buoyed her spirit.

Winter dragged on and the stark outline of the leafless trees on Oaklawn seemed to reflect John's mood.

But one Saturday in February, the sun shone all day and the temperature reached a record-setting sixty-seven degrees. John felt his spirits rise with the mercury, especially when Ellen suggested on the spur of the moment that they invite her closest friend, Sandra, to have dinner with them.

"I've been wanting to try a new recipe I saw," she told John.

"Why don't we just put something on the grill," he offered, knowing that Ellen would most likely not be up to cooking when the time came to actually do so. She'd always tended to bite off more than she could chew, and her illness had only intensified that trait.

Ellen and Sandra had been friends since they'd taught together during Ellen's first year at Calypso Elementary. Sandra Brenner's husband had left her after six years of marriage, leaving her with two small daughters to raise. Her girls were grown and married now. One a lawyer and the other a nurse, they were a walking testimony to the sacrifices their mother had made for them. Sandra had made the best of a difficult situation and John had always admired the courage and tenacity that were so incongruous to her petite, pixielike appearance. She was frank, and she could be brash, but those qualities had served her well. John couldn't help liking her.

He was turning burgers on the grill in the backyard when Sandra came out on the deck. John could see Ellen through the kitchen windows chopping vegetables for a salad.

Sandra didn't mince words. "John, what is going on with Ellen?"

He hesitated. "What do you mean?"

"Hey, if it's none of my business, just say so, but don't try to act like everything is hunky-dory when we both know it's not."

John looked through the window. Ellen was still at the counter, oblivious to their conversation. He let out his breath.

"Sandra, Ellen...she's not ready to talk about it. It would be better for everybody if she *would* talk to you." He paused, trying to decide how to phrase his comments in a way that didn't betray Ellen. "Listen, I know you have a pretty good idea what's going on, but it's not my place to break this news. The details will have to come from Ellen. Have you asked her about it?"

"I've hinted. She's not taking the bait."

He gave her a sheepish smile. "It's not like you to just hint around...."

She glared at him.

"I don't know what to say, Sandra. But..." He blew out his breath in a torrent of frustration. "I think if you confront her with your suspicions, she might be willing to talk to you."

"Yeah, if she can remember who I am." Her tone was caustic, sarcastic, but her voice trailed off when she heard the door slam and saw Ellen come onto the deck.

"Are the...the...hamburgers...almost done, John? Everything's ready in the kitchen." Ellen was in a cheerful mood, oblivious to the exchange she'd interrupted.

John shrugged behind Ellen's back, giving Sandra a "what can I say" look. He followed the women into the kitchen.

Dinner was a disaster. The first forkful nearly choked John. Ellen had salted and peppered the salad until it was inedible. He pushed it aside without comment, feeling guilty for not warning Sandra before she took a bite.

But she was saved from the salad when Ellen knocked her can of Coke over, sending a stream of the dark, fizzing liquid onto the floor. This type of thing was happening more and more frequently. The doctors had told them that Ellen would eventually lose her muscle coordination, but John thought this was more a matter of forgetting where she had set things. Usually he just cleaned things up, and they tried to pretend it hadn't happened. In front of Sandra, the humiliation seemed magnified out of proportion. Ellen burst into tears and ran from the room.

John wiped at the sticky puddle under the table with a kitchen towel and motioned for Sandra to go to Ellen.

He cleaned up the mess, then followed the women's voices down the hall to the bathroom. He stood outside the door and watched helplessly as Sandra ministered to his wife.

Ellen was huddled on the tile floor of the bathroom. She clumsily blotted at a dark stain on her blouse with the damp washcloth clutched in one fist.

Sandra glanced up at John before kneeling down beside Ellen on the cold tile.

He nodded his tacit permission and stepped back.

Sandra put her arm around Ellen. "What is it, Ellen? Please tell me."

Oblivious to John, Ellen looked up into her friend's eyes, her face a mask of despair. "I can't even feed myself anymore, Sandra. I'm a pathetic mess."

"Ellen, what's wrong? What is it?" Sandra repeated. "You can tell me."

"It's…I have Alzheimer's," she choked. "Oh, Sandra, I have Alzheimer's disease. I'm going crazy!" It was almost a scream.

As Sandra comprehended the truth of Ellen's words—a truth John guessed she'd suspected all along—her face contorted and the tears came. Sandra wrapped her friend in a hug. "Oh, Ellen…"

Ellen's voice rose hysterically, and her words came out in agonized sobs. "Oh, Sandra, how can John stand me like this? How long can he put up with this? I need him, Sandra. I need him. I love him."

John's heart lurched. He started to go to her, comfort her, but then she lashed out, turning her diatribe heavenward.

She shook her fists and raged, "God! Help me. I need help. God? Don't do this to me. Where are You? Where? Where?"

Sandra waved John away. "Let me talk to her," she mouthed.

He tiptoed down the hall to the den. But he left the door open, listening as his wife sobbed out her anguish.

After a while, their voices turned to an indistinguishable murmur, and when Ellen had seemingly been drained of every word, the two women appeared in the doorway of the den.

"Sandra knows everything, John. I told her everything."

"Good," he said, offering a weak smile. "You needed to tell someone."

Ellen and Sandra went on down the hallway, chatting and giggling as though their little gab session had healed Ellen.

But John sat behind his desk for an hour, pondering a future he dared not imagine. It was a relief to have someone else to share this horrible burden of knowledge. Now that the kids knew, and especially now that Ellen had confided her fears in Sandra, some of the pressure was off him. He was guiltily grateful.

But there was worse to come.

Chapter Twelve

Shortly after ten o'clock one night, the phone rang. John was in the den watching the news. Ellen had gone to bed half an hour before, claiming exhaustion. He grabbed the remote and turned down the volume, then picked up the cordless phone with his other hand. He punched Talk, hoping the extension in their room hadn't awakened Ellen.

"John?"

"Yes?"

"John, hi. This is Carolyn Linmeyer. Is Ellen there?"

Carolyn was the principal at Calypso Elementary.

"Well, yes, but she's gone to bed. I can wake her if you need to talk to her."

Carolyn cleared her throat, sounding decidedly nervous. "No, no... Actually, it's you I need to talk to. I just...well, I wanted to make sure Ellen wasn't standing right there."

John's palms went clammy, and he felt the adrenaline begin to flow. He could have written the script for Carolyn's next words. They chilled him just the same.

"John, this is really difficult for me. I'm not sure how to put this, but...Ellen has been having some real problems at school." There was a long pause on Carolyn's end.

John forced the recliner into its upright position and pushed himself to his feet. The silence dragged between them as he paced the length of the room. He felt cruel for putting the burden on Carolyn, but he was at a loss how to respond. Finally, he managed to form a sentence. "What kind of problems, Carolyn?"

"Well, frankly, I'm worried about Ellen. She seems like she's under a lot of pressure lately. I don't know how to describe it, but she just isn't herself. Not at all. I don't want to alarm you, but…she's done some really…well, *strange* things the last few weeks. I know this will sound crazy, but she's even gotten lost in the hallways at school—more than once. She forgets to send her class down to lunch…."

John stopped pacing. He shook his head against the receiver and closed his eyes.

Carolyn's voice droned on. "Yesterday in a staff meeting she just blanked out when I asked her a question. It was like she didn't even hear me. She just sat there and stared at me, even after I repeated the question. It was very uncomfortable, very odd. Some of the other teachers questioned me about it later. I'm not sure Ellen was even aware of what happened."

Carolyn's voice picked up steam as she recited a litany of Ellen's violations. She finally caught her breath and her voice turned contrite. "I hope I'm not out of line, John, but we're all very concerned about her. And it seems to be getting worse. I—I just felt like you needed to know."

John slumped back into his chair, struggling with what to say next. He had put Carolyn in an awful predicament. He was her boss, and she had been forced to tell him that his wife was incompetent. He and Ellen had agreed they would not tell anyone else about her diagnosis until it was absolutely necessary. It seemed that time had come.

Feeling like a traitor, he took a deep breath and plunged in. "Carolyn, I'm sorry this has put you in such an uncomfortable position. I'd like this to stay completely confidential until Ellen and I can discuss it, but I feel you deserve to know what's going on here." He paused, trying to decide where to begin. "Do you remember last March when Ellen took those three days of leave?"

"Yes." Curiosity and concern were mixed in her voice.

"Well, Ellen had been having some problems with her memory, some problems sleeping…some other symptoms. Our doctor sent her to a specialist. She went through some extensive testing. She was in the hospital those three days…and what they came up with… Well, they think Ellen has Alzheimer's disease."

"Oh, John! Oh no. I can't believe it. I am so sorry. But…she's so young!"

"I know. It usually doesn't strike people Ellen's age, but nevertheless, that's what they think we're dealing with. I know we should have told you sooner, Carolyn. It wasn't right to make you deal with this. Things have been bad enough here at home. It was foolish of me to think they'd be any better at school. I…I guess I haven't wanted to admit just how serious this is getting. I'm so sorry, Carolyn. I'm sorry this has fallen on you. But… well, Ellen didn't want to tell people yet. We're…we're struggling to keep things as normal as possible."

"Oh, I understand. Oh, John, I can't tell you how sorry I am. This is just terrible."

"It has been pretty devastating."

At that moment, he made a decision. He moved to his desk on the other side of the room and pulled out the chair. It seemed so strange for him to be making plans that would alter Ellen's life forever, without even discussing it with her. But he knew what he had to do.

He raked a hand through his hair. "This is going to be very difficult for Ellen, but I think it would be best for everyone concerned if we get a substitute for her the rest of the week and—" His voice caught and he faked a cough to hide his rising emotion. "I think we should start looking for a replacement immediately. I could never forgive myself if…well, if anything happened."

Carolyn started to protest, but John spared her the half-hearted attempts. It was obvious there were no other options.

"We need to be very sensitive how we present this to Ellen's class. It won't be easy to explain to second graders. I'll trust you to handle that, Carolyn. If you have any questions, don't hesitate to call me. Maybe we can buy some time with a substitute and wait until next week to tell everyone. That'll give me a chance to break the news gently to Ellen."

"Oh, John, I can't imagine what you must be going through. Both of you."

"I appreciate your concern, Carolyn. I know it wasn't easy for you to call me. I shouldn't have let it go so long."

"I don't know what to say…I think I'm still in shock. But please, please know that we'll be praying for you both. And the kids, too."

"Thank you, Carolyn." He was touched and his voice broke. "That means a lot."

John laid the phone down and sat at the desk, unmoving. From the other end of the room, the sound of the TV sportscaster droned on and on, the volume barely audible.

How could he have let this go on? He had put Ellen's coworkers in a thorny position. He had forced Carolyn to make this difficult phone call, had possibly even put children in danger.

Was he blind? Couldn't he see that Ellen was long past the stage of being able to do her job safely? He would never have forgiven himself if he'd allowed a tragedy to happen because of his misjudgment. He had put his own job in jeopardy with his foolish— Was it denial? Is this what denial was like? He'd been so blind!

Finally he got up, switched off the TV and climbed the stairs to their attic bedroom. His feet were like lead, and his bones felt a hundred years old. He tried to pray. He knew he needed strength he didn't possess, but his lips could form only one word—*please.*

Ellen lay curled up in bed, clutching the blankets under her chin. Even in sleep her fists were clenched, and her face wore an expression that was almost a grimace. There was no peace

for her, even in her dreams. John watched her chest rise and
fall under the layers of quilts. He wished he could crawl into
bed beside her and never wake up.

Ellen cried the next morning when John told her about
Carolyn's phone call. He sat on the bed beside her, caressing
her face, as if his warm touch could soften the blow of his
words. She saw in his eyes that it killed him to have to reveal
the humiliating things that were being said about her at
school.

But in a moment of clarity, she also realized that she would
never have accepted his gentle ultimatum—that she simply
could not teach any longer—if he had not given her the stark
truth. She had always been strong and self-assured. She
wasn't used to having John make decisions for her. A year
ago she would have argued with him—perhaps even defied
him and gone to work anyway. But now she could only weep.

How many more things would be taken away from her before this was all over? She was just beginning to grasp the
reality that her future had been stolen from her. And now her
present had been taken as well.

With mournful reluctance, she was letting go of her
dreams of watching her children grow and marry, of enjoying the grandchildren they would have given her. She had said
goodbye to the dreams she and John shared of traveling together.

Now she needed to tell John goodbye, as well. The single
redeeming thing she had discovered in the chasm of this disease was that she had been given an opportunity that most
deaths did not allow. She had been given a chance to say goodbye, to voice all the things that death too often left unsaid. As
she felt herself gripped ever tightly by the claws of dementia,
she began to feel panicked that she might let that opportunity
slip away, that she would be swallowed by the abyss before
she had declared her love for John—her precious John.

Somehow, today, seeing him so vulnerable and broken

as he gave her the news about Carolyn's call, Ellen knew it was time.

She dried her tears on the sleeve of her nightgown and sat up in bed, reaching for John. He put his arms around her and pulled her to himself. She burrowed into his chest.

In words that she realized were neither eloquent nor precise, she tried to make him understand her sorrow for what they were losing, and the deep love she'd always felt for him.

"John…John. Oh, how I've loved you. I…I'm so sorry for this. I'm so sorry to…to…" In her mind, the word *disappoint* was sharp and clear, but she could not get it to move from her brain and form on her lips. She felt the frustration begin to rise, but she forced it back and pushed on.

"You've been so good, John. So good to me…to the kids. I…I can't believe this is happening to us…I can't…" The tears overtook her again.

John stroked her cheek and tried to quiet her with gentle murmurs of "Shh. Shh. Shh."

"No, John. No! Don't hush me. I want to tell you. I want to love you. I want…I want…" The familiar fog of confusion began to creep up on her, and desperately she struggled to finish her thought. "Please, John. Don't forget me. Don't let the kids forget me. Please, John, will you tell my grandchildren about me…tell them how much I would have loved them."

John squeezed her so tightly she winced in pain. Yet the pain gave comfort somehow.

His voice in her ear was gravelly with emotion. "Ellen, how could I ever forget you? You're the love of my life. Don't you know that, honey? I could never forget you," he whispered.

"I do know it. I do." The fog grew thicker, and Ellen let it overtake her. She knew she had made him understand, and now she rested in the shelter of his arms.

John

Chapter Thirteen

Their secret was out. The first time John went to a basketball game after Ellen quit teaching, he discovered that the whole town of Calypso seemed to have heard the news. "Ellen Brighton has Alzheimer's." It screamed like a newspaper headline.

As he and his friend Alexander Billman, the high school principal, made their way into the gymnasium, John was stopped by two teachers collecting admission fees at the entrance.

"I'm so sorry to hear about Ellen, Mr. Brighton." Jody Denton's eyes reminded John of the scrawny puppy the boys had brought home a few years back.

He hadn't let them keep the dog, and Ellen had made him feel guilty for it. Now he squirmed under Jody's sad gaze, feeling an emotion akin to that old guilt. Maybe they didn't think he should be here in light of Ellen's situation.

Beside Jody, Marsha Sprague added her condolences with those same droopy puppy-dog eyes.

He wanted to tell them that Ellen was home, happily working on a scrapbook when he'd left the house, and seeming more normal than she had in days. A startling thought pricked his conscience: maybe he *should* have stayed home. Who knew how many more nights he and Ellen would have when she was "herself."

He mumbled a thank-you and picked up a program. Alexander was waiting for him at the bottom of the bleachers. He gave his friend an embarrassed shrug, and followed him up the bleachers two steps at a time. But even though he tried to avoid eye contact, as he made his way up the bleachers, he was greeted with half a dozen more offers of sympathy.

"You've been in our prayers, John."

"Sure sorry to hear the news. Hang in there, buddy."

"We're thinking about you."

He merely nodded his acknowledgment. He did appreciate their concern and sympathy, but it was as though people already considered Ellen dead. He hated it.

Finally he extricated himself from the murmurs of sympathy and made his way down the row where Alexander was saving him a seat.

While the crowd around him cheered the double-overtime game, John watched the action in silence. He rose with the crowd, taking his cues from Alexander, but when the buzzer sounded, he couldn't have told anyone the final score.

"Everything okay, man?" Alexander asked, as they walked to the parking lot afterward.

"I'm fine."

Alexander clapped a hand on John's shoulder, then quickly removed it. "If you want to talk, you know I'm here."

Alexander had lost his wife to cancer five years earlier. John knew his friend understood what he was going through better than most.

He forced a note of cheer into his voice. "Thanks, Alex, but I'm okay."

Maybe someday he'd feel like talking about it, but tonight his thoughts were too raw to be expressed.

The following week, John brought Ellen to a basketball game with him. Now, strangely, he caught people turning away, avoiding his eyes and whispering behind their hands as he and Ellen passed.

From then on it seemed that if people couldn't avoid running into the Brightons altogether, they would stumble through uncomfortable, halting conversations aimed at John, and all but ignoring Ellen.

"I feel like a leper," she told John one night after they'd been obviously shunned by some acquaintances at a restaurant.

He understood. He was leprous by association. At the office, a tangible hush descended on any room he entered. He didn't miss the sorrowful whispers that followed him down the hall or the street downtown.

The doctors had said to keep things as normal as possible for Ellen. They hadn't mentioned that this would be impossible to do once everyone knew her plight.

Sandra was a godsend. She offered Ellen sincere sympathy, then proceeded to cheer her up with her offbeat sense of humor. Ellen's friend somehow made it okay to joke about the crazy things Ellen did, to talk when she needed to—on the days she was able to articulate her thoughts—and to be silent without discomfort when words were too difficult.

John found himself looking forward to the evenings when Sandra visited. It was good to converse with someone who could give him a simple answer without a struggle. She became a buffer between John and Ellen, defusing the frustration they felt in trying to communicate with each other.

And Sandra could always make him laugh. He liked the way she made him feel. There was precious little laughter in his house these days.

John sat at the kitchen table dressed for work in a suit and tie. The sun had awakened him earlier than usual, so he was enjoying a rare second cup of coffee with the morning newspaper. The sun was rising earlier each day and spring was making itself evident with a myriad of signs. The forsythia bush outside the kitchen window burgeoned with fat ocher buds. If the temperature rose into the sixties as the forecast predicted, the bush would be a riot of yellow by the time he got home from work.

He was struck by the irony of it all. Such incongruity. The earth was bursting with new life, while Ellen was fading away. The days became longer as her memory grew shorter. New birth exploded in the world all around him, but in his home, life slowly decayed.

He had spent every day of the past three months regretting they had ever told anyone that Ellen had Alzheimer's. It seemed that the day they admitted the truth, she had begun a helpless slide down the cliff of insanity.

He knew his thoughts were irrational, but he felt sure that had they kept their secret, somehow it would not have become the grisly reality it now was.

In a strange reverse of nature, Ellen became more child-like as each day passed. She was temperamental and impatient—the total opposite of her true personality. It was like living with a stranger. A stranger he didn't particularly like.

Ellen wandered about the house with no direction and seemingly no goal. John brought her books from the library, but after reading only two or three pages, she lost interest.

She developed a strange habit of hoarding things, hiding small objects throughout the house. She packed tea bags, still in their paper wrappers, into her jewelry box. She took pens and pencils from the desk by the phone and tucked them under the cushions on the sofa.

If John caught her in the act of squirreling away some mundane treasure, it angered her. So now when he came upon her secret caches, he put the contents away without comment. Two calculators were still missing from a desk drawer, and yesterday his favorite tie tacks and his wedding band had disappeared from the valet on his dresser. His wedding ring was loose, and he wore it only occasionally. They had never replaced the inexpensive bands they'd exchanged at their wedding, so the ring was valuable only in sentiment, but he hoped she hadn't hidden it too well.

With John's prodding, Ellen managed to keep the laundry done and the house fairly tidy. For the first time in the busy years since she'd become a teacher, she seemed to take pleasure in these familiar, methodical tasks. But John did most of the cooking. Ellen had ruined many meals before they'd decided the kitchen was best left to him.

Besides, he was afraid for her to use the stove. Just yesterday she'd left a pot of soup simmering on the stovetop until it boiled almost dry. He had smelled it the minute he stepped into the house. Ellen was in the next room, sorting through some collection of worthless treasures.

"Ellen? There's something burning. You left a pan on the stove!"

She looked calmly up at him as if he'd just commented on the weather. "Oh. I did?"

"Yes. Didn't you smell it?"

She sniffed the air. "No. I don't smell anything."

"Well, it's there. Come and look. You could have burned the house down."

"Well, I didn't mean to," she huffed. "You don't have to get so angry."

He just shook his head and went to clean up the mess.

So now he had taken over the kitchen, too. It was a difficult adjustment for both of them. Ellen had always loved to cook, and John, though he'd become comfortable in the kitchen, had plenty of things he'd rather do. Sometimes he felt like he was caring for a toddler.

John hired a woman to come in once a week and do the heavy cleaning, but he made every effort to involve Ellen in the everyday household tasks. She rode with him to the grocery store, and he asked her for suggestions when they planned menus and made shopping lists. In truth, it would have been infinitely easier to do it by himself, but he remembered the doctor's exhortation that he allow her to do as much as she could for herself for as long as possible.

The doctor had said John should be grateful Ellen was still able to care for her physical needs, but it seemed to him that she had regressed at an alarming rate. Her memory seemed to fade daily—especially her recall of things they had done or discussed just moments before.

Brant called one night and talked to his mother for half an hour. Twenty minutes later Ellen turned to John and wondered aloud, "We haven't heard from any of the kids in ages. Why don't they ever call anymore?"

She grew apathetic and listless, sleeping late and retiring early. The *joie de vivre* that had been so much a part of her personality was discernible only in rare, fleeting glimpses. John tried to keep their life busy and stimulating, but Ellen seemed content to sit at home night after night. She'd had some embarrassing moments of forgetfulness and clumsiness in public, and though she denied it, John felt certain part of her reluctance to be with their friends—or in any public setting—was fear of further humiliation.

She went through periods of deep depression when she seemed barely able to pull herself out of bed in the morning. John tried to get her to talk about her feelings, to get her pent-up anger and fears out in the open, but the frustration of trying to voice her feelings only made matters worse.

He prayed with her—for healing sometimes, but more often for patience and peace. And for *time*.

Though she never said so, John sensed that Ellen was angry with God. He didn't blame her. If he were honest with himself, his faith had been shaken, too. Not that he'd doubted God's existence for a minute. Even before he'd given his life to the Lord, John had always believed in the concept of God. He'd never understood how man could see nature—the beauty of the landscape, the perfection of the workings of the human body, the amazing cycle of life—and not believe in God on some level. But now, in some ways, it would have been easier if he had lost all faith. It hurt to think that the God he loved had deserted him. Had betrayed Ellen. The thought startled him and, for some reason, brought Oscar and Hattie to his mind. How he longed to have the dear couple to talk to now. They would have offered comfort from the Scriptures, and wise words of counsel. Maybe they could have made some sense of it all for him.

But they were gone and he was left alone.

Chapter Fourteen

On the morning of the two-year anniversary of Ellen's diagnosis, the telephone rang while John and Ellen were sitting at breakfast. Ellen nearly jumped out of her skin. "What?" Her gaze darted wildly around the room. "What in the world... what *is* that?"

John saw genuine fear in her eyes. At first he didn't know what she meant. When the phone rang again she pointed urgently into the air, vaguely in the direction of the ringing. "That! That! Did you hear it?"

"The phone, you mean?"

"What is that?"

"The phone? Ellen! The telephone...you know, you talk to people on it." He was incredulous that she could not know something so basic. But when he realized the stunning truth—that she truly didn't remember what a telephone was—he patiently took her to it and explained to her how it worked.

By this time, the caller had given up and the bell was silent. But John was so upset he couldn't have spoken to anyone anyway.

Though Ellen couldn't identify a common everyday object, she seemed to sense how disturbed John was. She wrung her hands and paced the floor, a habit that had become far too frequent.

John insisted they go to worship services each Sunday morning as they had for all of their married years. Though Ellen seemed as apathetic about church as she was about everything else, she usually didn't argue when John reminded her that it was time to dress for church services. Their closest friends were there—Rob and Cathy McLaughlin, and Alexander. Even Sandra had started attending sometimes. John drew strength and comfort from the encouragement they offered. It was one of the few places he felt Ellen was accepted and treated as though she were still an adult…still human.

Often, after church, their friends would stop by the pew in the back row where the Brightons sat, offering their greetings and concern. Ellen rarely responded with more than a nod or a wan smile, and John suspected it was because these people had become strangers to her. He rarely saw recognition in her eyes anymore for anyone other than close family members.

Sandra was the exception. Ellen always knew her and was happy to see her. And while she was no more vocal with Sandra than with John, she seemed to feel comfortable in Sandra's presence. Sandra tried to keep conversation a part of their relationship, but when Ellen clammed up, or when her speech made no sense, Sandra would turn on the TV while the three of them sat companionably together.

Sometimes John and Sandra would talk quietly over Ellen's head. It helped him to have someone to talk to. He hadn't realized how important it had been to have Ellen listen to him rehash his day at work, or think aloud through his problems. Not just listen, but offer feedback. Help him see things from a different perspective. Now Sandra began to take on that role in a small way.

John was touched by the sacrifices Sandra made for both of them, and from her he learned much about relating to this new, silent Ellen.

Strangely, the jumbled words that had been such a glaring warning early in Ellen's illness manifested themselves less frequently now. John wondered if he had merely grown used to them, or if perhaps the mixed-up words abated simply because she was so silent now. Their fiery conversations and heated debates had virtually ended, and John missed them desperately. He made a conscious effort to describe his workdays to her in detail, to keep up his end of the conversation. But it was difficult when Ellen had become such a passive listener. And he feared that on the rare occasions when she was sane enough to understand him, it was too painful for her to hear news of the schools and teachers she'd once been so involved with. It seemed no matter how carefully he weighed his words, everything he said contained a blatant reminder of all Ellen had lost.

Her silence soon begot his.

Chapter Fifteen

Jana and Mark came to Calypso nearly every weekend after they found out about Ellen's illness. John was grateful for their company, and in the beginning Ellen seemed to enjoy having them there. But as she retreated further into silence, it became difficult for everyone. In one coherent moment, Ellen declared it was like a wake, only everyone was waiting for the corpse to die.

On the weekends John felt an obligation to entertain Mark and Jana, to cook for them and be the charming hostess that Ellen had once been. This did not come naturally to him, and he found himself becoming increasingly resentful—not of his daughter but, unreasonably, of his wife for failing him in this department.

He saw the strain it put on Mark and Jana's marriage, as well. They both worked long hours and their weekends were precious. Mark was a generous, caring man, but John could see that it was beginning to frustrate him to have to share his wife weekend after weekend. John heard them arguing one Saturday night when they thought he had already gone up to bed. Their overheard words cut him to the quick; yet he understood.

"I just want one day alone with you, Jana. Is that too much to ask?"

"This isn't fair and you know it, Mark. You're asking me to choose between you and my mother. I love you, but Mom needs me right now."

"I need you, too, Jana! Your mom doesn't even know you're here half the time." Mark's voice rose in anger.

John heard Jana start to cry. "That was cruel, Mark! How can you be so heartless?" She spat out her words in choking sobs.

John heard the back door slam and then Jana's muffled cries as she ran upstairs to the guest room.

The next morning John talked to Jana over coffee. "There's no reason for you guys to come next weekend," he said gruffly.

"But Dad, what will—"

"I need some time alone. And you guys probably do, too."

"Dad, really…we don't mind."

"I appreciate it, Jana, but I'm serious. You can come the weekend after that if you want to." He twirled a spoon in his coffee cup before meeting her eyes. "I think you need to spend some time with your husband."

Her cheeks flushed pink, and she furrowed her brow. "Did Mark say something to you?"

John shook his head. "No. I'm just putting myself in his place. And I heard you arguing," he admitted

"I'm sorry, Dad. Mark just doesn't understand. He—"

"Jana, I think you're the one who doesn't understand. You're asking a lot of your husband right now."

She arched a brow. "How can you say that, when Mom is so sick. She needs me. *You* need me."

He chucked her under the chin. "I appreciate your efforts, baby girl, but you know your mom. She would be madder than a wet hen if she thought you were neglecting your marriage for her sake."

Jana gave a sheepish grin. "Okay. But we'll stay close to home in case you need us. Just give us a call. We can be here in an hour."

"No. You guys go do something. Get away together. Get out of the house at least."

Jana argued halfheartedly, but John hushed her and closed the topic to discussion.

When Friday arrived and their car didn't pull into the driveway, John was surprised to find how much he missed them. The house was so quiet these days, and they'd filled it with pleasant noise again. But soon his loneliness was filled with a good book, an hour spent puttering in the garage and a leisurely walk through the neighborhood with Ellen.

Jana called John after supper, and though the topic was left unmentioned, the warmth in her voice let him know that everything was all right between them.

Ellen had not attempted to drive since the day she "lost" her car at the mall. It wasn't something they had discussed, but there was an unspoken agreement that she would not drive again. Like every little task, this too required a time of evaluation, a decision about what was safe, what was best for Ellen.

This loss of Ellen's independence was difficult for both of them. John knew Ellen felt she was burdening him, always having to be driven wherever she went. And yet neither of them was willing to risk the danger Ellen might be behind the wheel.

As long as they'd lived in this house, she'd walked to school when the weather permitted, relishing the exercise. She had continued to do so until she was forced to quit working. By then she had become withdrawn and antisocial, rarely going outside their home anyway, so John tried not to resent the times when he had to play chauffeur.

Late one spring afternoon when he was driving Ellen home from a dentist's appointment, she suddenly reached out and touched his arm. They were approaching the entrance to the Calypso Park, where they'd spent many an evening when the children were young.

"Oh, honey. Stop!" Ellen gestured animatedly. "Stop here. Let's stop here…at the…the…"

"The park?"

"Yes! The park. The park." She rolled the word around her tongue as though she were learning it for the first time.

John slowed the car and looked at Ellen. "You want to go to the park? Why?"

"I don't know. It just…it just…it sounds…fun. It's been a long time, hasn't it, honey? Or have we…have we…?" He knew she was unsure of even her memories now.

He was tired and had work to do at home, but she looked so hopeful he couldn't deny her. The park was inviting, with the trees wearing their new spring greens. He turned into the last entrance and parked the car near the playground. Without a word she got out of the car and walked toward the swings.

He followed, hurrying to catch up with her. By the time he reached the sandy area where the swings were, Ellen had seated herself in the farthest swing and was pumping her legs, trying to get the swing in motion. John went around behind her and gave her a gentle shove.

"Hang on!" He pushed her again.

She squealed like a gleeful little girl. "Higher! Higher!"

How long had it been since they had laughed together like this? John's heart was full as he pushed her higher, faster. A gentle breeze rustled the giant maples shading the park, and the waning sunlight cast bright, flickering shadows through the leaves.

Finally he let the swing die down. Tenderly he brushed the windblown curls from Ellen's face. He leaned over and took her head in his hands, planting an upside-down kiss on her lips. She pulled his head down again and again to her own, kissing him hungrily.

He wanted to stay here forever.

They lingered in the park—sitting side by side on the swings with fingers intertwined, swaying gently back and forth—until dark shadows fell across the grass, and the air grew cool.

Reluctantly John took her hand and they strolled back to

the car. He'd been refreshed by the gift of this sweet interlude, and yet a cloak of gloom settled over him.

Though their love for each other never faltered, nothing was really the same anymore.

Chapter Sixteen

The seasons passed and together John and Ellen learned to live with the daily inconveniences. There were rare days when he could almost pretend everything was back to normal.

But when the boys came home for the Thanksgiving break, John realized just how much had changed. Brant and Kyle had been home that summer, but it was obvious by their stunned faces that they were shocked at how much their mother had deteriorated in just three months.

After Ellen had gone to bed that first night, Kyle stormed into the den where John was paying bills at his desk.

"Dad, why didn't you tell us it was this bad?"

"What do you mean, Kyle?" John was truly puzzled.

"Dad! She's a total zombie!" His face contorted and a sob escaped his throat.

John realized then that the changes which had come more subtly for him, seeing Ellen every day, must have seemed monumental from Kyle's perspective. Also, John had tried to shield the boys from the truth. Whenever they called home, he made light of Ellen's problems and left out especially painful details. He knew now that he'd been wrong to do so.

"Oh, Kyle." He got up and came from behind his desk to

embrace his son. He held Kyle while he poured his grief out in tears that stained John's shoulder and stabbed a knife in his heart.

"Kyle, I'm sorry. I…I didn't realize that you weren't seeing how bad it's gotten day by day. In some ways, it's happened so gradually. But I know the last time you guys were home it didn't seem like Mom was all that confused."

"Dad, is she…is she always like this?" His voice cracked the way it had when he'd hit puberty. "Does she ever have good days anymore?"

"Not really, Kyle. For a while she did, but it's been a long time…a long time."

John heard footsteps in the hallway and Brant appeared in the doorway of the den. He took one look at Kyle's ruddy face, and he broke down, too. It was all John could do not to join them. But tonight they needed him to be strong.

"How can you stand this, Dad?" Brant swiped at his damp cheeks with a balled-up fist.

John reached over and quietly shut the door. Even if Ellen didn't understand what was going on, it would upset her to see her boys like this.

"Can't the doctors do something?" Brant shouted. "This is like a nightmare. She's so…she's just not even my mom anymore."

John put an arm across his broad shoulders. "I know, Brant. I know. All we can do is love her. Mom can't help this. It's not her fault. We have to keep remembering that. We have to remember her the way she was."

Father and sons stood in a three-way embrace, drawing strength and solace from one another before they went up to their separate rooms to wrestle with their own private agonies.

The newest development in Ellen's decline was a small thing, but it bothered John immensely.

Ellen had always taken pride in her appearance. In many

ways, John thought she was more beautiful in her forties than she had been when he met her. The beauty of her youth had mellowed into an elegance he found utterly attractive.

But Ellen had worked at it. She put on makeup and fussed with her hair and clothes every morning—even if it was Saturday and they had nothing more planned than to putter around the house or work in the yard.

She had loved to shop, and though she never spent a great deal of money on her wardrobe, she had impeccable taste and had managed to look stylishly chic even back when they were living on schoolteachers' salaries. He had always felt proud to have Ellen at his side.

Now, unless he reminded her, she forgot to even comb her hair in the morning. Fortunately, the last few years she'd been wearing her naturally curly hair in a tousled style, so a quick comb through was usually all it took to make her hair look presentable.

But her makeup, if she remembered to apply it at all, was harsh and sloppy, her lipstick uneven and sometimes staining her teeth.

She had taken to wearing sweatpants and mismatched shirts, pulling on whatever was handy and, John suspected, whatever had the fewest buttons or zippers to wrestle with. He had started laying out an outfit for her each day, and she was usually cooperative, dressing herself. But by the end of the day, her clothes would be rumpled and stained from her carelessness. John felt guilty letting this relatively minor thing disturb him so intensely. It was just that so much about his wife had changed that this sloppiness added embarrassment to his deepening pain.

Once again, Sandra came to the rescue. She picked Ellen up one afternoon early in December and took her shopping. They came home with several colorful, casual outfits that were easy to get in and out of. Sandra had also taken Ellen to the cosmetic counter and helped her choose new, paler shades of makeup that were more forgiving of Ellen's unsteady hand.

It was an improvement, but it still wasn't the Ellen that John was used to. But then nothing about her was the same anymore.

Though Ellen accepted his affection, she rarely initiated it. He made an effort to embrace her, to greet her with a kiss each morning as he always had, and to hold her hand when they walked together in the evenings.

The latter had become a necessity, to keep her from tripping on the uneven sidewalks. They walked almost every evening, just as they had for most of their marriage. It had been a time to catch up on the day's news and to connect with each other at the end of a busy day. It had also been a romantic time for them, walking hand in hand, sharing their love. But it was becoming wearisome for him to give and give, and receive so little in return.

He felt his love for her slipping away, and it terrified him.

He was becoming increasingly concerned about Ellen's safety around the house. He had no choice but to leave her alone while he went to work each day. He came home over the lunch hour and fixed her a sandwich or a salad. If Ellen was having a difficult day, or John was caught in a meeting, Sandra could sometimes get away from work to check on her.

Mrs. Dobbs, the cleaning lady, had been persuaded to come for two half days rather than one full day, so there was rarely a time when Ellen was alone for more than three or four hours. But so much could happen in those few short hours, and John knew the time was coming when he would have to get someone to stay with Ellen every day while he was at work.

The time came sooner than he'd anticipated. A staff meeting ran long one morning, and it was almost twelve-thirty when he finally got home for lunch. He parked in front of the house and ran inside, calling Ellen's name, worried that she would be hungry and fretting about his lateness. Usually she was sitting in front of the TV in the living room when he came home. And usually, in answer to his voice, she rose silently and came into the kitchen.

But today she did not appear. John searched the house, climbing the stairs to the second floor, then to the attic, calling for her with rising panic.

He ran out into the yard, screaming her name, not caring what the neighbors might think. He couldn't see her in the yard or the wooded area behind the house.

He ran back into the house through the garage, not sure where to turn next. Then he stopped short. In the dim light that filtered through the single window, he saw Ellen's profile behind the wheel of the car that had been hers.

He yanked open the car door, and with misplaced anger he pulled her roughly out of the seat.

"Ellen, what in the world are you doing?" he shouted.

She looked at him, perplexed. Then he saw the keys in her hand.

John grabbed the keys from her, then struggling for control and realizing it was himself he was angry with, he pulled her into his embrace. She started to cry. Over and over she wailed, "I thought I'd go…go…go… I thought I'd go…and go…"

He gently put his hand over her mouth to quiet her. "Ellen, you mustn't ever, ever get into the car when I'm not with you." He forced her to look at him. "Do you understand me? Never!" He scolded her like he had Jana when she was a toddler. And yet he knew that, unlike little Jana, Ellen would never learn another lesson. Her mistakes would never again be teachers.

John led Ellen into the house and fixed her a sandwich. He spent the rest of his lunch hour fixing the door to the garage so it could be locked from the outside.

The next morning he made arrangements with the school board to take a two-week leave of absence and after that, a schedule of shortened hours at the office for "as long as he needed it."

He also arranged for a woman from their church to come

in to stay with Ellen during the mornings. It was far from ideal, and it wouldn't work indefinitely, but for now, it was all John knew to do.

Just after Christmas, on a beautiful, crisp evening, John bundled Ellen up, and they walked several blocks around the neighborhood. He'd been feeling cooped up and in need of fresh air, and it felt good to get out in the brisk night air. It had been weeks since the weather was warm enough for them to take a walk.

Tonight, the sky was clear and full of stars, and Ellen seemed nostalgic. In fragmented sentences she recounted aloud their first days living on Oaklawn. While she couldn't remember the current day of the week, sometimes she could recall events of their past—often in surprising detail. This was ground on which John could meet her. He was feeling cheerful and optimistic with reminiscence.

They came back to the house, and standing by the closet in the front hall, John began to help her out of her coat and gloves and scarf. Her face was flushed from the cold, and she looked like the Ellen of old. She flashed a winsome smile, and suddenly, he was overcome with desire for her. He dropped her coat to the floor and took her in his arms and kissed her hungrily. She didn't resist him, but looked at him questioningly. He took her hand and started up the steps to their bedroom.

Suddenly, Ellen sighed heavily, contentedly. Then in a clear but childish voice she crooned, "Oh, Daddy. So fun… fun. Can we go again? Walking? Maybe Mommy can come, too…walk on the farm."

John stopped in his tracks. He turned, sick at heart, and looked down the steps at Ellen. Her eyes were gazing far away into the past. Her expression, her voice, were those of the child she had been forty years before. And in a moment of horrible realization, he knew that in Ellen's mind he had become her father. How could he take her into their marriage bed?

He turned slowly and guided her back down the steps. In the kitchen, he fixed her a cup of warm milk, and while she sat at the table sipping contentedly, John went to make up the twin beds in the bedroom on the ground floor.

The room had most recently been Jana's. The wallpaper was a pale peach to match the ruffled comforters. The furniture was French provincial—a young girl's dream room. He brought down a few of Ellen's things from the bathroom and carried their alarm clocks down and plugged them in. Then he went to the kitchen and led Ellen to her new bed. He tucked her in and gave her a chaste kiss.

She seemed unaware that anything was amiss. With a sigh, she burrowed under the blankets and closed her eyes.

John turned out the light, and with leaden feet, he climbed to the attic. There he unplugged their lamps and gathered the contents of his night table drawers. He took their toothbrushes and toiletries from the bathroom and moved these things down to the bathroom across the hall from Jana's room.

He went back to the attic and gathered the clothes from Ellen's closet and drawers. Burying his face in the soft fabrics, he breathed in the faint scent of her perfume that lingered there. He arranged her things in the downstairs room and returned once more to the attic stairway and climbed it slowly.

At the top of the stairs, he stood in the doorway and looked around the room, now lacking their personal items. Through misted eyes, he saw the history of their love in this room. Sweet, intimate scenes floated like ghosts before him in the emptiness—a young couple sharing tender, romantic moments. Was that him? And Ellen? And now it had come to this?

His throat was so full with emotion he felt a physical pain. John pulled the door shut, and with finality he put the time-worn key in the lock and turned it.

The next morning John awoke slowly. With half-closed eyes he looked groggily around the room, trying to remember why he was here on a narrow bed in Jana's old room. He turned over, squinting to block out the blinding sun that streamed in the east window. In a halo of sunlight, he saw Ellen's auburn curls spread on the pillow in the bed next to his, and it all came back to him with terrible clarity.

He had said goodbye to his lover last night. Never again would he know the intimate touch of her hands on his body. Never again would they share the oneness that had healed so many differences…the communion that had been such a joy to them for a quarter of a century.

Today he awoke to a new role. No longer friend and equal. No longer lover and confidant. Today he would begin to learn to be Ellen's protector…her keeper…her defender. Today she had become his child.

The weight of the task before him was oppressive. He felt small and unworthy. And worse, he wasn't sure he wanted the awesome responsibility—however precious his charge.

He threw back the covers and rose to face the morning. He would live one day at a time. It was an old cliché, but never had he understood its meaning so clearly.

Ellen stirred beside him. Barely acknowledging him, she sat up in bed and looked around the room. Amazingly, she didn't seem to see anything amiss. After a minute of stretching, she crawled out of bed and stumbled toward the kitchen.

John followed her, pulling out a chair at the kitchen table for her, patting her shoulder as she sat down. He started coffee brewing and put two slices of bread into the toaster.

And so together—with much difficulty and many blunders—they began to learn how to live with this terrible thing called Alzheimer's.

Spring came again, a long summer passed, and when autumn once again caused the leaves to drop from the trees, when everything shriveled and died, John finally felt that nature reflected Ellen's perverse metamorphosis. However, there was a beauty in nature's dying that John could not find in Ellen's.

Like the leaves falling one by one from their branches, Ellen died a little each day. A memory gone here, a sparkle of laughter there, until John hardly recognized the woman he loved.

Julia

Chapter Seventeen

Martin Sinclair was buried on a cold day in October. The wind swept through the trees in sporadic gusts, carrying the last dead leaves of autumn in frenzied circles, dipping and diving between the marble gravestones.

Julia Sinclair, Martin's young widow, sat under the canopy with the casket, her eyes red-rimmed, the skin around her nostrils ruddy and raw. She had shed a myriad of tears in the past three days; no amount of makeup could hide that fact. But her eyes were dry now, her demeanor dignified.

She sat erect, her short dark hair brushed away from her face, her slender hands clasped in her lap.

The air was gray with a dense fog that muted the colors of the landscape to muddy greens and browns. The cemetery was wrapped in the stark tracery of a black iron fence. Against this backdrop her beloved husband, the father of her sons, was laid to rest.

The minister wore traditional black over his starched clerical collar. He stood before the people, intoning the ancient psalm: "'The Lord is my shepherd; I shall not want. He maketh me to lie down in green pastures; he leadeth me beside the still waters. He restoreth my soul…'"

The contingent of mourners swayed imperceptibly, a sea

of dark coats on the side of the hill. The silence was broken now and then by muffled crying, the dark fabric relieved by the white flash of handkerchiefs.

"'Yea, though I walk through the valley of the shadow of death, I will fear no evil: for thou art with me; thy rod and thy staff they comfort me.'"

But there was no comfort for Julia, or her young sons, who stood protectively by her, one on either side of her chair.

Julia's silence was incongruous with the voice that cried out in her mind, struggling to fathom the reality of this funeral. It was still like a dream. The phone call…the panicked trip to the hospital. The words played an abrupt staccato in her mind: "Rain-slick roads…an accident…nothing we could do…Martin…gone…so sorry."

With agonizing pain, she saw again the stricken looks on her son's faces as Sam and Andy absorbed the news that their beloved dad was gone.

At fourteen, Sam had tried valiantly to be brave, and Julia marveled at how he'd comforted her that first awful day. But he couldn't contain the sobs that racked his adolescent body as he lay in his room that night. Julia stood at his door and prayed to be given some perfect words that would make his pain go away.

Andy, not yet twelve, was the tender one. He fell into her arms and cried inconsolably when she told him the news. It made Julia feel stronger, for the moment anyway, to be needed by someone hurting so badly.

She watched her sons now as the coffin was lowered into the dank hole. Sam's face was unreadable, but she feared she saw anger in Andy's eyes and in his posture. A crazy thought flitted through her mind: *Martin will know how to handle this.*

"'Thou anointest my head with oil; my cup runneth over. Surely goodness and mercy shall follow me all the days of my life: and I will dwell in the house of the Lord forever.'"

Oh, Martin. It's true. You're really gone. How will I ever make it without you? How will these boys live without their father?

The final prayer was offered, and the pallbearers walked out from under the canopy. The mourners swarmed slowly toward the row of seats where Julia and the boys, her parents, and Martin's mother and brothers were seated.

As the people passed by wearing sober frowns like masks, she nodded a mute reply to each expression of sympathy. She was moved by the sheer number of friends who had come to pay their respects to her husband. Martin was so loved.

She felt small, each condolence given from a height above her. At one point she tried to stand, but the ground beneath her was spongy under a grass carpet. Her heels sank into the uneven sod, and her legs would not hold her. She fell back onto the hard chair and buried her head in her hands, trying to compose herself before the next mourner paraded by.

Julia's parents had flown in from Indiana for the funeral. They stayed at the apartment with Julia and the boys for a week. On the morning they were to fly back home, Julia woke with a start a few minutes before five o'clock. Martin's antique alarm clock ticked a steady cadence, and the old refrigerator hummed out in the kitchen, but the rest of the house was quiet.

She tried to go back to sleep, but it was no use. Slumber eluded her. Finally she threw back the covers and crawled out of bed. Pulling on a robe, she padded into the kitchen and started a pot of coffee brewing. As much as she had needed her mother and father at her side during these difficult days, she knew the real work of grieving Martin could not begin until her parents had gone home. She was anxious to tell them goodbye and begin the unavoidable task.

She carried a steaming cup of coffee to the table by the big kitchen window and sat down. The apartment that had been her home—their home—for over a decade was a renovation in Chicago's old Lakeview neighborhood, one that the real-estate listings had touted as having "lots of character." And in spite of the temperamental plumbing and the inefficient utilities, Julia had grown to love the rooms' high ceilings and creaking hardwood floors. She looked through the kitchen into the open living and dining areas beyond, and memories came flooding back.

It seemed to her that Martin had been gone forever—and yet it also seemed as though he might walk into the room at any moment, his booming voice holding a smile that one could hear.

"Up so early?" Her father's voice startled her, brought her back to the moment. He was freshly showered and smelled of the spicy shaving soap he'd used for as long as she could remember.

"Oh, I couldn't sleep. I'm sorry if I woke you."

"It's okay. I couldn't sleep either."

"Here…I'll get you some coffee."

She started to rise, but he waved her away and went to pour himself a cup.

He brought the carafe and refilled her cup before sitting down across from her to doctor his coffee with sugar and creamer.

She felt his eyes on her as he stirred.

"Are you okay, sweetheart?"

She sighed and took a cautious sip. "I'm dreading this day… I'll miss you and Mom. And yet…I know that until I face this apartment alone and see how the boys are really handling all this, I can't begin to…to recover."

She broke down then, putting a tight fist to her forehead. "Oh, Dad…how can I ever recover? I just never thought this could happen to me. I never thought I'd be alone." Panic rose inside her as she faced the reality of the life before her. "I can't raise these boys by myself! I can't do it, Dad! They need a father! They need Martin!"

Her father pushed back his chair and came around to stand behind her, placing his hands firmly on her shoulders.

His voice was thick with emotion, but he spoke with the strength that Julia remembered from her childhood. His words poured over her like a soothing ointment. "Julie…oh, Julie."

He hadn't called her that for twenty years. "Honey, I don't know why God has seen fit to put you through this. If I could take away the hurt…if I could bring Martin back, you know I'd do it in a heartbeat. But I can't."

He appeared to be wrestling with his own emotions, and when he spoke again, Julia knew the strength came from somewhere outside of himself. "I know this, though, you're not in this alone, honey. You know that God is able, above and beyond all that you can imagine, to take you through this. I have not a doubt that Mom and I are leaving you in good hands when we get on that airplane today. Don't you forget that."

"I know, Dad. I know. Just…please pray for me."

"Oh, honey. We'll be praying for you every single day."

She stood to meet his embrace. "Thank you, Dad. Thank you for everything." For more than forty years her daddy had always been there when she needed him, and never had she needed him more than today.

Six months later Julia stood in the same kitchen surveying the apartment through new eyes. Her father's words had proven true. Though there had been times of despair, the Lord had comforted her in miraculous ways. But the memories of Martin were painfully close here in these rooms they had shared.

At first it had comforted her to be reminded of him at every turn. She'd tried to keep their family traditions alive—taking the boys to breakfast at the Pancake House before church each Sunday, grocery shopping together every Wednesday night, out for pizza afterward. She had renewed their season tickets to the symphony and invited a friend to use Martin's ticket. She had continued to jog the route they had jogged together each morning.

But now she had begun to be angry that he wasn't there

sharing these places with her. She'd begun to resent whatever friend sat in Martin's seat at the symphony. She dreaded the jogs because they only reminded her of how lonely she was.

The apartment was full of Martin. He'd had such a presence about him. Without being obnoxious or overbearing, Martin had held court in any room he entered. He was charming and affable, and he had been the indisputable head of the Sinclair family.

Three months after the funeral, Julia had cleaned out his closet and packed up his toiletries from the bathroom. In a fit of anger, she'd rearranged the furniture in their bedroom, grunting and huffing to move the huge bed by herself. She took his sailing trophies off the mantel and threw them in a box. How dare he leave her alone like this! How dare he leave his things to remind her, everywhere she turned, of the great love they'd shared. But try as she might to banish his ghosts from the apartment, his presence permeated every room.

The boys were haunted by memories, too. Sam and Andy both refused to sit in Martin's big recliner in the living room. It had been "Martin's chair." When he was alive, the boys had argued over the chair if Martin wasn't home, and wouldn't have dared to sit there if he was. Now that they were free to take it over, it was as though the chair was abhorrent to them.

Not understanding their feelings, Julia had made a terrible mistake about that recliner one night.

The three of them were watching a movie in the living room when Sam and Andy started to argue over the couch they were both sitting on. Sam sprawled across the length of it, and plopped his huge feet on Andy's lap. When Andy complained, a shoving match ensued, and Sam pushed him to the floor. This made Julia furious.

"Sam, if you want to stretch out so bad, sit in the recliner. It's sitting there empty—the best seat in the house. You can stretch all you want."

"No, Mom. I was here first."

"Fine. Then sit up so Andy will have a place to sit."

"Why don't you make *him* move?"

"Because he's not the one who wants to hog the entire couch."

Sam ignored her and stayed recumbent on the couch.

"Sam, get off right now."

No response. The movie blared in the background, and Sam feigned interest in the action on-screen.

"Hey!"

He sat up, eyes wide. She had his attention.

"Don't make me tell you again, Samuel James. Go sit in the recliner."

"Forget it. I'll sit up." He made a halfhearted effort to start moving.

"No," she said through clenched teeth. "It's too late now. You just lost your couch privileges, buddy. You sit in the recliner."

He stood and started to move a straight chair from the table in the adjoining dining room, dragging it off the rug and across the bare wood.

"Sam! Stop it. You're scratching up the floor. Don't drag that in here. What's wrong with the recliner? Just sit there."

"No!"

He was so adamant she should have sensed it was something more than just losing his place on the couch. But she only heard his defiance. He was standing right in front of the recliner now, and she gave him a shove that neatly seated him in the big chair.

The anguished cry that rose from his throat was barely human. It was the wail of an injured animal. No, she realized too late, it was the wail of a boy who had sat in the lap of a ghost.

Sam struggled to pull his gangly body from the chair and fled to his room, sobbing.

Julia was shocked. She turned off the TV and stared at Andy as though he might have an explanation. He started crying then, too. Through tears he tried to make her understand.

"Mom, you shouldn't have made Sam sit in Dad's chair. That's *Dad's* chair. He should be sitting there. It's not fair."

Julia pulled his head to her shoulder and sat with him until his sobs subsided.

She ruffled his hair affectionately. "You'd better get to bed, bud. We'll finish the movie tomorrow, okay? You gonna be all right?"

He nodded.

She steeled herself and went down the hall and knocked softly on Sam's door.

His reply was a muffled "Yeah?"

He was lying on his stomach in bed, the pillow bunched into a ball under his chin. She rubbed his back tentatively, testing his response. He didn't reject her.

"Sam, I'm sorry…it wasn't about the chair, was it?"

"Uh-uh."

"It's about Dad? That's what Andy says."

"Andy's pretty smart." He rolled over and gave her a sad half grin, then turned serious. "Mom, I'm kinda mad at God. I don't understand why He let Dad die. You and Dad always told us that God loves us, that He wants what's best for us. But I don't see how it could be best for us to lose Dad. No way."

"Oh, Sam." Julia sighed and sent up a quick prayer— an SOS to heaven for the right answer to give this searching young man. "Honey, I was mad at God for a while, too. And I won't pretend to understand why this happened to us. I'm like you…I can't believe God thought it was best for Dad to die and leave us to go on without him. But I think it's what we do now that it has happened that is important. Maybe the laws of nature are more to blame for Dad's death than God is."

"What do you mean?"

She scrambled to piece her thoughts together in a way that might make sense to him. "I truly believe God is great enough that He could have reached down and saved Dad from the wreck—if He had chosen to. But for some reason we'll probably never understand, He didn't. And we have to go on from there. The Bible says that all things work together for good to those who love God, and I'm just trusting that that's true." She rubbed her son's back as she spoke and prayed that God would meet Sam with the answers she couldn't provide. Strangely, she had tried to comfort herself with those same words, but they had not taken root in her heart and mind.

They talked for an hour then—mother and son. Sam spilled out hurts and fears that had been locked inside for all the months since he had lost his dad.

And late that night, alone in bed, Julia made the decision to leave Chicago. They would go somewhere—away from this city of memories. After Christmas she would start looking for a job outside the city. It was time to build new memories of their own.

John

Chapter Eighteen

Christmas had become a time of great sadness at the Brighton house. John dreaded it for weeks beforehand and could not bring himself to decorate the house in any way. It seemed sacrilege to adorn the house for celebration when there was more cause for mourning.

When Brant and Kyle came home two days before Christmas, they went to the garage for the ladder and boxes of lights, and without consulting John, they spent the afternoon stringing lights on the house and hanging their stockings on the mantel. They put the tree in its stand in the front hall, but decided to wait until Mark and Jana came to hang the ornaments.

John tried to allow their loving efforts to lift his own spirits, but he felt powerless to escape the depression that engulfed him. The battle to reconcile his present circumstances with God's goodness had exhausted him. He knew, in a place deep within himself, that God was in this trial somewhere. Or at least God was with him through it.

When he and Ellen had buried baby Catherine, they had known the assurance of blessing even in the sorrow. That blessing had come in the formation of a greater bond of love between husband and wife, and in the fulfilled hope of more children. But Ellen's disease offered neither the bond nor the hope. He toiled to find even a hint of God's hand in all this, but he came up empty. Yet somewhere, somehow, that deep river of faith continued to flow in him, keeping him from utter despair.

Jana and Mark arrived on Christmas Eve afternoon. A few hours later, they were putting the final touches on the Christmas tree when Howard and MaryEllen pulled into the driveway. With MaryEllen's arrival, the kitchen became a haven of homey sounds and spicy aromas.

Jana had grown close to her grandmother since Ellen's illness, and John knew both women relished this time together. Jana still needed her mother, and sensing this, MaryEllen had become the confidante Ellen could no longer be. They baked cookies and breads, talking as fast as they stirred.

Ellen sat at the kitchen table and watched, but she showed no interest in joining them. Still, it seemed a comfort to her mother and her daughter to have her nearby. From his desk in the den down the hall, John could hear her speak quietly now and then, as if to herself. And though he knew Jana and MaryEllen could make no sense of her words, they responded whenever she spoke and tenderly included her in their conversation.

Around nine o'clock that evening, John went out to the kitchen and led Ellen in to get ready for bed. She fell asleep almost instantly, but he lay awake and listened as grandmother and granddaughter talked late into the night.

The next morning he awoke to plump loaves of bread cooling on the kitchen counter, and the aroma of roasting turkey. MaryEllen was already bustling about the kitchen.

Later, they laid a feast on the oak table in the dining room. The table was set with Ellen and John's wedding china and an elegant centerpiece of holly and tall white candles that Ellen's mother had brought.

There was much love around that table, and John felt his spirits begin to lift. Ellen seemed oblivious to the faces gath-

ered around her, yet in their own way, each of them ministered love and acceptance to her. They were trying so hard to
break through—to reach her in whatever faraway place she
dwelled. John willed her to acknowledge them, to show some
glimmer of recognition. It would mean so much if she would
just give Jana a smile, or give the boys that teasing grin she
had always reserved for them.

But Ellen existed on another plane. After dinner she sat on
the sofa staring at the TV while the guys watched a football
game. Then she got up and paced between the kitchen and
the conservatory. She had developed a shuffling gait that
made her look older than her fifty years. It made John ache
to see her that way. Yet in repose, her face was still beautiful—as smooth and free of creases as someone ten to fifteen
years younger. Her youthful beauty made her affliction seem
all the more cruel.

Today, as he did every morning, John had lovingly applied
lipstick and blush to Ellen's passive face. She was wearing
the pale violet dress he'd laid out for her that morning. He
had brushed her hair till it shone, and except for the vacant
stare that marred her eyes, she truly looked beautiful. If it
meant nothing to her, it comforted him to have her look pretty
and well kempt.

In the afternoon when it was time to open gifts, John
coaxed Ellen to sit in the overstuffed chair near the fireplace.
The family gathered around her as though she were the centerpiece of this celebration, and in a subdued spirit, they
opened their gifts.

Ellen began to open the brightly wrapped packages that
John put in her lap. Painstakingly she took off each ribbon, and
taking care not to tear the paper, she removed it, folded it neatly,
and stacked it by her chair. She held each item up and inspected
it quizzically, as though wondering what to do with it.

She opened a bright blue sweat suit from John and tried
to pull it on over the clothes she was wearing. John gently
took the outfit from her, and with a quiet explanation, he

folded it and laid it beside her chair. Ellen opened night-gowns, a sweater, and from Jana, a little porcelain bird for her collection. This made her smile, pleasing Jana immensely.

As she opened each package, John patiently explained who it was from until Ellen nodded a response. She laid down the last gift in the small pile that had collected at her side. Then she looked around the room, a tiny smile of recognition flashing in her eyes. "Thanks you…thanks you to…to…. Good. Good…" Her words crashed into one another the way they'd come to do of late.

But then, to John's astonishment, Ellen bowed her head and began to pray. With clarity and eloquence, the muddled syllables were suddenly replaced with clearly enunciated words of praise. "Oh, Father, thank You," she prayed, her voice bubbling up half an octave. "Thank You for this day You have made. Thank You for this love You have given us. Thank You, Lord… thank You…" Her words trailed off, but a serene smile remained on her face.

John was stunned. He looked around the room, wondering if anyone else had heard her. The tears that cascaded down Jana's cheeks, the emotion on the faces of his sons and Ellen's parents, told him he wasn't imagining it.

Not wanting to spoil the reverence of the moment, but needing to understand what had just happened—wondering even if a miracle had taken place, a healing of some sort—John touched Ellen's hand.

She looked up at him, but his hopes sank as he saw the vacant confusion still in her eyes. The smile she gave him was not one of recognition. John's momentary disappointment was quickly replaced with a sense of awe. He had witnessed a miracle. While Ellen's mind was wasting away, he—they all—had been offered a glimpse of the spirit within her that communed with an eternal God. It was an answer to John's prayer. She had acknowledged their presence. She had felt their love. And she still knew her God. It was enough for John.

Chapter Nineteen

John punched his pillow and rolled over in the bed for the tenth time in as many minutes. Light from March's full moon streamed in through the thin curtains, glaring harshly in his wide-open eyes. He flopped onto his back and yanked on the blankets, pulling them over his face. He expelled a breath that came back on his face hot and moist.

In the bed beside him, he heard Ellen's even breaths as she slept peacefully—a mixed blessing. Chances were she'd be up and wandering the house about the time sleep finally overtook him.

Ellen had caused him yet another dilemma. He sighed again. That wasn't fair. Poor Ellen couldn't help what had happened to her. But that didn't change the fact that John was in a quandary. The district conference for school administrators was to convene in Springfield early in March. John planned to leave after work on a Wednesday and would not return until Sunday evening. It struck him that in all the years since Ellen had become ill, he'd never once left her for more than a few hours.

At the beginning of February Ellen's condition had deteriorated to the point that John had hired two retired nurses from their church to come in and stay with her part of each

day. Sandra offered to come and stay with her on the evenings when John had school board meetings.

He was still working full-time most weeks, but his social life—and Ellen's—had virtually come to an end. To
make matters worse, their bank account was dwindling at
an alarming rate.

The school district had been incredibly supportive, giving
him time away from the office when Ellen's needs were his
first priority. But John felt he could not continue to give his
job such halfhearted attention and still feel worthy of keeping it. And this conference was not optional.

He considered driving Ellen to the Randolphs' to stay for
those few days, but MaryEllen had fallen on an icy sidewalk a few weeks ago and broken her wrist. Even if she
hadn't had the accident, it wouldn't have been fair to place
the burden of Ellen's care on her mother. In spite of their
good health, Howard and MaryEllen were, after all, both
almost eighty.

Sandra offered to take a few vacation days from her job to
stay with Ellen, but John didn't feel right about that either. Sandra had already sacrificed so much for Ellen—for him, really.

He didn't even tell the kids about his conference. He knew
each of them would, without hesitation, offer to make arrangements to get off work or school and come as soon as
they could. He didn't want the burden on them either.

But the weight of his responsibility left him physically exhausted and mentally beaten down. He finally drifted off, not
one step closer to a solution than he'd been when the inter-
minable night began.

The week before John was to leave for the conference, he
finally called a number that he found in the Yellow Pages for
a home-nursing service. The price was higher than they could
afford, but on Monday morning the agency would send a registered nurse out who could stay with Ellen the entire time.
She would cook for Ellen and do her laundry, as well. He de-

cided the peace of mind was worth it. Besides, what choice did he have?

On Wednesday the doorbell rang at exactly 6:00 p.m. John opened the door to a cheerful, grandmotherly woman. He'd been expecting the traditional white uniform and nursing cap, but the woman was dressed in casual street clothes.

"Hello." John extended his hand. "I'm John Brighton. Please come in."

"Thank you. Anne Grady with Homecare."

"Nice to meet you. I'm very grateful you could come. Come on in, and I'll introduce you to my wife. They did tell you that Ellen has Alzheimer's?"

"Oh yes. I have all the information right here." She patted the bag that hung heavily from a strap on her shoulder. "I've worked with quite a few Alzheimer's patients before, Mr. Brighton. I'm sure everything will go just fine. How long has your wife—may I call her Ellen?"

"Yes, please. She'll be more comfortable with that."

"How long has Ellen been ill?"

"She was diagnosed about three years ago. But we were beginning to see symptoms probably a year or more before that."

"Is she still coherent? Does she recognize people?"

"Not very often. Once in a while she seems to know the kids when they come home. I think sometimes she knows who I am…or at least I'm a familiar face to her. But she rarely calls any of us by name or even speaks directly to anyone anymore. She's fairly quiet, actually. When she does speak, we usually can't make any sense of what she's saying."

He led the way back to the kitchen. "The doctors say Ellen is in the early stages of dementia, if that tells you anything. They tell me I'm fortunate that she's so quiet and subdued." He shook his head. "*Fortunate* seems a strange word for it." He didn't mean to be maudlin. He murmured an apology and continued with his instructions.

"Ellen does still take care of most of her personal needs.

She dresses herself if I lay out her clothes and keep reminding her to get dressed. She can bathe herself if I run the bath water. You'll need to stay with her, though. She fell asleep in the tub once…. I don't trust her alone." He felt panic rising in his throat. There was so much information Mrs. Grady needed to know. What if he forgot to tell her something important?

He raked his memory. "Let's see…what else do you need to know? Her medications are on top of the kitchen cupboard, and I've written down the schedule and dosages. She feeds herself, but she won't eat unless you put the food right in front of her, and sometimes even then you have to keep reminding her to eat. She seems to be getting thin, so I try to give her frequent snacks. There are sandwich fixings in the refrigerator and plenty of soups in the cupboards. Ellen likes salads for lunch and there are vegetables in the crisper for that. Please make yourself at home. I hope I've stocked the cupboards with some things you like."

"Oh, I'll be fine. Don't worry about me. Would you have any objections if I took Ellen out in my car?"

"Not at all. She would enjoy that."

"Does she need help walking?"

"We usually walk each evening—just around the neighborhood. She likes to hold on to my arm. She won't break any records for speed, but she does pretty well. Around the house she gets along fine on her own."

"She goes to the bathroom by herself?"

"Oh, yes. Really, except for cooking and bathing she does amazingly well. I do help her with her hair and put a little lipstick on her. She was always so careful about how she looked."

They'd come to the living room where Ellen sat staring at the television. John went over to her and touched her shoulder. She looked up at him blankly.

"Ellen, this is Anne Grady. She's going to stay with you while I'm in Springfield. Remember, I told you I have some meetings there?"

In spite of his conscious efforts not to, John had begun speaking to Ellen in the tone one would use with a small child.

Anne Grady sat down beside Ellen and took her hand. "Hello, Ellen. How are you?"

Ellen looked at her but did not respond.

"I'm Anne. I'll be here if you need anything, okay?"

Ellen turned and looked up at John. "Oh, oh, oh, oh, okay."

So often now, her speech sounded like a broken record. She would speak a syllable and then couldn't seem to turn it off. It irritated John more than any other symptom of Alzheimer's.

Anne Grady reached over and patted Ellen's leg affectionately. Ellen quieted and turned back to the TV.

The older woman rose to her feet and smiled. "I think we'll do just fine, Mr. Brighton. Now if you would show me around the house, I'll get settled so you can be on your way."

It felt strange to be on the road. Except for short trips to visit the kids or the farm to see Howard and MaryEllen, John and Ellen had stayed close to home for the better part of the past three years.

When they'd first found out Ellen was sick, John had offered to take her to all the exotic places they had dreamed about—Europe, the Caribbean—but Ellen told him she just wanted to be home. So they had made the most of every minute in the house they both loved. Now, he felt oddly vulnerable without her by his side.

Despite the three pages of detailed notes and phone numbers he had left with Mrs. Grady, he kept thinking of additional things he should have told her. At the last minute, he had called Jana and told her about the arrangements so she wouldn't worry if she tried to call home and got no answer. Still, he was afraid he had forgotten something important.

As soon as he checked into the hotel where the conference was being held, he called home to see how things were going.

Since everything seemed to be under control, he relaxed a little. He slept better that night than he had in a long while.

He enjoyed the following morning's meetings immensely and felt guilty when he realized that he had managed to put Ellen out of his mind.

When he got out of his last meeting at five o'clock, the weather was beautiful, so he went for a run on the hotel's jogging path that followed the curving course of a man-made lake. Surprisingly, the path was deserted this late in the early evening. As John breathed in the air that blew across the water, he breathed in a freedom that he had forgotten existed.

How liberating to have a few days laid out before him—hour upon hour—with obligations to no one but himself and the job he loved. He felt physically lighter with each step he took, as though a great load were being lifted from his back. It came as a revelation—just how desperately he needed this hiatus from the grave burden of Ellen's care.

He went back to his room, showered, and walked down to the hotel restaurant for a late dinner. He read the newspaper over chicken cordon bleu, lingering at the table, relishing each precious second of time that was his alone.

After an hour, he paid the tab and started back to his room. Before getting on the elevator, he stopped by the desk in the lobby to inquire about the next day's schedule.

But when John mentioned his name, the concierge turned to the large board behind him. "Oh, Mr. Brighton. I believe we have a message for you." He handed John a folded slip of paper bearing his room number.

John opened the paper and read the ominous words: "Call home immediately."

He'd turned off his cell phone in the meetings this morning and hadn't once thought to turn it back on. Now he jabbed at the keys, checking for messages. He had six of them. He dialed Jana as he jogged toward the elevator. No answer. He pushed End and called home.

The elevator seemed to take forever to arrive at the lobby

and there were half a dozen other people waiting to get on. John rushed past them and stepped inside. He blindly pushed the button for his floor, not caring if he appeared rude.

What could have happened? Was something wrong with Ellen? Had Mrs. Grady backed out on him? Knowing John's circumstances, no one would leave him a message like this unless it was truly an emergency.

"Oh, dear God. Let it be a mistake. Please let it all be a mistake."

The phone started to ring, then lost reception as the elevator crawled to the fourth floor and opened onto the long corridor. John flipped the phone shut and ran down the hall, fumbling in his pockets for his room key card. He unlocked the door and went to the phone on the bedside table. The message light was blinking red. He stabbed at the buttons on the phone, trying to get an outside line. Finally he heard the tone. With a deepening sense of foreboding, he punched in the number for home.

Jana answered the phone.

"Jana?" Why was she there? "It's Dad. Is everything okay?"

"Oh, Dad! Thank goodness you called!" Her voice wavered. "Mom's…gone."

"What? What are you saying, Jana?"

"The nurse was fixing Mom a snack in the kitchen this afternoon, and when she came back to the living room Mom wasn't there. She looked everywhere in the house and outdoors, too, but Mom was just gone. We've been trying to reach you since about five." Her words tumbled out in a rush. "Oh, Dad, I'm so worried. Everybody in the neighborhood is looking for her, but we don't have a clue where she might be. Nobody has seen her."

"You mean she just walked out of the house by herself? She's never done that, Jana. Are you sure she's not hiding in the house there somewhere? Or out in the yard? I can't imagine her going off on her own like that. She's never done that before," he repeated.

"Mrs. Grady said the front door was open when she came to give Mom a snack. I don't know what else could have happened."

"Have you called the police?"

"Yes. They said they would put out an alert, but we haven't heard anything from them yet. Oh, Dad, what are we going to do?"

"I don't know, Jana. Do the boys know?"

"I just got hold of Brant, and he's going to try to find Kyle and come home right away. Mark is out searching with the neighbors. She couldn't have gotten very far, could she, Dad? She can't even walk that well."

"I don't know, honey. Hang on…" He checked his cell phone. "Let me call you back on my cell." Without waiting for a response, he dropped the receiver into its cradle and dialed home on his cell. Jana picked up on the first ring.

"Dad? What happened." Her voice reflected the panic and helplessness he felt.

"I switched over to my cell phone." He clamped the phone between his shoulder and his ear, lofted his suitcase onto the bed and started tossing his clothes and a raft of papers from the conference into it. "Just try to stay calm, Jana…okay? I'm packing right now. I'll be home as soon as I can. It took me about three hours to get up here so it might be late, but I'll be there as soon as I possibly can." Then almost to himself he said, "I *knew* I shouldn't have left her. I can't believe this is happening."

Still balancing the phone on one shoulder, he went into the bathroom and swept his toiletries off the counter into his shaving kit. "Where is Mrs. Grady now?"

"We sent her home. She was really upset, Dad. She feels terrible. Do you think maybe she wasn't watching her very well?"

"I don't know, Jana. I can't imagine how this could have happened!" A cloud of guilt descended, nearly overwhelming him. How could he have left her? What was he thinking?

With difficulty, he composed himself. "Okay. I'm going to hang up and get on the road. You're doing great, honey. The cell service is lousy around here, but I'll try to keep checking in. Just stay by the phone…and pray. She'll have to show up soon."

"I know, Dad, but it's getting dark."

Macabre thoughts filled John's mind as he flew through the night toward home. He saw Ellen's twisted body lying in a ditch, or worse, floating on a black river. With each vision, he pressed his foot harder to the accelerator.

"How could I have let this happen? I never should have left her. Oh, Ellen…poor Ellen. Please, God. Wherever she is…be with her…help her. *Please.*"

John drove for miles berating himself. He remembered the day he had found her in the car in the garage, and he chastised himself for not taking the incident more seriously. Surely that had been a clue that she was prone to wander. How could he have been so stupid? Would his children ever forgive him if anything happened to their mother? Could he ever forgive himself? He alone was to blame. This was all his fault. He had no business running off so far away, lounging in a hotel when Ellen was so ill. What kind of husband was he anyway?

He was breaking the speed limit, and still the landscape seemed to crawl by. Every few minutes, he tried to call home to see if they had found her yet, but he couldn't get through. And he didn't dare to waste precious minutes stopping at a pay phone.

And so he drove on. "Oh, dear God. Is this how it's all going to end? No! Please…not yet! I'm not ready to lose her. Not like this."

Chapter Twenty

The clock on the car radio read ten thirty-five when John finally turned onto Oaklawn. Even before he was in sight of their house, he saw the line of cars parked on the street in front. He recognized Brant's car and Mark and Jana's. Even Howard and MaryEllen had driven in. Sandra's car was there and several other vehicles he didn't recognize.

All the lights inside and out were burning, giving the old house a festive look, as though a happy party were raging inside. He'd finally gotten through on his cell phone ninety miles from home, but there'd been no news to report.

He parked on the driveway behind Brant's car and ran up the front walk. Jana met him at the door.

"Oh, Dad. Thank God you're home."

"Did you find her yet?"

"No! Not a clue. The boys and Mark are still out looking, and some of the neighbors—the Grants and Bob Markham." She lowered her voice to a whisper and motioned toward the living room. "We finally made Grandpa come inside—we were worried about him. He walked the neighborhood for two hours. Dad, I don't know what else to do." She broke down and sobbed in John's arms.

"Jana, you've all done exactly what you should. I couldn't

ask for more. I'm going to make a couple of phone calls, and I want you to go up and try to get some sleep. We're going to have a long day ahead of us and—"

"Dad! You've got to be kidding. How could you think I could sleep at a time like this?"

He shushed her, waving his idea away. She was right, of course. He wasn't thinking straight. "I'm sorry. Forget it… Now, has anyone called the hospital to see if she's shown up there?"

"Yes. But that was a couple of hours ago. Do you think we should try again?"

"Yes. I'll do that. And I'm going to call the police department myself. You should at least lie down for a few minutes, honey."

"I'll try. But first I'll go make up the bed for Grandma and Grandpa."

John went into the living room and spoke with Howard and MaryEllen, Sandra and the others who had gathered to help. Without prompting, they gathered and circled the room, joining hands.

"God," John prayed aloud, "You know where Ellen is right now. Oh, Lord, we put her in Your hands. Please watch over her, and keep her warm, Lord. It's so cold out there tonight…" John's voice faltered, and he felt Jana and Sandra squeeze his hands on either side. Their touch strengthened him to go on. "And give us wisdom to know where to look for her. Please, God. We need You. We need You now."

They stood that way for a long time, heads bowed, bound together. Finally John cleared his throat and broke from the circle. There were no words to express his thanks, but he tried. He sent home the neighbors and friends who had gathered to help with the search. He told Ellen's parents that Jana had their bed ready, and they wearily climbed the stairs.

Sandra stayed, tidying up the kitchen and offering moral support while John went to the telephone and dialed the hospital. They had nothing to report. He was still making phone calls when the boys came in just before two in the morning.

Sandra gathered her things and left with a promise to return at daylight. The searchers had gone home for some rest and something to eat, and they had arranged to start again at daybreak.

The police came to the house and talked to John, asking him for a photograph of Ellen to fax to the surrounding towns.

John had called everyone he could think of who might have seen Ellen, but it seemed no one knew anything. Where could she be? Why wasn't anyone finding her. She surely hadn't been kidnapped. But maybe she'd been picked up by someone with evil intentions? He shuddered at the thought.

At 3:00 a.m. a light rain began to fall. John sat half propped up on the couch in the living room, hope deflating in him like a pierced balloon. He watched a silent television screen display the time and temperature. It was fifty-two degrees. John willed the thermometer not to drop any lower. And he prayed as he had never prayed in all his life. Finally his words dissolved into a four-word litany. *Be with her, God. Be with her, God.*

An hour later, he finally dozed off. And when the first gray light of morning filtered through the curtains, he woke with a start. He got up and took a quick shower to steel himself for the day ahead.

He tiptoed into the kitchen and put on a pot of coffee. Within minutes the boys joined him, and by the time they finished toast and coffee, the whole household was stirring and cars were pulling into the drive.

John called the hospital again. Still no luck. Then he called the police. They had no new information, but assured John they were doing everything possible to locate Ellen.

When the searchers showed up at sunrise, he left Jana and MaryEllen to manage the phone, and sent the rest of them in different directions throughout the neighborhood. They could cover the most territory that way. He asked Howard to search the large yard and surrounding woods once again.

When everyone had dispersed, John stepped out the back

door. The morning chill filled him with new terror. It was barely fifty degrees. According to Anne Grady, Ellen had been wearing sweatpants and a light sweatshirt. Could she possibly have survived a night in this weather?

John began walking the route he and Ellen usually took on their strolls through the neighborhood each evening. Never had he felt so solitary walking that path. He tried not to think that he may never walk this way with Ellen again. He longed for the warmth of her hand in his, the familiar weight of her body against his as he wended his way alone down this street they loved.

John walked to the point where he and Ellen usually turned back and started retracing his steps, straining to see what he might have missed on the first pass. In an odd trick of light, the gardens and yards where he and Ellen had always found such beauty now took on an ominous, foreboding aura. His imagination turned bent tree limbs into human limbs. He felt as though he were walking through the gates of hell.

When he walked through the front door of their house forty-five minutes later, the house was in bedlam. Jana was on the phone, tears of joy and exhaustion mixing on her cheeks. MaryEllen was trying to hush the cheers and excited questions of the others so that Jana could hear to write down a phone number. MaryEllen waved her hands futilely, her wrist still encased in a cast.

When Jana saw John, she shouted, her voice breaking, "They found her, Dad! They found her!"

"Where? Is she okay?"

With her hand over the receiver, Jana explained. "She was at the school. This is Mrs. Linmeyer. When she got to school this morning, she found Mom sitting on the front steps waiting for the doors to open." Jana broke down and handed the phone to her dad. "Here, you talk to her."

"Carolyn?"

As he listened to Carolyn's story, relief flowed through him and he felt the knots in his shoulders loosen a hitch. Ellen had wandered the twelve blocks to the school—a route she had walked many days when she was teaching—and apparently had spent the night on the steps. She was cold and wet, hungry and confused, but she was unharmed.

John and Jana drove to the hospital where Carolyn had taken Ellen. She was on an examination table in the emergency ward. Someone had called Dr. Morton, and he met John in the hallway.

"Hi, John." There was sympathy in his voice. "Pretty tough night, huh?"

John nodded wearily. "Pretty tough. Is she okay?"

"She's going to be fine. I'm having them start an IV right now—just as a precaution. She's really in pretty good shape considering what she's been through. She keeps saying she has to get to class—she was such a dedicated teacher."

John knew it was Jerry's way of giving dignity to the humiliation of the situation, and he silently blessed the man for remembering Ellen as she had been before.

He went to her then. He heard her voice before he saw her, and was amazed at the clarity of her words, however irrelevant they were.

Over and over she pleaded in a singsong voice, "Somebody, please, I've got to get to school. I've got to get to class. Please, somebody."

When she noticed John her eyebrows arched and she reached for his hand.

He went to her, took her hand in his. And then he fell apart.

John spent the days that followed in turmoil. He arranged to take yet another week's vacation from work. He could ill afford the time off, but there were decisions with far-reaching consequences that had to be made. Now he had seven short days to make them.

Ellen could no longer be left alone for even a minute. He

would never forgive himself if this happened again. Or, God forbid, something worse.

While Jana or MaryEllen sat with Ellen, he slumped at his desk writing out lists of options and alternatives, considering the advantages and disadvantages of each choice. He spent hours on the telephone. He searched his heart, trying to discern his motives. And after three days, he was no closer to an answer than he had been at the beginning.

In desperation, he dug through his desk drawer and found the sheet from Dr. Gallia's prescription pad that was given to him those few years back, which now seemed like an eternity ago. "The Alzheimer's Association" was scribbled on the note with a toll-free number to call. What could it hurt? John picked up the phone and dialed the number. When he finally worked his way through the maze of recordings and heard a human voice, John felt he had been thrown a lifeline.

Here were answers to some of his questions. Here were people who understood exactly what he was going through. Here were people who amazingly seemed to know Ellen. Through the referrals they gave him, John discovered there was a nursing care center right in Calypso that specialized in the care of Alzheimer's patients. He had driven past the sprawling complex of buildings a hundred times. The modern sign in front declared Parkside Manor—The Place That Cares. But never had John thought this place had any relevance to him. If he gave it any thought at all, he had pictured rows of rocking chairs, a wrinkled face and gray head nodding in each one.

Reluctantly, John made an appointment to speak with the administrator the following Monday. He learned that while there was a waiting list for private rooms, a semiprivate room was available within the month. But he would have to decide quickly.

On Monday, John took the tour. Parkside had a special unit for Alzheimer's patients, and John was impressed with the services that were available. The rooms were beautiful, the hallways clean and uncluttered. The nurses and aides were friendly and attentive. Only one thing tainted the professional environment—the residents.

If he had walked through these halls four years earlier, before need colored his view, he would have been sickened... appalled by this distorted segment of humanity that he had never before given a thought to. He saw a dozen Ellens—staring blankly at the television, walking down the hallways with that characteristic shuffle, mumbling to themselves as they paced the solarium. Through an open door he heard a belligerent voice screaming obscenities, and the calm, patient reply of an attendant. He saw men and women in their seventies and eighties, and a few, like Ellen, who looked barely fifty.

Could he bring Ellen to this place and walk away? Could he live with himself if he abandoned her here? Oh, of course, he would visit her every day. He would continue to care for her in every way he could, but would she see it as abandonment? Would she sink further into dementia in a place like this? Or was there help for her here? These questions clanged noisily in John's head, and he left the place deeply troubled.

The sound of breaking glass shattered the 2:00 a.m. silence. John sat upright and saw immediately that Ellen was not in her bed beside his. The door that he was careful to close tightly each night was ajar, and he heard Ellen's low moans coming from the kitchen. He stumbled through the dimly lit hallway and into the kitchen.

Ellen sat on the floor, blood from an ugly gash on the palm of her hand staining her nightgown. The jagged shards of a broken juice glass surrounded her, and she held her hand gingerly while she rocked back and forth, wailing like a frightened child.

John grabbed the broom and quickly swept a path for his own bare feet. Then he picked Ellen up and carried her to the safety of the living room. The wound in her hand was fairly deep and would need stitches. He wrapped a clean dishcloth around it to stanch the flow of blood and dressed her for the trip to the emergency room—her second one in just over a week.

In the waiting room, Ellen fell asleep on John's shoulder. There had been a car accident and the emergency room was full. They waited for nearly an hour before Ellen was ushered, groggy and confused, into a treatment room. John sat beside her and held her other hand while the doctor put eight stitches in the wound. The doctor gave her a sedative, and Ellen slept through most of the ordeal.

When they returned home, she was wide-awake and paced the hallway outside their bedroom, picking at her bandage and examining her hand as though it were a foreign object. John tried several times to get her to lie down, but each time she threw the covers off, climbed out of bed and began pacing again. Finally John gave up trying to get any sleep himself. The sun would be up in an hour anyway.

He took Ellen's hand and led her into the kitchen. He took a seat across the table from her, and there, as gently as though she could understand every word, he told her what he had decided to do.

"Ellen, I want to tell you something, honey." He hadn't used the endearment for so long that it sounded alien to him. "In just a few days we're going to take you to a beautiful place called Parkside Manor. They'll take good care of you there, Ellen."

A sob rose in his throat as the reality of his decision sank in. Ellen reached across the table and, with a detached expression, looked at John.

He stroked her cheek and she leaned into his hand, her cheek warm against his palm.

"I can't do it anymore, El. I'm sorry… I can't take care of you as you deserve to be cared for. But they have nurses and doctors there who can help you. They won't ever let you get lost or get hurt like you do here."

He wept openly now. "I'll come and visit you every day,

El. And we can still go for our walks in the evening. But you can't stay here anymore.... You just can't."

She stared at him, looking straight into his eyes—a rare thing. Then she reached up and, with her bandaged hand, gently wiped a tear from his cheek.

"Hurts...oh...oh...oh...hurts. Hurts! Away...away...away. Go away. No...no...no... Away...away...away...away... away...." Ellen's words were spoken in the lifeless, singsong voice that Alzheimer's had given her, but the words themselves were poignant.

Deep inside a tender place that had never been touched, John ached as he recognized the source of Ellen's words.

They came from her heart.

Chapter Twenty-One

With a heavy heart, John made the arrangements with Parkside and set the date for Ellen to move in. He called each of the kids and told them what he had decided to do. Brant and Kyle were upset. They hadn't realized John was considering such a drastic solution, but they seemed to understand their father's decision, and each in his own way gave John his approval.

Jana was silent when John told her. He tried to elicit a response from her, but she gave him a frosty "thank you for calling," and hung up on him. John heard the tears in her voice and knew it was more anguish than anger. He decided to give the news time to soak in before he tried to make peace with her and convince her that he was doing the right thing.

But he was upset to have Jana angry with him, and it ate at him all day. Making this decision was hard enough without having his children turn against him. Couldn't they understand that he was already eaten up with guilt?

He came home from work two days later and found a letter in the mail from Jana. He unfolded the letter and read the words written in Jana's precise, rounded scroll.

Dear Dad,
This is the most difficult letter I have ever written. You
are my dad and I love and respect you. I want you to
know that comes above everything else I am about to
say, but my heart is broken by what you have decided
to do. I'm sorry, but I don't understand how you can
put my mother in a nursing home. I know, Dad, that
these last few years have been very hard on you, and I
know Mom has been getting worse and worse, but still,
there has to be another solution. Honest, Dad, if she
were seventy or eighty years old I could understand it,
but she's only just fifty! I feel like it will literally kill her
to be thrown in there with all those old people.

No—I feel like Mom has already died. How will our
family ever be the same without Mom at the house? I
know you say we will bring her home for holidays and
for visits, but it won't be the same. Do you just throw away
someone you love because it gets a little inconvenient?

Dad, you know I've offered to quit my job and come
and help with Mom. I can't understand why you won't
accept my help. Mark promised he would support me
if that is what I decide to do. Will you please recon-
sider? Dad, I've never begged for anything in my life,
but I am begging you to change your mind. I don't know
what else I can say.

I will love you no matter what you decide, but I'm not
sure I can ever forgive you for this. I'm just being hon-
est.
Love,
Jana
P.S. I do love you, Dad. Please know that!

He put an elbow on the table and rested his forehead heavily
on the palm of his hand. Jana's words stung. Her postscript did
little to soften the blows she had dealt with her harsh words.
Yet John knew in his heart the decision he'd made was the right

one, and best for everyone. No, it wasn't ideal, but there was no other solution. Ellen would never have wanted Jana to leave her husband to care for her mother. And Jana didn't have a true picture of how bad things had become with Ellen.

He'd tried to be honest with the kids. Since the Thanksgiving when Kyle and Brant had been so upset about Ellen's deterioration, he'd been more careful to warn them of any new developments in her health. But unless one lived with Alzheimer's day in and day out, there was no way to really understand the horror of it. And the father in John wanted to spare his children the uglier details of their mother's decline. He couldn't bring himself to tell them that Ellen had occasionally begun to be incontinent; or that she practically had to be spoon-fed now. He felt bound to preserve some of Ellen's dignity before her children.

He rose and plodded into the den. Taking pen and paper, he started a reply to Jana's letter. He tore up his first effort and started again on a new sheet, but the words he could think to write seemed sterile and uncaring on paper. Finally he picked up the phone and called her.

"Jana, it's Dad."

"Dad, I—"

"Please, Jana… Let me finish what I have to tell you, then we'll talk."

"I'm listening."

Was that contrition in her voice?

"Honey, I really do understand how upset you are. And I don't blame you. But you need to know my side of the story."

He heard her release a slow breath. "Okay."

"I *have* looked at all the alternatives. I spent an entire week trying to find a way to keep Mom at home. There just isn't any way to make it work, honey. I can't keep my job and take care of Mom, too, and if I lose my job, I can't afford any kind of help for Mom. As it is, I've already taken a deep bite out of our savings."

A long pause. "I…I didn't know."

"I know you didn't, honey. Listen, I appreciate your offer and Mom would have, too—I know you made it out of love. But I also know that she would never have allowed it. You belong with Mark. Mom would have absolutely hated the thought of her sickness causing you two to separate. Or even if she knew it had put any kind of strain on your marriage."

"It's not, Dad. Mark understands. He'll be okay with it."

"Well, he's been great, and I appreciate all he's done. Both of you." He hesitated, not sure how to persuade her. He was pretty certain his daughter was in denial. Mark *had* been a prince, but anyone with eyes could see the strain this had put on the young marriage.

"I don't want to sound cruel, Jana, but Mom has reached the point where I don't think it's going to make much difference where she lives. As long as we go see her, and as long as she is being taken care of, I think she's as happy as she'll ever be. And it'll be a lot easier once she gets a private room. Then we can go sit with her and visit as long as we want."

He paused, waiting for her response, but she was silent on her end. "I'm glad you let me know how you're feeling…I really am…but I want you to understand that I haven't made this decision selfishly. I've thought and prayed about this long and hard, and I truly feel this is the best thing we can do for Mom right now. I just don't know any other way, honey."

For a long time Jana didn't say anything. John didn't try to fill the void with further reasoning. What more was there to say? Finally, he said simply, "Jana, I'm asking you to trust me, and if you still think I'm wrong, to forgive me. Do you think you can do that?"

A shuddering sigh came over the line, and she began to cry. "Oh, of course I forgive you, Dad. And I do trust you. I'm not sure I understand all your reasons, but I trust you. I do. I know you only want what's best for Mom, too." She paused, then her voice broke. "I'm sorry about the letter. I wish I could take it back. Can you…can you forgive me?"

"You didn't do anything wrong, honey. You were just being honest. It's okay."

"Thanks, Dad. I love you."

"I love you, too, honey. We'll see you next week, okay?"

Her sobs started anew, but through her tears she managed to tell him goodbye.

He hung up the phone, too weary to feel anything but gratitude for a quick reconciliation. It would take time for Jana to work through her resentments, but he needed everyone behind him to go through with this.

Too soon the day arrived to take Ellen to Parkside. The kids wanted to be there. None of them were happy about John's decision, but they were supporting him, and they wanted to help.

Until Ellen got a private room, there wasn't much to take except her clothing and a few personal items. John really didn't need the help, but he let his children come anyway, and he was grateful for their company.

They gathered at the house early on a Monday morning. John had already packed the clothes and toiletries Ellen would need. Jana went through the motions of looking through her mother's closets and drawers, but the only thing she added to the items John had already packed was a little porcelain bluebird she had given her mother for Christmas one year.

When Jana was small, Ellen had given her the coveted privilege of helping dust the collection of fragile little birds. John thought to offer the collection to Jana, but it seemed too morbid for a day already fraught with finality.

The boys put the two small bags in the trunk of John's car, and Jana helped Ellen into the passenger seat beside John. Then, with the three kids in the backseat, they began the short drive to Parkside.

As John backed out of the driveway, he glanced in the rear-view mirror. Reflected there, like ghosts from the past, were his three children—Jana, with a brother on each side—just the way it had been for so many years. His family, all piled in the car together, appeared to be off for a day of adventure. Who would have thought it would end like this?

He swallowed the lump that lodged in his throat and tried to concentrate on the road in front of him.

While the nurses helped them put Ellen's things away, she sat in the chair by her window and stared outside. A curtain divided the two halves of the room, and the beds were bulky and institutional. The room was large and brightly lit, but it still had the feel of a hospital room. There were only two other pieces of furniture in her area: a small bedside table and a chair upholstered in leatherlike vinyl.

John spread a favorite afghan of Ellen's—one MaryEllen had crocheted—across the foot of her bed and hung her bathrobe on a hook near the closet. Jana put the little bird on the windowsill in front of Ellen. Unfortunately, these additions did little to make the room seem like home.

Ellen's window looked onto the crowded parking lot, but she didn't seem to mind the view, and John was grateful that at least she had something to look at besides the stark interior of her room.

They had her settled in less than twenty minutes, and then John and the kids stood awkwardly around her chair. John watched her face. Did she understand what was happening? He would have given anything to know her thoughts, just for that moment. But her eyes gave nothing away, and her voice had long been silenced of any language that John could comprehend.

Ellen's roommate was a sweet woman in her eighties. Like the other residents on this wing, she had Alzheimer's. Ellen was assigned the bed by the far wall, so they had to walk through Stella's half of the room to get to Ellen's side. Stella had a friendly smile for them each time they walked through, but she also had something to say to each one, and none of them could make sense of her disjointed comments. It was awkward and embarrassing.

When they had stayed for an uncomfortable half hour, John kissed Ellen goodbye and casually told her that he would see her tomorrow. The kids followed his lead and gave her farewell hugs. Ellen seemed oblivious to her new surroundings, and she made no reply to their goodbyes.

Brant and Kyle had to get back to Urbana early in the evening, but John took Jana out for pizza before she headed for Chicago. They talked about Jana's job and about the weather, carefully avoiding the one thing that was foremost in both their minds. It was an uneasy, painful time, and John was relieved when the waiter brought the check.

John invited Jana to the house, but she made excuses and started back to the city, saying her goodbyes in the driveway. Though Jana was making an effort to be supportive of John's decision, he sensed her lingering resentment toward him. And he understood that it was simply too difficult for her to go back into the empty house now.

He expected it to be hard for him, too. He parked the car in the garage and went in through the kitchen. The house looked the same. He walked down the hallway to their bedroom, testing his emotions. Ellen's bedside table was empty except for the alarm clock that he had decided she wouldn't need. Other than that, nothing was different in here either. Since that cold night when he had moved their bedroom down from the attic, he had felt like a stranger in his own home.

John waited all evening for the impact to hit him. For the guilt to overwhelm him. For the sadness to creep in. But all he felt was relief.

Ellen was safe. He could sleep in peace tonight for the first time in many months, knowing that she was being well cared for. He'd made the most difficult decision of his life and he was convinced he'd done what was best for everyone.

Tomorrow evening he would take flowers to his wife, and together they would walk a new path.

Julia

Chapter Twenty-Two

Julia Sinclair stood at the kitchen counter up to her elbows in the sticky bread dough she was kneading. Little clouds of flour puffed out with each turn of the lump, dusting Julia's navy sweatshirt with a fine white powder.

The phone rang from the den. With a groan she raced to beat the answering machine, wiping her hands on a dish towel as she ran.

"Hello. Sinclair residence."

"Yes, Julia Sinclair, please."

"This is Julia," she said cautiously. *So help me, if this is another sales call, I'll scream.* She had been interrupted twice in the space of an hour, and her patience was beyond thin.

"Yes, Ms. Sinclair. This is Paul Cravens at Parkside Manor. You submitted an application a few weeks ago…?" His voice trailed off in a question. "I apologize that it's taken so long to get back to you. I guess I should ask you first of all if you're still interested in the job?"

Julia had mailed the application almost two months ago and had given up on getting even a negative response. But, yes. Yes, she was very interested. She told him so.

"Good, good. Well, I must say we were very impressed with your résumé. We'd like to set up an appointment for an interview. Now we do have a couple other people we are considering for the job, but those interviews haven't been scheduled yet, so the calendar is pretty wide open."

They agreed on the following Monday morning, and Julia quickly arranged to get the morning off work. She'd been up front with her boss about this job search. She liked her accounting job at the small medical clinic, but she became more determined each day to get the boys out of the city.

The school year was quickly coming to a close, and a sobering look at her financial state decreed that the boys could not go back next year to the private school they now attended. Martin's insurance had been generous, but Julia was acutely aware that the funds would have to stretch over many years—until the boys were on their own. College expenses alone were going to kill her. She pushed the thought from her mind. They still had many years of private schooling to fund before that. To her, it was unthinkable to throw the boys into public school in this city after their sheltered years at St. Mark's.

She had applied for jobs in several small towns in the surrounding communities, but so far nothing had panned out. The prospect of this job and the small-town life that would accompany it filled her with optimism. She sighed and returned to kneading the pliant dough. It was so good to be looking forward to something instead of looking back.

As she patted the dough, mindlessly forming the fragrant loaves, her thoughts delighted in the possibilities ahead, and her voice whispered a prayer of hope.

Julia hurriedly parked the car, gathered her purse and tote bag from the seat beside her and wobbled on a new pair of heels toward the door of Springhill Medical Clinic. Of all the days to oversleep!

It was her last day of work at Springhill, and she met it with ambivalent feelings. She had loved this job. Some of her closest friendships had begun in this office. Of course she would keep in touch with her friends here—Calypso wasn't that far from Chicago—but she knew things would never quite be the same. Without the bond of working in the same environment, without the shared problems of the workplace, it was inevitable that friendships would change and perhaps even fade.

She would have dreaded this day had she not been so excited about the new job awaiting her in Calypso. The independence she felt in making this decision for herself and her sons was exhilarating. The boys' lack of enthusiasm tempered her own a bit, but Sam and Andy were young; they would adjust quickly. She honestly felt this move would do all of them a world of good. It was time for a change.

She hung her jacket in the cloakroom and opened the door to the accounting office.

"Surprise! Surprise!"

She looked up to see the office decorated with streamers and balloons. A computer banner spanned one wall, declaring, "We'll miss you, Julia! Best wishes on the new job!"

Her eyes burned and the faces of these people she loved like family shimmered liquidly before her. She grinned through her tears, at first embarrassed by her show of emotion, then suddenly unconcerned if they saw her break down.

There were hugs all around, and Julia was led to a table laden with cakes, punch and a beautifully wrapped gift. She was overwhelmed. She'd never considered they might do something like this for her.

"Oh, you guys! I can't believe this." Her voice grew stronger as she teased them about the fuss they'd made over her. "Mindy Durham, did you have anything to do with this?"

"Wouldn't you like to know?" But Mindy's grin told the truth.

"You sneaky little thing, you. I didn't have a *clue*. I can't believe you pulled this off."

The emotion of the moment gave way to jovial laughter,

joking and the warm camaraderie of friends in the work-place.

Over cake and coffee they presented Julia with the gift. "Ooh, this is almost too pretty to unwrap." She slid the lamé bow off and ran her fingers gently under the seam of the gilded wrapping paper, being careful not to crush it. The paper fell away to reveal a thick white box. She removed the lid with candid curiosity.

Inside was the oak mantel clock she had coveted ever since she saw it displayed in the window of an exclusive gift shop down the street from the clinic.

The tears started anew. "Oh! It's beautiful. I've wanted this so badly! But…how did you know?"

Then she recalled that several of her coworkers had seen her admiring the clock when they walked by the shop together after lunch one day. She noticed a card attached to the back of the clock, and she opened it and read the blurring words of the inscription. "To Julia…a time for everything."

Though the lump in her throat kept her from speaking for a minute, the emotion she felt was like a warm quilt around her shoulders. This had been the most difficult time of her life, yet through it all she had been taken care of. She knew it was the hand of God that had carried her through the valley of grief, but she marveled that He had done it in such tangible ways—through the arms of her parents, the joy of her sons, the perfect fitting together of circumstances. And now through the love of these friends who surrounded her. She felt her faith swelling in slow motion, as though she were witnessing the unfolding of a flower through a time-lapse lens.

In the weeks following Martin's death, she had struggled to see a speck of truth in the biblical promise that "all things work together for good." Now the meaning of those words was coming into focus, clearer and sharper each moment, and she felt blessed beyond imagining that the promise was for *her.*

She spent the rest of the day relishing precious last moments with her friends. When she cleaned out her desk that afternoon, her sadness was defused by a sense of gratitude, purpose and joyful anticipation for the future.

John

Chapter Twenty-Three

For John Brighton, the weeks filed by like marching soldiers, and life settled into a neat, cheerless routine. He came home from work each evening and changed clothes. Then he went to Parkside, usually arriving just in time to walk Ellen back from the dining room.

Occasionally he brought Chinese takeout to her room and ate there with her for old times' sake. The China Garden had closed down years ago. The restaurant had changed ownership several times over the subsequent twenty years, and the food never was as good as it had been when it was "their" restaurant.

He smiled, remembering how Ellen had actually shed tears that long-ago afternoon when they drove by and saw the boarded windows and the "Closed" signs plastered across the doors of their old haunt. Still, now and then through the years they had ordered egg foo yong at a new Chinese place, just for tradition's sake.

Now John doubted his feeble effort to continue the habit made a whit of difference to Ellen. He was pretty sure she didn't remember the significance of the feast he brought. But somehow, it comforted him to keep alive a tradition from happier days.

Only two months after Ellen moved into Parkside, a private room became available. The room was large and full of light, with a view of the residents' enclosed courtyard. The walls were papered in a soft shade of yellow, and the draperies were a cheerful floral. Much effort had been made to avoid an institutional look. It was a huge improvement over the sterile shared room, and John felt incredibly fortunate that it had become available so quickly.

At first he was grateful mostly for the kids' sake. And they were happy and relieved to have more privacy with their mother. But after Ellen was settled in the new room and they'd brought in some furniture, paintings and the rest of Ellen's little collection of porcelain birds, John realized how much easier his own visits had become. He could bring a book, lounge on the couch and read. He didn't have Stella to deal with; he didn't feel as though he were in a fishbowl with everyone watching to see how he was handling everything. His time with Ellen felt more like companionship now that her room felt more like home.

He walked with her nearly every night. When the weather was warm, they went outside and strolled along the sidewalks on the grounds. When it was chilly, they walked the long corridors inside the building.

Almost weekly, John saw a decline in her physical state. She had increasing difficulty getting around, her steps an uneven little shuffle. But her doctors said she should continue to walk as much and as often as possible. So John tried not to miss, except for the nights he had school board meetings or other obligations with his job.

After spending an hour or so at Parkside, he usually went straight home to fix a light supper, and then read or watched TV until the news was over. His last thought before sleep overtook him each night was that he would wake tomorrow to a day no different than this one had been.

He tried not to dwell on his circumstances, tried not to feel sorry for himself. It wasn't easy. He was starved for companionship, hungry for conversation.

Except for Alexander, John had no one at all in whom he could really confide. Alexander was a godsend—a good listener, a respected source of advice and one of the few people in Calypso who could beat John at tennis. But Alexander had a busy life of his own, and John tried not to burden him with his woes too often. Most of the time, it just felt good to play a challenging game of tennis and talk about nothing more than the weather or the football game the night before.

John's job became his lifeline. He wasn't sure he could survive the loneliness without it.

One morning late in July, John arrived at the office to find that his secretary had scheduled an early appointment for him.

"I apologize, Mr. Brighton," Barbara said. "I told the woman you may not be in, but she was very insistent that she see you right away. I hope there's no conflict."

Barbara seldom made appointments without checking with him first. "No problem. Did she say what she wanted?"

"Something about transferring her kids to Calypso schools. I believe the family is moving here from the city. I told her she needed to file the applications with the principals, but she insisted that she speak to you personally. She was very persuasive."

"I see." John curbed a grin. Barbara was not easily persuaded. "Well, I have to run over to the high school for a few minutes, but I should be back by eight-thirty or so. It shouldn't be a problem."

When John returned, the door to his office was open, and he saw that someone was waiting in the upholstered chair in front of his desk. He cleared his throat to announce his arrival, shrugged out of his suit jacket and hung it on the hook behind the door.

The woman fumbled with the purse in her lap and started to stand, but John motioned her to keep her seat. He extended his right hand.

"Hello, there. Sorry to keep you waiting. I'm John Brighton."

"Good morning. Julia Sinclair."

"Good to meet you. How can I help you, Mrs. Sinclair?"

"Julia, please."

She had a warm handshake and a friendly smile. She spoke in a low, melodious voice. He guessed her to be in her mid-thirties, and while she wasn't classically beautiful, there was an aura of confidence and poise about her that was very striking. She was simply but stylishly dressed in a pale blue skirt and matching blouse. She wore her dark hair smooth and straight in a short, no-nonsense cut. She wore no jewelry save for a simple gold band on her left ring finger. John noticed because Julia Sinclair spoke with her hands. Her fingers were long and slender, and her hands were as expressive as some women's eyes.

"Well, Julia, what can I do for you? My secretary tells me you're moving here from Chicago?"

"We hope to. That's why I wanted to talk to you personally. I realize that enrollment usually goes through the principals, and I apologize for taking your time about this, but you see, we'll be in two different schools here, and I want to be certain we can get both boys enrolled in the district even though we're not officially residents yet."

She smoothed a crease in her skirt. "I've just started working at Parkside Manor—I'm an accountant there—and we do plan to move to Calypso as soon as possible. Unfortunately, there's no guarantee we'll have found a place to live by the time school starts."

The reference to Parkside startled John, and he struggled to concentrate on what she was saying.

"I've just started house hunting. My two sons have been attending a private school in Chicago, but I would like them to be able to start school here in the fall. Sam will be a sophomore and Andy an eighth grader. I really hope we'll be moved by then, but there aren't many houses on the market here right now."

"That's for sure. We've had so many people moving into Calypso recently. Your husband's job is in Chicago?" he asked.

"Oh, I'm sorry. I should have explained. My husband… passed away. It's just the boys and me." Julia swallowed hard. Her grief was obviously still fresh.

"Oh, I'm so sorry."

"Martin was killed in a car accident. It'll be two years ago in October. It's been pretty tough." She swallowed again, blinking back tears. "It's been especially rough on Andy—my eighth grader—but we're managing okay now. I want to get the boys out of the city. I can't afford their private school any longer, but I just can't bear to put them in public school in the city. They've never known anything but small classrooms and a private school setting. I feel very fortunate to have found this job at Parkside. It's a really nice place, and they've been very understanding of my problems with the commute and the boys' schedules."

John could have reaffirmed her praise of the facility, mentioning his connection to Parkside. But he found himself drawing back—pointedly dodging the subject. *Why?* Then it struck him: most everyone in the small town knew his situation with Ellen. This was the first time he'd been faced with an opening for explaining his circumstances to a stranger. Was he ashamed of Ellen?

He fought to focus on the woman's words.

"So, what do I need to do to get the boys enrolled for the fall?" she asked.

John cleared his throat and forced himself to concentrate and answer her question. "Well, assuming you find a house, just show up for enrollment next month. I'll send you a schedule as soon as the dates are set. Unfortunately, we do have a large number of requests for out-of-district enrollments, and with the influx of new people we've had into town, enrollment is up anyway. So just in case you haven't moved by then, we'll get your name on a waiting list. Of course, you're at an advantage getting your name in early, and we'll definitely take into consideration your plans to move here and your employment here."

She graced him with a relieved smile. "Oh, that's good news."

"And if I can brag just a bit," he said, "Calypso is ranked as one of the best school districts in the state. My three children all graduated from CHS, and from a parent's point of view, I can't say enough good things about the district.

"We'll have you fill out an application here today, which we'll file with the school principals. Then after the regular enrollment is tabulated, the board will decide how many out-of-district applications to accept. Unfortunately, that cuts it pretty close for those who are rejected. Um…if you could possibly find housing in the district—even just a rental—that would guarantee the boys' enrollment. In the meantime, we'll see what we can do. I think we can probably work something out."

Julia thanked him again and filled out the necessary forms. They chatted amiably while she wrote. Her eyes sparkled when she spoke, in spite of the sadness that hid behind them.

When she left, John felt a disquieting mixture of emotions. He'd experienced a strange elation at meeting this warm, candid woman. It had been a long time since he'd had a pleasant conversation with a woman who wasn't expressing sympathy for him over Ellen. He realized that pity, though well intentioned, was cloying. It had been refreshing to relate to someone without the specter of his tragedy coloring their exchange.

And yet, he felt guilty that he had been so reluctant to mention Ellen. He had consciously avoided any mention of her, when under other circumstances, her name would have come up several times. No doubt about it: what should have been an unremarkable encounter with Julia Sinclair had been strangely unsettling.

When John got home that evening there was a message on the answering machine from Brant. His voice had a hint of urgency in it, though his message was nonchalant.

"Hey, Dad. Brant. Uh, give me a call when you can. I've got to work tonight, but I should be back by nine or so. Catch you later."

At nine-fifteen John dialed Brant's number.

He answered on the first ring.

"Hey, you're home. What's up?"

"Dad! Thanks for calling back. What's up? Well, um… quite a bit, actually." He sounded embarrassed. John could almost hear him squirm.

Finally Brant blurted, "What would you think if I told you Cynthia and I are going to get married?"

"Are you serious? When?" John was incredulous. He hadn't expected this.

"Well, we're talking about next winter. Cynthia has always wanted a winter wedding. And, well…" He launched into what sounded like a well-rehearsed speech. "I know it will be hard when Cynthia still has so much school left. I'd probably have to get a second job, and I know money would be tight, but… well, we think it will be easier if we're married and not using up so much energy thinking about each other all the time and trying to get together. We think we can make it work." He paused and caught his breath. "You have any opinions on that?"

"I sure do. I think…" John tried to sound stern and paused for effect, but he was sure the smile in his voice would give him away. "I think you're absolutely right. You two have gone together for a long time, and I know you wouldn't make a decision like this without thinking it over carefully. I'm happy for you."

He could hear Brant's relief on the other end.

"I have to tell you, son, the first time you brought Cynthia home, your mom and I told each other we hoped you wouldn't let her get away. She's like family already."

"You really think so?"

"You know I do, Brant. I want you to know that you two have my blessing."

"Thanks, Dad."

"Dad?" Brant's voice broke. "Do you think Mom…do you think she should come to the wedding?"

Emotion hung heavy between them, silence filling the lines.

"Oh, Brant." John sighed heavily. "It's up to you and Cynthia, but I'm afraid it would be hard for everybody. Mom doesn't know anyone these days. By next winter…" He let his voice trail off. He couldn't bring himself to predict how bad things might be by then. "You know Mom would have given you and Cynthia her blessing before she got sick. She'll be with us in spirit no matter what you decide."

"Thanks, Dad."

"Hey…" He attempted to steady his voice. "You tell Cynthia congratulations. And give her a hug for me. I'm very happy for you two."

Julia

Chapter Twenty-Four

Midmorning, on the tenth of August, a large moving van pulled up to the curb of the apartment building at Lakeview. Sam Sinclair, who had stood sentry at the front window all morning, announced its arrival with a shout.

"Mom! They're here."

"Okay, let's get busy," she hollered down the hallway. Andy?"

"I'm in my room...."

"Hey...let's go." She clapped a warning. "Come on! They're here."

"Okay, okay, I'm coming." His tone was surly, and he slammed his bedroom door defiantly behind him. Andy had been dragging his heels about the move ever since Julia had announced it to the boys. Martin's death had changed everything, and Andy was angry that he was being torn from his friends and the only home he'd ever known.

As he came plodding down the hallway to get his "marching orders," Julia ignored his rudeness and mustered a cheerful grin. "Ready?"

She didn't wait for an answer. "Okay. You and Sam start closing up those boxes in the kitchen—use the packing tape and make sure they're secure—and I'll find out which room the movers want to haul out first."

They worked steadily through the morning, and by noon the apartment was empty, and the van was on its way to Calypso. Julia loaded her houseplants and a small box of fragile items into the back of the car. While the boys vied for space in the cramped backseat, Julia walked through the rooms to be sure they hadn't left anything behind.

Her heels clicked on the bare wood floors and echoed through the hollow rooms of the apartment. It was an effort to remain matter-of-fact about this final walk through the old apartment that had been her home for a dozen years. These rooms held so many memories.

She walked into Andy's bedroom, and through eyes moist with remembrance, she saw it, not as the recent haven of an almost teenager, but as the nursery it had once been.

She and Martin had brought Andrew David Sinclair home from the hospital to this room. She could still see the cloud blue curtains at the window and hear the plinking metallic notes of his little clown-shaped music box. "Send in the Clowns" played over and over in her mind, and she longed to hold in her arms the chubby infant it had soothed. She closed the door silently and walked down the hallway.

She poked her head into Sam's room and then the master bedroom, and, seeing both were empty, closed the doors. It was not their bedroom that evoked memories of Martin. It was the bathroom. A large old-fashioned room, she had always loved its pedestal sink and deep, claw-footed tub. A clerestory window let in sunlight that showed off the rich patina of the dark oak wainscoting. How many mornings had she leaned against this door frame—a thick terry bathrobe wrapped snugly around her, her hands warmed by a steaming mug of coffee—watching Martin shave? She had never grown tired of watching his ritual. It was the one time she had him captive…his lips silenced by a thick lather of shaving cream, the boys still asleep in their beds, and the phone quiet in the early morning. It had been her favorite time of day, and she realized that since his death she had not once thought of it until today.

She closed the bathroom door. It was hard to say goodbye to this home—to turn the final pages of the story she and Martin had written together.

The blast of the car horn shook her back to the present…to reality. She didn't know how long she'd been standing here, but the boys were growing impatient, and it was time to be on the road.

John

Chapter Twenty-Five

John was shopping for groceries on a sultry evening in August when he rounded a corner by the produce aisle and nearly had a head-on collision with Julia Sinclair. She was dressed in jeans and sweatshirt, her hair tucked casually behind her ears. Her grocery cart was piled almost to overflowing.

"Well…hello, there," John stuttered, when he recognized her.

"Oh, hi."

"Does this huge mound of groceries mean you're an official Calypso resident now?" he teased.

She laughed. "As a matter of fact, it does. We just finished moving the last load from the city yesterday, and the house looks like a tornado went through it. We've got stuff sitting all over the house in boxes, but growing boys have to be fed whether the kitchen's in order or not."

"How well I remember. We couldn't keep enough food in the fridge when our kids were that age. So, you found a house, then?"

"Yes." She was beaming. "Do you know where Sweetbriar Lane is?"

"Isn't that just south of Broadway?"

"Yes. Our house is on the far east end of Sweetbriar. It's a nice neighborhood. I think I got a good deal. It's a two-story with a two-car garage, so we have lots of room. And the boys are thrilled because there's a basketball net in the driveway. They weren't too happy about leaving all their friends in the city, but they've already made friends in our neighborhood. I think we're going to love small-town life." Her enthusiasm was contagious.

"That's great. Well, welcome to Calypso." He extended a hand and she shook it, smiling. He started to push his cart away, then remembered something. "Oh, hey. We're gearing up for enrollment on the tenth. Did you get the information from our office?"

"To tell you the truth, I haven't looked at the mail for two days. We had another stack a mile high at the post office this morning, and I haven't sorted through that yet either, but it's probably in there somewhere."

"Well, if you don't find it, just give the district office a call, and we'll get something in the mail to you. Boy, it doesn't seem possible that school will be starting in a couple of weeks. This summer has sure flown by."

"Tell me about it. I just hope we're settled in before school starts."

They stood in the aisle, cart to cart, and visited for another twenty minutes. Conversation came easily with Julia, and John had the impression she was flirting with him. He was guiltily afraid he was reciprocating.

Finally, in midsentence, she looked down at her cart and gave a little gasp. "Oh, my ice cream is melting! I'd better get home and feed the troops. Nice to see you again."

"You, too. I'm glad you found a house. Good luck with the settling."

He waved, surprised at how reluctant he was to end the conversation. They headed in opposite directions and again, John felt that uncomfortable mix of emotions—boyish anticipation at the possibility of seeing Julia again, and a stirring of guilt that he had enjoyed their encounter so much.

He finished his shopping and went home to put the groceries away.

But all evening long, images of an attractive dark-haired woman flitted through his mind as he replayed their conversation over and over. He felt like a silly teenager with a first-time crush. "This is ridiculous." He spoke the words aloud, then felt foolish. He willed himself to think about something else, but ten minutes later there she was, messing with his mind again.

He went to bed that night more acutely aware than ever of just how lonely he was.

The next few weeks were busy ones for John. School started and with it all the headaches of getting the term running smoothly. There were some curriculum changes that weren't working out as well as he had hoped, and a high school English teacher had a heart attack the second day of school and was under doctor's orders to lay off work for at least six weeks. It was early in October before John felt as though things were on an even keel, and he could cut back to regular hours and relax a bit.

He volunteered to help in the press box at the high school football games simply so he could feel justified in attending the games. Though he knew probably no one judged him more harshly than he did himself, he feared what people might think seeing him enjoying himself at a ball game. He still felt guilty for allowing himself even the smallest pleasure when Ellen was so bereft of any joy at all.

He had not played tennis or jogged since late July, and the bathroom scale was starting to creep up at an alarming rate. He knew he should be more careful how he ate, too. Ellen had always been adamant about getting plenty of fresh vegetables and fruits in their diet. She'd scolded John if he hit the doughnut shop too often on the way to work. Now he found himself grabbing fast food several times a week because it was too much trouble to cook for one. But it was all starting to catch up with him, and he resolved one morning—after discovering yet another pound had crept onto his frame—to make time to get out and exercise now that things had settled down at school.

He came home early from work and changed into shorts and a sweatshirt. The temperatures were still in the sixties during the day, but the late afternoon air was ten degrees cooler—perfect for jogging. He headed out the back door feeling proud of himself for finally taking the initiative to get out and run.

It felt great to be outdoors. He ran at a brisk pace for the first half mile, but then he felt the long hiatus from exercise catching up with him. By the end of the first mile, he was out of breath and sweating profusely in spite of the brisk air. He slowed to a walk.

He had run from Oaklawn to the large park where he and Alexander played tennis. There was a jogging path that ran the circumference of the park, and if he circled this twice, he would have his four miles in by the time he jogged back home. He broke back into a slow run, embarrassed to be so winded after such a short time.

As he started his second jaunt around the track, he came up behind a woman in blue shorts and a hooded sweatshirt. She moved to the side of the narrow track so he could pass. He turned around, still at a jog, to acknowledge her courtesy.

"Mr. Brighton!" It was Julia Sinclair.

"Oh, hi!" He slowed down to match her pace and pointed to her covered head. "I almost didn't recognize you with the hood. Hey, call me John, please. I don't feel like Mr. Brighton on the jogging track. Especially when I'm about to keel over." He rolled his eyes and clutched his throat with an exaggerated gagging sound.

She laughed. "To tell you the truth," she admitted with a quirk of her lips, "I couldn't remember your first name. John." She said it with a thoughtful nod, as though committing it to memory. "You must hate running as much as I do."

"Well, if I hadn't let myself get so out of shape in the first place, I'd probably be enjoying this." He rolled his eyes. "It's been weeks since I did anything remotely athletic."

"Me, too. It really ticks me off how quickly I get out of shape if I don't keep at it. Do you always run here…in the park?"

"Oh, I try to keep it interesting and go someplace different once in a while. I like to run here because I don't have to fight the traffic, and it's easy to keep track of how far I've gone. I don't know why it really matters, but somehow I feel better if I can come home and say I ran four miles or five miles or whatever."

"Wow. Do you always run that far?"

"Well…" He tried to look appropriately sheepish. "Five might be an exaggeration. But I try to get in at least four. I figure as long as I'm out here anyway, I may as well make it worth my time."

She rolled her eyes. "I'm doing well if I make it two or three."

John shrugged. "Hey, at least you're running."

"Well, I'm probably slowing you down."

"No, no, that's okay. I'm going about as fast as my lungs will let me right now." He didn't want her to get away, and scrambled to think of something to say…anything to keep the conversation going. "So… How are the boys liking school by now?"

"Oh, it's going well. Sam is having a blast playing football. He kind of hated those early-morning practices the first couple weeks, but the games make it all worthwhile."

"He's got some talent. I don't get to very many of the junior varsity games, but I saw him play against Hanover and he looked great. He's really got speed. Has he gotten to play quite a bit?"

She beamed proudly. "He started the last two games. He's thrilled about that. He's already planning a big career with the Bears." She laughed, then cringed. "He'd kill me if he knew I told you that."

"My lips are sealed." Julia was getting winded.

John slowed to a fast walk. "What about Andy? Everything going all right for him, too?"

She sighed. "He's doing okay. Everything is always harder for Andy. I don't know if it's the whole adolescence thing, or if it's just his personality. He seems to take everything so seriously."

"Some kids are made that way."

"Yes, but Andy was always so happy-go-lucky before Mar—before his dad died. Sometimes I feel like that accident robbed me of more than a husband." A faraway look came to her eyes. Then just as suddenly, she seemed to come back to herself. "I'm sorry, John. You don't want to hear all this."

"No, no, that's okay. If there's anything I can do to make things easier for Andy, I want to know. I really do appreciate you sharing this with me. If you don't have any objections, I'll make his teachers aware of the situation. They might have some insights to offer."

She slowed to study his face, as if assessing his sincerity. "Thank you. I didn't mean to put this on you. I know that's not at all a part of your job."

"Hey, I've always felt like anything that affects the kids *is* my job. I taught for quite a few years before I became superintendent, and I have to say one of the things I miss about teaching is that one-on-one contact with the kids."

"I appreciate that, John. I'm doing double the worrying about the kids now that I'm both Mom and Dad. I know Andy will be okay…with time. He's already made a couple of friends in our neighborhood. It's just that he doesn't feel like he fits in at school yet. But if eighth grade is still anything like it was thirty-some years ago, *nobody* thinks they fit in."

He did some quick math. "If it was thirty years ago, you must have been about five years old in eighth grade." He was fishing brazenly.

She smiled. "I'm forty-three, John. I don't mind telling my age."

"I'm sorry. That was pretty obvious, wasn't it? Well, you don't look as though you could be thirty, let alone forty-three."

Her cheeks flushed pink. "Well, thank you. I appreciate the compliment."

They jogged side by side in companionable silence until they came to the park benches at the end of the path. "Wanna cool down for a little bit?" John risked.

"Sure."

They sat down and a full hour passed before John thought to look at his watch. Julia made him realize afresh how much he missed this easy, familiar conversation. He'd accepted the silence in his life because he had no choice, but now he felt years of suppressed thoughts and emotions welling within him, begging for expression. He felt he could talk to her forever.

He hurried home, started a load of laundry and showered, whistling all the while.

That fresh air did me a world of good, he thought to himself. *I need to run more often.*

He dressed and drove to Parkside. Ellen was still in the dining room when he arrived. The evening meal was served at exactly five-thirty at Parkside, and John rarely arrived in time to share supper with her. Tonight the table where she sat was crowded, so he kissed her on the cheek and told her he would come back for her when she was finished eating. She looked up at his face, but her expression did not acknowledge him.

John went down the hallway to her room. He threw out a wilted bunch of chrysanthemums he'd brought from the garden at home the week before. He rinsed the vase and set it on the bathroom counter to dry and made a mental note to bring another bouquet when he came tomorrow night.

He straightened the books on her night table. He was fairly certain that Ellen had lost her ability to read, but he continued to supply her with a new large-print book every few days, just in case.

Absentmindedly, he leafed through the album of family pictures he and the kids had fixed for her. Though Ellen rarely looked at the album, he knew the nurses and Ellen's other caregivers did. He hoped it would give them a sense of who she had been. Before.

He glanced at the clock. She would be finished eating by now. He closed her door behind him and hurried down the hall to the dining room.

Ellen was sitting alone at the table, tapping a fork against her coffee cup. The busboys were clearing the tables, carrying on a loud conversation across the room. John went up behind Ellen and put his hands on her shoulders.

"Ready to go back to your room, Ellen?" He asked the question as always, expecting no answer in return.

Without speaking or looking at him, she pushed her chair clumsily away from the table and took his waiting arm. Together, they walked slowly down the corridor to her room.

John spent the next hour beside his wife on the sofa in her room, but his mind was a million miles away in rapt conversation with one Julia Sinclair.

John ran into Julia in the park again just a week later. As before, they fell into easy conversation, jogging to the end of the path, then claiming a park bench and talking until the sun disappeared behind the trees and he could find no excuse to stay longer.

He discovered that he and Julia shared many of the same values and philosophies, yet there was an edge to their conversation that gave it an excitement he couldn't quite explain. Though he tried to push the comparison from his mind, it reminded him of the stimulating exchanges he and Ellen had always enjoyed. He didn't want to compare Julia to Ellen. It seemed disloyal to Ellen—and unfair to Julia. But he couldn't seem to help himself.

It was becoming an effort to keep their conversations centered on Julia's life. He walked a precarious tightrope in order not to reveal too much about his situation. He hadn't told her about Ellen. He talked about his grown children, but he didn't mention his marital status.

He told himself that he was keeping Ellen a "secret" because he didn't want Julia's sympathy…and because he didn't want to burden her already heavy heart with *his* woes. He didn't want her to pity him, as did virtually every other person in his life.

That was part of what drew him to Julia—she didn't know he was deserving of pity.

But in the early-morning hours, in that unsettled sleep just before awakening, he admitted the truth to himself. He was a liar. He was deceiving Julia as surely as if he looked squarely into her beautiful eyes and told her a bald-faced lie.

Julia

Chapter Twenty-Six

The administration offices of Parkside Manor were in the east wing of the sprawling complex. The inside wall of the director's office was actually a huge window that overlooked the residents' lounge and offered a view of the two hallways that forked from the lounge. The accounting offices and the employee entrance, however, were at the back of the building. This was partly a matter of convenience but mostly a matter of security. Every entrance accessible to the residents of Parkside was locked at all times and equipped with a sophisticated alarm system.

On a chill November evening, in her small but nicely appointed office, Julia Sinclair sat at her computer working on the month-end billing. In spite of the overtime she was putting in this month, she was enjoying her new job immensely. But more than that, she was loving her new life in the suburbs. The small-town friendliness that had endeared Calypso to her from the beginning was exemplified by the people who worked in her office. They had made her feel at home here, and it was nice to look forward to work each day. It had been a good decision to move away from Chicago.

Julia felt settled in the house she'd bought, though she was looking forward to doing some redecorating when she had time—and when money wasn't so tight. To her relief, the boys finally seemed to be feeling they fit in at school and in the neighborhood. She, too, was making friends here. And yet, Chicago was close enough that they could drive in for a visit with old friends and still come home to Calypso the same day.

Home. This really did feel like home now.

With a sigh of contentment, she closed the file she was working on, shut down her computer and locked up.

It was almost dark outside and she switched on the car lights as she backed out of her parking space. Turning the car toward the exit, she eased past the front of the building.

She watched a man open the door to the front entrance, juggling a large vase of flowers. As he turned to slip through the door, she recognized his face. It was John Brighton.

"Hmm…that's strange," she murmured to herself. "He must have family here." It was odd he'd never mentioned it. They'd talked about her work at Parkside often enough that she thought he would have mentioned it if he knew someone who lived here. She shrugged it off. He was probably visiting a family member of a school-district employee.

But she thought about it again as she fixed leftovers for the boys. She wondered about it throughout the evening, then puzzled over her own curiosity. Why did she care so much?

The next morning while going over some billing statements, she impulsively called up "Brighton" on the computer.

The screen flickered as it ran the search. Then there it was. *Brighton, Ellen. Room E147. Bill to John Brighton, 245 West Oaklawn, Calypso, Illinois.* That was strange. John was paying the bills. It must be his mother or grandmother. That made it stranger still that he hadn't mentioned it to her before.

Julia hadn't admitted, even to herself, how interested she was in John Brighton. But their warm conversations had given her hope that someday she might be able to feel about another man the way she'd felt about Martin.

More than two years after Martin's death, she was just beginning to come to terms with her grief. It still hurt to be alone, and it was an incredible burden to be both mother and father to their boys. But she was starting to be able to look back on the memories with fondness. In fact, they became a comfort to her rather than a torment. Lately she'd begun to reflect on marriage in general and had concluded that it was a wonderful institution, one she would like to enter into again if the right man ever came along.

After her encounter with John in the park, she'd entertained hopes that he might call to ask her out. She felt as though she may be ready to date again.

Feeling embarrassingly coy, she had purposely gone jogging in the park where they'd run into each other, hoping to see John again. When that didn't happen, she reminded herself that she really didn't know much about him at all. She knew he had children because he mentioned them often. Knowing Julia was a widow, he surely would have said something if he, too, had been widowed, so she assumed he was divorced. The fact that he never mentioned his children's mother sent up danger signals, but she didn't wish to pry into something he wasn't comfortable talking about.

Julia fretted over her discovery all morning, and over her lunch hour she made a rash decision. Feeling guilty and a little ridiculous, she left the office area and headed down the corridor toward room E147. She didn't have any idea what she would do when she got there, but her curiosity had gotten the better of her.

As an accountant at Parkside, Julia rarely had contact with the residents or their families. She knew the people in the institution served only as names and numbers on a computer printout. In fact, on the rare occasions she had to walk through the wings of the complex where the residents lived, she was always startled to realize that this was her place of employment. The atmosphere of the accounting department was much like any other office Julia had worked for—very practical and professional. Not at all a reflection of the human drama that played out every day on the other side of these walls.

The door to Ellen Brighton's room was ajar, and Julia could see at first glance that it was a cheery, sunny room. There were vases of flowers on an antique table in front of the window, and the upholstered furniture and botanical prints on the wall gave the room a stylish, yet homey look.

At first, Julia didn't see anyone in the room. Then, just as she was about to turn and walk back down the hall, the door to the room's private bath creaked open, and a woman with curly, pale auburn hair shuffled out slowly. Julia watched her from the doorway. When the woman turned and sat down in a chair by the window, Julia almost gasped aloud. The noon sunlight illuminated her face, and Julia saw that she was beautiful. She couldn't have been much older than Julia herself. Though she wore no makeup or jewelry, there was a faded elegance about her that was incongruous with this place where she lived. The woman stared out the window, and even from a distance Julia could see the haunted look in her eyes. She was unmistakably a patient here, unmistakably demented. But beautiful in spite of her insanity. What a sad story this must be.

Momentarily, she forgot that the woman had a connection to John Brighton. Julia was caught up in the novelty of the woman's youth and beauty in a place like this. She toyed with the idea of going into the room and speaking with her. But what would she say? She had no business here. She felt mildly ashamed of herself. Her curiosity was gratuitous, bordering on obsessive.

She turned quickly and hurried back to the office. She finished her lunch and got back to work but couldn't keep her mind on the figures before her. Maybe Ellen Brighton was John's sister. But a sister would probably have been married, and few women her age kept their maiden names.

Impetuously, she called up the Brighton file once again and accessed more information.

Brighton, Ellen... Bill to John Brighton... Occupation: Superintendent of Schools... Relationship to patient: Husband.

Husband? Julia felt as though she'd been struck. John was married!

But why should she have assumed otherwise? She broke into a cold sweat, her stomach roiling. What a fool she had been. She'd imagined he was flirting with her. And—how humiliating—she had flirted back. She flushed with embarrassment at the very thought of her shameless coyness with him. How could she ever face him again?

But *he* hadn't been right in this either. Why hadn't he admitted that he had a wife? A wife who lived at Julia's very place of employment! He had every opportunity to mention it. What was he trying to pull?

"Hang on, Jul," she chided herself. "It's not like he ever asked you out or anything. You probably just imagined the flirting. You're the one who made a fool of yourself. He didn't owe you his life story." She suddenly felt a horrifying sense of disloyalty to Martin.

She dropped her head to her desk. She was so confused.

She stewed over her discovery all afternoon, and when she got home that night, she was preoccupied and snappish with the boys.

A week passed, and finally, gradually, the obsession, the embarrassment lessened. In its place was a vague sense of disappointment. She had to admit, she'd had hopes for John Brighton.

"Okay, so life goes on. Get over it, Jul. It's no big deal."

The Calypso Public Library was quieter than usual on a Sunday night in February two hours before closing time. An older couple browsed the stacks, and in the study carrels several high school students did last-minute homework.

Julia had come to the library out of boredom. Even after all this time, it was still hard to get through the weekends. Martin had worked long hours, and they barely saw each other during the week, so they had relished their time together during the weekend. She still missed him terribly, but never as much as when Friday night rolled around.

She was looking through the new fiction, trying to find a good novel to read. She loved to read, but lately it seemed every book she started wound up depressing her. She needed something light and funny. She'd rejected a dozen books already on the basis of the jacket flaps' synopses. Too much death, too much loss, too much angst. Maybe a good mystery…no, too scary to read in the house alone. Even when Martin was alive, she had not read a mystery unless he was sitting in bed beside her. Silly…

The elevator across from the shelves where Julia stood came to a squeaking, grinding halt and the doors slid open.

Julia froze as John Brighton stepped out of the elevator, his head bent over the sheaf of papers in his hand. Before Julia could turn away, he looked up and spotted her.

"Julia! Hello!"

She hesitated. "Hello."

"Sunday night at the library, huh?"

She gave a halfhearted laugh. "Yeah, I guess so." She didn't know how to be with him. How to let him know that his secret was out.

He seemed not to notice her coldness.

"I'm doing a little last-minute research." He waved the papers with his explanation. "We're still trying to get the school-bond issue passed. I was hoping to find, somewhere in all the city's archives, a surefire way to convince the community to vote in favor of it." He motioned to the elevator. "There's some amazing history stored in that basement. I could have spent all evening down there. Did you know that Calypso's first school was in the old Lutheran church?"

She was having trouble being friendly, but he seemed oblivious. He went on, enthusiastically explaining his ideas for the public forum the school board had scheduled for the following week.

John's eyes sparked with passion as he spoke about the school-bond issue, and somewhere along the way, he won her over and she forgot about her discovery about Ellen Brighton. She found herself listening to him with increasing interest. Being a newcomer to the community, she was in the dark about some of the politics that had preceded this controversial election. It was all rather fascinating.

Before she knew what was happening, John had steered her to a comfortable lounge area in the corner of the nonfiction section, and they fell deep in conversation as though they were old friends.

Finally, he stopped talking. An awkward wedge of silence slipped between them.

"I'm sorry," he said, "I'm probably boring you to tears. It's just that I'm so wrapped up in this thing right now, it's all I can think about."

"Oh, no…it's interesting…really. Especially since I don't know very much about Calypso. I feel like a very well-informed voter now." She smiled. "I guess I'd better get down to city hall and register to vote now, huh?"

John burst out laughing. "You mean I just sat here and wasted my two-hour lecture on somebody who can't even vote?"

"Hey, don't you worry. By election day I'll be a bona fide registered Calypso voter."

There was an easier silence between them now. Julia's reservations about John had vanished in his presence.

He turned in his chair and leaned closer to her. "How is Andy doing these days? I remember he was struggling the last time we talked."

The genuine concern on his face warmed her. "Things are getting better. We're not home free yet, by any means, but we're making progress. His teacher told me you talked to her. I really appreciate that, John. You went above and beyond the call of duty, if I can use an old cliché."

He waved her thanks away. "Hey, it was no big deal. Like I told you, anything that affects the kids is part of my job."

"You love kids, don't you?"

He shrugged and flashed a self-effacing smile. "I have ever since I started teaching. I know it sounds crazy, but I didn't decide to go into teaching because of my love for children. That came later. I was an only child, so I didn't know anything about kids. Teaching seemed to be a noble thing to do. My father…"

He paused and looked at his lap, brushing at an invisible wrinkle in his pants leg. "My father was a lawyer who chose his profession for the money it would bring in. I guess teaching was my way of rebelling against him. He ended up dying before I got my degree, so it didn't matter anyway."

Looking up at her, he grinned. "Just so you know, I've tried to redeem my wrong motives, and I think I'm in this field for the right reasons now. I really have come to love the kids."

Julia seized the opening. "Tell me about your own kids. Here you practically know Sam's and Andy's life histories, and all I know is that you have three kids. But I don't know anything about them."

"Well, Jana is married and lives in Chicago. She works for an advertising agency there, and her husband is in engineering. Brant and Kyle are both at the university in Urbana. Brant is a grad student. He just got engaged to a very sweet girl. And Kyle is doing his student teaching this semester. We're—" He stopped midsentence. "I'm—I'm thrilled about that, of course."

Julia could tell by his suddenly flustered manner that John had slipped. Julia was silent, giving him a chance to explain himself. He said nothing.

"What about their mother, John?"

"What?" He was floundering.

"I'm sorry," she said, waving her hand as if to dismiss her own question. "It's none of my business. I have no right to pry."

John sighed. "No…no." He put his head down, obviously upset.

But finally, haltingly, he told Julia what she already knew.

"Their mother…she… My wife has Alzheimer's disease, Julia." The words came out in a rush now. "She doesn't live at home anymore. She's in the advanced stages, and she doesn't even know me anymore."

"Where does she live, John?" Julia felt deceitful asking a question to which she knew the answer, but she was determined to carry this conversation to its bitter end.

"She's at Parkside."

"Why haven't you mentioned that before, John?" She heard the hurt in her own voice and saw in his eyes that he understood it.

He shook his head. "I'm not sure. I'm really not sure. I don't know if I could tell you if I did know the reason."

"What do you mean by that?"

He reached out and put his hand lightly on her arm. It was a familiar gesture. Too familiar. She sat motionless waiting for him to explain.

"Julia, I'm a married man, and I love my wife, but I'm lonely. I know you can understand that. I didn't mean anything by keeping this…by keeping Ellen from you. I guess…I was afraid I would lose your friendship if you thought I was married."

"You mean if I *knew* you were married," she snapped. She couldn't suppress her anger another minute.

He sighed and gave a contrite nod. "Yes. If you knew I was married."

"You should have told me, John. I don't appreciate being toyed with."

"Hey, it wasn't like that, I promise. I enjoy your company. More than you'll ever know."

Julia brushed his hand from her arm, gathered her purse and jacket and stood. "I have to go now."

"Julia, wait. Please, don't leave like this."

She longed to hear him out, to find an excuse to stay here with him. But she didn't dare. Without another word, she ran through the library and darted through the front entrance into the cold black night.

John

Chapter Twenty-Seven

John saw Julia several times in the following weeks. They passed each other in their cars as she was leaving Parkside and he was arriving to visit Ellen. She pretended not to see him, ostensibly adjusting her rearview mirror as their cars met on the narrow drive. But he knew she had recognized him. It hurt that she wouldn't even acknowledge his presence.

Never in his life had he experienced such deep regret about something he could have changed. If only he'd been honest with Julia from the beginning. They could have been friends if not for his misguided attempts to avoid speaking of Ellen's existence. He knew he hadn't done it to protect Julia. If he were honest with himself, he had to admit that he'd been playing with fire. His motives hadn't been evil—truly they hadn't. He only wanted their friendship to go as far as propriety would allow.

But that had been terribly unfair to Julia. She was completely innocent in her ignorance of his marriage. He hadn't considered her feelings at all, hadn't allowed her to decide if she was comfortable being his friend under the circumstances. If only he could be given a second chance with her. If only…

The following week, John saw Julia at parent-teacher conferences across a crowded corridor at the high school. This time she couldn't run out on him. But her greeting was cool and distant, and she hurried on down the hallway, obviously anxious to avoid any further conversation.

Twice in the week that followed, he picked up the telephone to call her. To try and explain…to make excuses. But both times he ended up hanging up before he'd dialed the last digits. It was no use. Everything he thought to tell her would only further tangle the web of deceit he'd woven.

So he tried to put her out of his mind. The school bond had finally passed, and there was much work to be done with plans for the new school and reorganization of the other buildings in the district. He was thankful for the busyness that kept his mind off of Julia.

And off of Ellen, too.

Recently, Ellen had taken what John thought of as "a turn for the worse." Physically, she was much the same. But the quiet, subdued manner that first characterized Alzheimer's for Ellen had been replaced with one of agitation and frustration, manifesting itself in loud outcries. Ellen's words were not merely fractured English, but alien, cacophonous babbling that John could hardly bear to listen to.

At times she was so crazed that she beat on him, her thin arms flailing impotently at his chest, as though he were to blame for the ghosts that haunted her. When her tantrums were over, she would sit and weep for hours at a time, as if she understood and felt remorse for what she'd done. Where she got the strength for her frenzied outbursts, John couldn't imagine. She was a pale skeleton, and her eyes had a sunken, bilious look to them.

It became torture for John to walk through the wide doorways of Parkside each evening. No longer could he come and stay for an evening of reading and quiet companionship with Ellen—the one thing they had left. Now, he brought his offerings of flowers, fresh laundry or a dish of ice cream, then made his escape as quickly as decorum would allow.

John was not the only one who found it difficult to visit

Ellen. Many of her friends from church and her fellow teachers at school had come often in the beginning. They sat quietly with Ellen, or they came in twos and threes and visited among themselves, keeping Ellen company with their conversation. But she had inflicted her tirades on them, as well, and one by one they drifted away. Some sent a card now and then, but most had completely abandoned Ellen. And because of this, they avoided John, as well.

John didn't fault them. He, of all people, knew how difficult it was to be with Ellen now. In reality, he didn't think Ellen even understood that the visits had stopped. But John knew, and he felt the rejection keenly, as though he were the rejected one.

Even Sandra could no longer stand to see Ellen the way she had become. She called John occasionally to ask about Ellen, but their conversations were strained, and John could hear the guilt in her voice. A part of him wanted to tell her it was okay and that he understood. But another part wanted her to suffer, too, and to feel shamed for forsaking her best friend. John hated the feelings this whole miserable situation forced upon him.

Even the children's visits had tapered off. Of course they had farther to drive, and they were understandably busy with school and their jobs. But John didn't miss their veiled excuses. Sometimes he suspected them of using their fancy answering machines and caller-ID service to avoid his calls, as well.

Only Howard and MaryEllen remained completely faithful. They came each week, without fail. The trip was difficult for them, and seeing Ellen deteriorate week after week only increased their pain. But John knew better than to ask them not to come. For them, it would have been unthinkable.

Ellen's sisters came when they were in the state. Kathy, who lived in Indiana, came fairly often, but Diana and Carol had moved out of state and rarely got back for a visit. It was especially tough on them because they saw great leaps of decline in Ellen each time they came. John knew the sisters carried a measure of guilt because they couldn't be closer to help out. He didn't fault them for it, and yet, it would have been nice to have someone else to share the burden.

One particularly difficult evening when Ellen lashed out at John, none of the usual "remedies" seemed to calm her. He'd tried to coax her into a walk. He read to her, then tried to distract her with the television. He had taken her tightly into his arms, only to have her bite him.

In desperation, he fled her room, not knowing anymore how to cope with her outbursts. Shaking, he had the presence of mind to stop off at the nurses' station and ask them to give her a sedative.

He didn't wait to see that it was done, but strode on down the hall, away from Ellen's room.

What good did all his attention do? Most of the time, she didn't even know who he was; when she did, she seemed to hate him. Was Ellen any better off for the things he did for her? In his heart he knew she wasn't to blame for her actions. He knew she could no more control them than she could stop the Alzheimer's itself. But it seemed impossible not to take it personally when the woman he had loved more than half his life behaved with such violence toward him.

These questions besieged him as he pushed open the front doors and breathed in the brisk air of the coming night. More and more it was sheer relief to walk out those doors.

With his head down, he started toward his car in the parking lot. It was chilly even for March, and he pulled the collar of his jacket up around his ears. In the dusky light of evening, he saw a familiar figure leaning over the hood of a car several rows down from where he was parked. He was already headed toward her car ready to offer help, when he realized it was Julia.

She was wrestling with something on the hood of the car, and she seemed distressed.

John approached her, clearing his throat loudly to announce his presence.

"Julia?"

She looked up. Her shoulders slumped as she recognized him.

"Hi! You having car trouble?"

She seemed exasperated and embarrassed. "I think I locked my keys in the car." She gave a little groan and rummaged in her purse, which was flopped open on the hood of the car. "Stupid keys! They're not in the ignition, and I've dumped my whole purse searching for them, but they're not here. I must have put them under the seat."

"Oooh, boy. Do you have a spare set anywhere?"

"At home in my desk. A lot of good they'll do me there. I kept promising myself I'd get a spare set for my billfold, but I never got around to it." She straightened and rubbed at her neck. Meeting his eyes for the first time, she gave him a crooked smile. "Of course, with my luck, then I'd probably lock my whole purse in the car."

He laughed. "I know what you mean. In fact, I did that one time—locked my keys in my car, and thought I was so smart to have a spare in my wallet. Then I looked in the car and there sat my wallet on the console."

She smiled up at him and sifted halfheartedly through the contents of her purse again.

"Hey, listen…I'd be glad to drive you home to get your extra keys and bring you back here."

"Oh no. That's okay. You don't need to do that. I'll figure something out."

"Seriously, Julia. I don't have a thing going on tonight. It wouldn't be any trouble at all. Besides, it's too cold to stand around here for long."

She hesitated. "Oh, John. I don't know. I hate to put you out. Are you sure?"

"Absolutely. No problem. Come on, I'm parked over here."

She quickly stuffed everything back into her purse and followed him to his car. John unlocked the passenger door for her, then came around and got in behind the wheel.

"Let's see… Sweetbriar Lane, right?"

"Yes, all the way east on Sweetbriar. I think it's quickest to take Third Street over to Broadway."

"Okay."

He turned onto the highway, and they rode in awkward silence for several minutes.

Julia broke the stillness, putting her hand to her mouth with a gasp. "Oh, John. I can't believe I'm so stupid. My house keys are on the key ring with my car keys. I'm not going to be able to get into the house. Andy is spending the night with a friend, and Sam won't be home till after supper tonight." She put her head in her hands. "This is embarrassing. I am so sorry to cause all this trouble."

"Julia, don't worry about it." He started to reach out and touch her arm, then thought better of it and ostensibly adjusted his rearview mirror. "Let me think… Do the boys have keys?"

"Yes. Sam has both house keys and car keys. He's at Brian Baylor's house. I'd have you take me there if I knew where Brian lived. Do you know him?"

"I know who he is, but I don't have any idea where he lives. Can you call him?"

"I don't have his number, but I could call information. But I don't have a cell phone. Haven't moved into the technical world yet," she joked.

He laughed. "Well, I have, but it doesn't do much good if you forget to carry your phone. But it's okay. We can swing by my house, and you can call Sam from there and we can go pick up the keys."

Julia was nearly squirming with embarrassment. "I should have called from Parkside. Would you mind taking me back there? I'm sorry to make you go so far out of your way."

"I don't mind at all, but I live just four blocks from here. It's a lot closer, and you'll have a comfortable place to wait."

"Okay," she said, resignation plain in her voice. She paused, as if trying to decide whether to say something or not, then she sighed and plunged in.

"John, I am really uncomfortable about this. I wouldn't blame you at all if you thought it looked like I set this whole thing up. But, honestly, I didn't."

"It never crossed my mind. Although if I'd had some time to think about it, it might have." He grinned at her, teasing, trying to put her at ease.

She didn't return his smile, a frown wrinkling her forehead.

He turned serious. "Hey, I believe you, Julia. I'm just kidding. Honest. Listen, if anybody needs to do any explaining here, it's me."

He was silent for a minute, trying to compose his thoughts. Finally he plunged in. "Julia, I'm sorry for the things I said in the library the other night. I had no right to say what I did. And even more than that, I was very wrong for not telling you up front about Ellen."

Julia sat with her head down, preoccupied with a hangnail on one of her tightly clasped fingers. But he knew she was listening and he went on.

"I didn't want to say anything when we first met because I didn't want it to look like I was after your sympathy. Frankly, it was nice to relate to someone who wasn't always overcome with pity for me. Then, after we got to know each other, it seemed…well, I had let it go so long without telling you, I was afraid you would avoid me if you found out after all that time that I was married."

She turned and opened her mouth, but he held up a hand.

"Hear me out…please. I've thought about it a lot, Julia. I know I was being very selfish and terribly unfair to you. I needed someone to talk to, and I guess in that way, I used you. I want to be careful how I say this, but…as attractive as you are, and as much as I enjoy talking to you, I wasn't hitting on you. I promise you that. At this point it probably sounds trite, but I'm really a pretty decent guy." He smiled in the semidarkness of the car. She didn't respond, so he went on, determined to convince her.

"I love my wife, Julia, and I intend to stay faithful to her. I believe in the wedding vows…in sickness and in health included."

Now she turned to him, a gentle smile lighting her face. "Thank you, John. I appreciate your honesty. I'm sorry I didn't give you a chance to explain that night at the library. I shouldn't have run out on you like that. I was angry…and to be honest, I was disappointed in you. It bothered me a great deal that you led me to believe you were single—available. And then out of the blue I find out not only do you have a wife, but she lives at Parkside. It just seems like the subject might have come up once or twice before it did." She gave him a chastening half smile.

"You're right," he said. "I plead guilty." They were approaching the driveway to his house and he depressed the brake pedal. "Julia, I don't know if you will believe this, but I'm not usually a liar. I know I was deceitful about Ellen. I realize now how terribly wrong that was, and I'm truly sorry. I've asked the Lord's forgiveness, and if you can forgive me, I'd like to start over." He got out of the car and went around to open her door.

He bowed as he opened her door and made his voice prim and proper. "Good evening, ma'am. I'm John Brighton. I live right here at 245 Oaklawn. My wife, Ellen, lives at Parkside, and we have three beautiful children together." He knew it sounded corny, but he wanted to make her laugh, to lighten the moment.

She rolled her eyes, then grinned up at him. Extending a hand, she followed suit. "Julia Sinclair. Nice to meet you, John." She let him help her from the car, and followed him up the walk to the front door.

He unlocked the door and stepped back to let her in first. As he led her through the main rooms on the first floor, she admired the old house. They chatted cordially while John gave her a brief tour. While she oohed and aahed, he bragged about Ellen's taste in decorating the house. It felt good to be open with her about Ellen, to not have to weigh his words so carefully.

"Would you like something to drink? Iced tea?"

"That'd be great. Don't go to any trouble though."

"No trouble. I made sun tea this morning. Do you take sugar?"

"Mmm. Sounds great. No sugar though, thanks."

While Julia tried to reach Sam, John poured tea over ice in tall glasses and brought them into the living room.

Julia hung up the phone and reported that the boys were playing basketball, but Mrs. Baylor wasn't sure where. They weren't due back for another hour. Julia explained the situation to her and arranged to call back later.

"Why don't we go get a bite to eat while we wait? There's a great little diner just a couple blocks down the street."

"Oh, John. You don't have to do that."

"I don't *have* to, but I'd sure enjoy the company. You haven't eaten have you?"

"Well, no." She looked at her watch, then at him, her brow knitted. "If you're sure you don't mind."

He smiled and jingled his car keys at her. "Let's go. I'm starving." He led the way to the front door, feeling happier than he had in a very long time.

Chapter Twenty-Eight

At the café near John's house, they ordered burgers and fries. Conversation came easier now that they'd cleared the air. Wanting to begin anew in complete honesty with Julia, John told her about the rough day he'd had with Ellen. He poured out the whole story from the beginning, concluding, "It's just devastating to have her vent her rage on me. I honestly don't think she has any idea who I am…. I know I shouldn't take it so personally, but still, it's hard not to. I feel so frustrated for her."

The waitress brought their food and they picked at it in silence for a few minutes. It seemed neither of them were hungry after all—except for conversation.

Julia wiped her mouth on the paper napkin and shook her head sympathetically. "Oh, John, I just can't imagine how awful it must be to have someone fade away before your eyes like that. You know, I was so angry because I didn't get to tell Martin goodbye, but this must be so much worse. You have to say goodbye every day."

Julia's face softened, and John could hear in her voice that her kindness was genuine.

"That says it perfectly. I feel like Ellen has died over and over. In many ways it would have been easier if she had just suddenly died one day. This has been…I don't know…a walking death, I guess. Ellen has been dying a day at a time. We've lost one thing after another, and I know it will continue that way, until finally, there's nothing left at all. This is a terrible disease, Julia…it's simply terrible." He stared into his coffee mug, afraid of breaking down in front of her.

When he looked up, he saw there were tears in her eyes. He went on, emboldened by her attentiveness and sensitivity. "First I lost my confidante. Communication was always such an essential part of our relationship. Ellen and I talked all the time—about everything. There was nothing we couldn't tell each other. It seems so cruel that one of the first things Alzheimer's took from her was her ability to speak—or at least to speak sensibly." John shrugged and shook his head, feeling anew his confusion at the way things had turned out.

"After that, things went downhill in a hurry. I lost my helpmate. Ellen was a teacher, and we frequently worked together on projects at school—things that involved the students. Only a year after she was diagnosed with Alzheimer's, she had to quit teaching. Of course, she'd had it much longer than that. We just didn't know what it was. About the same time, I started doing all the cooking and shopping. We finally hired someone to clean when she couldn't handle that anymore. Of course, eventually, we needed someone at the house all the time."

He told her then about the awful day that Ellen had wandered off, and about the excruciating decision he'd had to make to put her in Parkside.

John struggled with how much he should say. Julia was so understanding that it was tempting to tell her more than he should. But he went on, avoiding her eyes. "Then I lost my lover. When Ellen didn't know me anymore—or worse, when she thought I was her father or one of the boys—it just didn't seem right to…well, you know what I mean." He paused, overcome with emotion. Though he willed the tears

away, his eyes burned with them. "When Ellen first moved
to Parkside, at least she was still a companion to me. I could
go and just sit with her. I felt it meant something to her…that
I was helping her by being there. And it eased my loneliness,
too. But now, I don't even have that. I just don't have any
part of her anymore, Julia."

"You still have the memories, John," she said quietly.

He paused, thinking about her comment. "I do. We made
some good memories. But I have to work so hard to conjure
them up, it sometimes doesn't seem worth it. The truth is,
Ellen is a totally different person now. I feel as though my
Ellen has been dead for years."

"Oh, John." Julia shook her head slowly. "I'm so sorry."

"Alzheimer's is a cruel disease. It has totally robbed Ellen
of her personality. There's nothing left of the old Ellen—the
one I loved." His eyes were unfocused, staring into the face
of the past. He tried to remember now, and the remembering
was easier because Julia was there to share it.

"Ellen was funny and smart and strong. She loved to 'debate,' she called it—" he chuckled as he suddenly saw Ellen's
furrowed brow, and the expression she always wore during a
good argument "—but she never held a grudge."

His thoughts carried him to the past. "Ellen was such a
good mother. We lost a baby at birth—our first—and I think
Ellen treasured the other three that much more because of it.
It makes me angry that she'll never be able to see what our
kids have become. We had so many plans for these years. We
wanted to travel. She always wanted to go to Europe…." His
voice trailed off again, remembering.

Julia didn't try to fill the silence.

"I'm grateful this happened after the kids were grown and
living away from home," John said. "It would have been far
worse to deal with it while they were still home. But, oh, I'd
give anything if Ellen could see how happy Jana is…how
much Brant likes his job…how excited Kyle is about student
teaching. I think you probably understand more than any-

one how the joy diminishes when you can no longer share these things with the one you love—the one with whom you gave life to your children."

"I do understand that, John. I would never tell my children this, but when Martin died, it was as though their lives became a little less, somehow. It's hard to explain, but their father was so much a part of them, and even though I see him in both of the boys, it's not the same now that he is gone. It's like he was the standard for comparison, and now there is no standard. Does that make sense?"

"I think so."

"Martin was such a strong person. He wasn't perfect, and I've tried to be careful not to put him on a pedestal like so many widows do. But he had a…a presence about him—a strength. The boys don't have it, at least not yet. I think sometimes I fault them for that. Maybe it would have been easier if we'd had girls. Maybe I wouldn't have expected so much from Martin's daughters."

"And maybe you would have expected more. One thing I've learned, Julia, is that it doesn't pay to play the 'if only' game. It's hard enough to get through what is, without worrying about what might have been."

"I know you're right. But that's something I've always found difficult. I'm too analytical, I guess. And I do play the 'if only' game. Oh, I lay awake those first nights torturing myself. If only I'd insisted we get new tires on the car. If only I hadn't told him that morning to hurry home…" She paused, obviously lost in her memories of the past.

John waited for her to come back from her reverie.

"I was so lonely—so terribly lonely. You know, when Martin went away on a business trip—even a long one—I often thought, 'this isn't so bad…I think I could survive as a widow.' But I had no idea…*no idea* of the loneliness, the emptiness you feel when someone you love is gone forever from your life."

She looked at John, her brows arched, as though a revelation had struck her. "That's how it is with Ellen, isn't it? She's...she's gone forever from your life."

He set his jaw and nodded.

They barely touched their food, taking sustenance in the conversation instead. The waitress cleared their dishes away, and John paid the check. It was dark when they got in the car, and as they drove back to his house, talking of less serious things, John watched Julia's expressions in the ebb and flow of the yellow light cast by the streetlamps they passed. With fascination, he saw her hands echo the words she spoke. He remembered now that it was one of the first things he'd noticed about her that day they'd first met in his office.

Back at his house, Julia called the Baylors again. She relayed to John that Sam was back, and he heard her make arrangements to meet him at their house.

When they pulled into Julia's driveway ten minutes later, Sam wasn't there yet, so they sat in the car and continued their conversation.

Julia began to talk again about the dreadful day Martin had been killed. Her voice was detached, as though she were telling someone else's story. John could see by the faraway look in her eyes that she was reliving the day in her mind—going to school to get the boys...the horror of telling her sons that their father was dead.

"That was the most difficult thing I have ever done in my life. I went to Andy's class first. I'm not sure why. Isn't that strange? I don't remember why I went there first." Her voice rose with emotion and questioning, and she looked up at him.

Then her eyes glazed over again. "I remember Andy came bounding out of the classroom with a huge smile on his face—like I'd come to bring him a wonderful surprise or something. I—I don't remember what I said, but I didn't want to give him the news inside the school, so I made him come outside with me. Then he was *sure* I had a surprise for him. I must have been calm because he...he was babbling on trying to guess the surprise. He thought we had a new car. He guessed that we were going to visit his grandparents. He guessed a pony! A pony! I—I couldn't make myself tell him to stop the guessing. And then…then I had to tell him his daddy was gone forever. I've never felt like such a traitor. I will never forget the look in his eyes…." Suddenly, her voice broke. She put her fist to her mouth, but the sobs came anyway. She wept bitterly, unable to speak.

John was overcome with compassion for her. He felt the well of tears behind his eyelids, hot and threatening to spill. Spontaneously, he leaned across the seat and took Julia in his arms. Tenderly at first, then with more insistence. Almost instinctively he took her face in his hands, felt the smoothness of her damp skin against his palms. Before she could wrestle free, he realized what was happening and backed away in horror at his own unbridled emotions.

"Oh, Julia. I am so sorry. Please, I didn't mean for that to happen. I had no right—"

But she was already out of the car running for the front porch. He got out of the car and ran after her. Halfway up the steps he grabbed her shoulders and turned her toward him.

He looked straight into her eyes and spoke firmly. "Julia, I was wrong. I promise you that will never happen again."

She was trembling. "It wasn't just you, John. I'm guilty, too. And you're right, it won't happen again."

They heard a car approaching, and John dropped his hands from her shoulders. The car slowed and turned into the driveway behind John's car. Sam got out and waved as the Baylors backed out of the drive. Then he ran up onto the porch.

"Hi, Sam," Julia said with obviously feigned cheeriness. "You know Mr. Brighton, the superintendent of schools? John, this is Sam."

"Sure, I remember Sam." John extended his hand.

Sam shook it, a questioning look on his face.

"I rescued your mom in the parking lot at Parkside. Seems she locked every key she owns in the car."

"Yeah, that's what Brian's mom said." Sam cocked his head, as though not quite sure he bought John's explanation. "Well, thanks a lot for bringing Mom home. I've got my keys." He waved them in the air as proof.

John turned to Julia. "Can I give you a ride back to your car?"

"No, thanks. You've done more than enough." She winced.

John pretended not to catch the double meaning of her words, but he cringed inside, as he waved off her thanks. "You're sure. How will you get to work in the morning?"

"I can catch a ride with a coworker. She just lives a couple blocks up the road." She motioned toward the street. "I do appreciate everything, John. Thank you. We'll be fine now." She dismissed him.

"Well, okay," he said, drawing out his words, reluctant to leave. "I guess I'll be seeing you."

Julia

Chapter Twenty-Nine

Julia watched John pull out of the driveway while Sam unlocked the front door.

"How was your day, Sam? Did you have a good time at the Baylor's?" She forced her voice to steady as she followed him through the living room to the kitchen.

She heard the teenage tenor of Sam's voice as he answered, but when she caught him staring at her with a puzzled expression on his face, she realized she had not heard one word of his response.

"I…I'm sorry, buddy. What did you say?"

Sam tipped his head to one side, his bangs falling across his forehead. "Are you okay, Mom?"

She felt her cheeks burn and was grateful she hadn't turned the light on in the kitchen yet. "Sure. I'm fine. You…you want something to eat before you go to bed?"

He shook his head, his bangs flopping. "Nah. We had pizza. You sure you're all right?"

She reached up to brush the hair out of his face. "We need to get you in for a haircut. How long has it been? I'll call for an appointment tomorrow."

But Sam wouldn't let her change the subject. "How come

Mr. Brighton brought you home?" There was a note of suspicion in his tone.

"Didn't we tell you? I locked my keys in the car."

"At work? What was he doing there?"

She turned her back to him and ran hot water over the dishrag. "He was visiting his— He has a family member there.
He was visiting." She wrung out the steaming rag and
scrubbed at a stubborn, invisible stain on the countertop.

"Oh. Well, you could have called me, you know."

"I tried. Nobody was home."

He shrugged. "Oh, sorry. I forgot we went to the park."

She looked pointedly at the clock. *You've got school tomorrow. You'd better get to bed.* She made excuses and hurried into the bathroom, locking the door behind her.

She rested her hands on the counter on either side of the
sink and stared at her reflection in the mirror. How had she
let that happen with John? One minute they were talking and
the next she'd suddenly found herself in the warm circle of
his arms. A knot settled in the pit of her stomach. What was
wrong with her? How could she have let that happen?

And Sam was no dummy. He'd obviously known something was amiss. Her stomach roiled, and for a minute she
thought she might be sick.

The wave of nausea passed, but the tears came on the next
crest. Julia turned on the sink faucet full force to mask her
cries. Then she slumped to the floor in front of the bathtub
and sobbed till her ribs ached.

John

Chapter Thirty

John drove home from Julia's house in a daze. He tried to make sense of all that had happened, but was more confused than ever.

One thing he knew for certain: he did not want to have to dread running into Julia the way he had after their confrontation in the library.

When he felt sure that Sam would be asleep, he dialed her number. She answered on the second ring.

"Julia. Hi, it's John."

"Yes?" Her tone was understandably frosty.

"I just wanted to make sure everything is okay between us. Are you all right?"

"I think so. I'm…I'm still trying to sort things out."

"Me, too. But I don't want you to worry. What happened tonight will never happen again. Okay?"

"I trust you. We just got caught up in the emotion of the moment, that's all. And I was as much to blame as you, John. I'm sorry. Please don't feel guilty."

"Well, it's a little late for that. I do feel very guilty. But it's over now. Let's go on from here."

"Okay."

"Did you make arrangements for your car?"

"It's all taken care of, John." There was a definite chill in her tone.

"Oh. Good."

Silence.

"Julia, would you have dinner with me tomorrow night?"

"I don't think that would be a good idea."

"Well, how about going jogging with me tomorrow night? Would you feel comfortable with that?"

There was such a long silence that John wondered if they'd been disconnected. He held out an excuse. "We're both going to be running anyway."

He heard her sigh on the other end of the line.

"Julia?"

"Okay. I'll meet you at the park. What time?"

"Would seven-thirty be all right?"

"Okay. We should be done with supper by then. I'll see you then."

"Okay. Good night."

"Good night, John."

Running in the park became their habit. There they felt safe from their own emotions, and it didn't seem improper for them to be seen together in a public place. As wonderful as it was, Calypso was still a small town. John was well aware that gossip spread faster than wildfire here, and the last thing he wanted was rumor of a scandal. They were careful to come and go alone, and to keep their distance physically.

For a while John was elated with the headiness of their blossoming friendship. There were moments, though, when guilt bore down on him, like when he realized that his visits to Ellen were becoming more brief and less personal. He started forcing himself to stay longer each evening, and to endure Ellen's angry outbursts more stoically than before.

He rationalized that Julia's friendship fortified him for the agony he faced with Ellen. The promise of Julia's support and encouragement did help him bear the visits each evening. Knowing that in a few minutes he could pour out his anguish to Julia—or simply engage in some lighthearted chitchat—he found himself being more gentle and compassionate with Ellen.

He had never been in better physical shape in his life. They were running three or four miles several times a week, and only the foulest weather kept them from meeting at the park those evenings at seven-thirty. Often their cooldown time stretched into an hour of walking and talking.

Occasionally Julia expressed concern that she was spending too much time away from the boys. Still she was there each evening, waiting for him.

One night, though, she told him—rather evasively, he thought—that she wouldn't be there the next evening, a Friday night.

"Oh? Why, you have a date?" John teased her in the intimate repartee they'd grown comfortable with.

But she was serious. "Yes, John. I do."

He literally stopped in his tracks. He stood there, breathing hard, with his hands on his waist. "Are you serious?"

"Yes, I am." She kept running, and he had to hurry to catch up.

"May I ask with whom?"

"His name is Bill Morland. He works at Parkside."

"Oh." John didn't know what else to say. He knew Bill Morland. He was the assistant administrator of Parkside. He was good-looking, divorced and, quite honestly, John couldn't stand the man.

They jogged along in silence for almost a mile.

Finally Julia turned to him. "Why so quiet?"

"No reason."

She started in on him like a house afire. "John, you and I are just friends, remember? I would like to get married again someday. I'm finding that a little difficult to work toward when I haven't had one date since Martin died." Her tone had turned angry and sarcastic.

"Well, you could do a lot better than Bill Morland." His anger matched hers.

"Oh, give me a break! Who did you have in mind, Your Majesty?"

John threw up his hands. "Hey, it's none of my business. You go out with whoever you like." He pulled ahead of her then and sprinted back to his car.

When he reached the car he turned to see Julia gaping after him. He reached in through the open window of his car and pulled out a towel. He stood there swabbing the sweat from his face and neck, trying to cool off in more ways than one. Unsuccessful, he threw the towel to the floor of the car. He got in, revved the engine and screeched out of the parking lot. He knew he was acting like an immature, impetuous teenager, but he felt powerless to stop himself.

At home he got into the shower and let the force of the hot water soothe his anger. He was being ridiculous. He had no claim to Julia whatsoever. His little tantrum in the park had betrayed his true feelings for her, both to himself and to Julia. He owed her an apology.

He tried to call her all evening long, but there was no answer. At eleven o'clock he finally gave up and went to bed. But sleep eluded him and he lay awake wrestling with his conscience. When the sun streamed through his window hours later, he knew only two things: He did not want to lose Julia. And he could not have her.

Two weeks passed and Julia didn't show up at the park. John went jogging every evening, hoping against hope she would be there, but deeply disappointed when she wasn't.

One night almost three weeks after their fight, he got out of his car, and broke into a run as usual.

She materialized at his side.

"Well, look who's here," he said as casually as he could muster, trying not to give away the wild pounding of his heart.

"Hi."

"Julia, I'm sorry."

"Hey. Forget it. I shouldn't have gotten so mad. Let's just forget it and pick up where we left off."

"Umm…where we left off? I believe you called me 'Your Majesty,' and I peeled out of the parking lot like a spoiled brat."

She laughed. "Well, then let's start from the day before that."

"Deal."

They shook on it, and he fought the fierce temptation to pull her into a grateful embrace. His relief at their reconciliation was boundless. A nagging knowledge ate at him: they would eventually have to deal with this again. But he pushed the thought away determined to take each day as it came. No use trying to look too far into the future.

Christmas went by more easily than it had in four years. For the first time since Ellen had moved to Parkside, John didn't bring her home for the holiday. She had become calmer in the past few months, partly due to a new medication her doctor had prescribed. But now, any change in her routine seemed to cause her anxiety. The doctor recommended they bring Christmas to her rather than taking her home.

It was a nice Christmas, both at Parkside and back at the house on Oaklawn. The kids were all home, and Ellen's parents were there, of course. They had visited Ellen in the afternoon, taking the gifts there to be opened, but the real celebration took place at the house. It was almost as though they were weaning themselves from Ellen. Her absence wasn't felt quite so keenly now that everyone was accustomed to her being at Parkside and John being alone in the big house.

With Christmas over, the day of Brant and Cynthia's wedding was fast approaching. John was grateful for all the preparation involved in getting this son of his married. It took his mind off the worries about Ellen—and off his guilt over Julia.

He had no idea that the groom's parents had so many responsibilities. There were tuxedos to order, a rehearsal dinner to plan, gifts to buy. It was a bittersweet time. John remembered so clearly the joy he and Ellen had felt as they planned Jana's wedding. He longed for the old Ellen in a way he hadn't in many months—both for sharing the happiness of this occasion and for the practical help she would have been. He knew exactly nothing about wedding etiquette.

Jana was very helpful when she could find the time. If he asked for it, Julia offered wedding advice, too. But of course, her help had to be given from afar.

John and Julia had agreed it would be best not to mention their friendship to the children. Julia's boys—because their allegiance to their father was still so fresh—might not understand John's place in Julia's life. John's kids lived far enough away that there was no need to discuss it with them and risk a misunderstanding.

John felt somewhat troubled that he and Julia had this secret to keep. It seemed to degrade their friendship. But they had talked about it at length and both felt it was best this way. So they continued week after week, meeting in the park, playing therapist to each other and growing closer day by day.

One evening as they jogged in the park, they came face-to-face with Sandra Brenner. John was embarrassed. Stuttering and stammering, he introduced the two women, deftly skirting any mention of his relationship with Julia.

Sandra shook Julia's hand warmly, and gave John a knowing smile before she jogged away.

That night when John was getting ready for bed, the phone rang.

"John, hi. It's Sandra."

He steeled himself. "Hi, Sandra."

"Hey, I just want to put your mind at ease. I know you were uncomfortable introducing me to your girlfriend. I just want you to know that I understand. And I'm happy for you. If any-one deserves to have some happiness, it's you."

"No… Sandra, you misunderstood." He was angry at her assumption. "Julia is a good friend, nothing more."

A long pause. "Somehow, I find that hard to believe."

"Well, don't go jumping to conclusions. That's not fair, Sandra."

"I'll take your word for it. But I think Ellen would under-stand if—what's her name? Julia?—if she were more than a friend. I don't think Ellen or anyone else would judge you if you found someone else. Ellen is the same as dead, John. I admire your devotion to her, but don't be too hard on your-self."

"Ellen is very much alive, Sandra. If you'd go visit her once in a while you might know that."

"I—I'm sorry, John." She sounded truly repentant. "I shouldn't have said that. But you know what I mean. She's not going to get any better. And, John, it's not as though you're going to hurt her. She won't know. I've visited her re-cently enough to know that."

"Well, thank you for your opinion—I think. But please don't start any rumors, Sandra. I assure you, Julia and I are friends—nothing more."

He slammed down the phone. It sounded so cheap to hear Julia called his "girlfriend." Could he trust Sandra? He'd told her the truth, and he would feel awful if rumors to the con-trary started going around town.

But Sandra had planted a seed in his mind. *Would* anyone judge him? Could he be justified if this friendship were more? He brushed the thoughts aside, but the seed germinated some-where in the back of his mind.

Chapter Thirty-One

John began to worry about Julia. She had been depressed since Christmas and had begun to drop hints that she wanted to break off their friendship. He knew she longed to be married again. Over the last weeks and months she had dated off and on, but hadn't met anyone yet that she wanted to date steadily.

She usually told John whenever she had a date, partly because she had to break their jogging dates. Sometimes she would report back to him about how the evening had gone. After all, they were just friends.

But he was miserable when he knew she was out with another man. *Another man,* as though *he* were her man. He pushed the thought from his mind.

He'd begun to do that a lot lately—push out all the thoughts that crowded in about them being more than friends. Because he was married, and they were just friends.

The morning of Brant and Cynthia's wedding, John woke to a gray fog hanging over Chicago. The January air was frigid, but Brant's spirits were buoyant.

John, Brant and Kyle drove to Chicago early in the day and dropped their garment bags and shaving kits off at Mark and

Jana's apartment. Then Mark took the guys to a basketball court at the community gym where they played a cutthroat game of two-on-two.

They came back to the apartment in high spirits and took turns showering, shaving and eating the sandwiches Jana had waiting for them. She clucked over them like a mother hen, straightening their ties and spit licking Kyle's hair till he threatened to do her bodily harm.

It heartened John to see his kids enjoying one another, looking forward to a happy occasion together. There had been too many somber meetings between them lately. And while Ellen's absence was keenly felt, John knew they had each come to terms with it in their own way.

Jana, especially, seemed to have a new peace about her mother. She drove to Calypso several times each month to visit Ellen at Parkside. She usually stopped by the house afterward, declaring to John how good all the staff were to Ellen and how nice her room was. John suspected she was still trying to convince herself that sending Ellen to Parkside had been the right thing to do.

Marriage agreed with Jana. He watched her bustling around their apartment getting ready for the wedding and pride swelled in him. Jana looked radiant in the cranberry-colored satin dress she'd bought for the wedding. Her hair was cut in a new shorter style, and John was startled by how much she looked like Ellen.

Finally it was time to leave for the church. The ceremony began promptly at four o'clock. Though the fog had not lifted, inside, the chapel was beautiful in candlelight and simple ivy greenery.

Brant and Cynthia had chosen to have a small wedding. Only Kyle and Cynthia's sister stood with them as attendants. Their families and closest friends waited expectantly, scattered throughout the first few pews.

John felt a surge of happiness for Brant as he met his bride at the altar. Cynthia was breathtakingly beautiful in the elegant white gown. Her blue eyes met Brant's, and the love they shared was unmistakable.

John's throat swelled with emotion—joy and pride in this handsome, noble son who stood before him, and great hope for the future Brant and Cynthia had ahead of them. Yet underneath the joyful sentiments lay a deep sorrow for what they all had lost. The contrast between Brant and Cynthia's closeness and John's utter loneliness was acute. And painful. If only Julia could be here beside him. What a comfort she would have been.

The thought startled him. Why was he thinking of Julia today? It should be Ellen—his wife, Brant's mother—who he was longing to have at his side.

Two voices began to quarrel inside his mind. He felt as though he stood on the brink of a crucial decision—perhaps a life-changing decision. Surely he deserved the love and companionship that Julia had added to his life. The thought of her brought a smile to his lips.

He knew he could not go on with Julia as they had been. The passion was too great. There was more—much more— simmering between them than friendship, and it begged to be fulfilled. He had grieved—oh, how he'd grieved for Ellen. But she was gone. She was virtually dead. There was so little left of Ellen's spirit—the Ellen that he had loved. It was hard for John to visit her anymore. He'd remained faithful to go to her nearly every day, but it had been months since she'd uttered his name. He couldn't remember the last time.

And though the tantrums had abated, her constant nonsensical jabbering repulsed him. It hurt to be repulsed by someone who had once been so dear to him. But *once* was the operative word. There was nothing left of Ellen that was dear to him now…nothing but memories. And even those were fading.

He felt like an old man when he was with Ellen.

It was Julia who was dear to him now. She was alive and vibrant and responsive. She made him feel like a twenty-year-old kid. *He loved her!* He hadn't really admitted it to himself until now. But he had no doubt that she loved him, too, even though they'd not yet dared to speak the words. He was certain she felt the same about him. And he needed so to be loved right now.

The organ stopped playing, and an expectant hush fell over the small sanctuary. The minister, his hair and beard white with age, but his voice rich and sonorous, began the litany of the marriage ceremony.

Cynthia's father gave his daughter's hand to Brant, and the couple turned to face each other. Brant repeated the vows after the minister. "I, Brant, take thee, Cynthia, to be my lawful wedded wife. To have and to hold from this day forward…"

Brant's next words gripped John like a vise, and the quarrel in his mind became fierce. "…for better or for worse…" He and Ellen had shared so many years of "for better"—but now he was living "for worse."

"…for richer, for poorer, in sickness and in health…" But this was a sickness that had no end, like a death. Ellen would never recover. Sandra was right. Ellen may as well be dead.

"…to love and to cherish from this day forward…" He had loved and cherished Ellen with all of his heart. He had been good to her. He had taken care of her—was still taking care of her. And he would continue to do so. Julia would help him take care of her. They would never let their love abandon Ellen.

Then Brant spoke the words that would forever transform John. "And to thee only will I cleave, as long as we both shall live."

Thee only…thee only…thee only—the words echoed over and over in John's mind—*as long as we both shall live.*

A wave of nausea washed over John as he watched Kyle and his bride light the unity candle. A snippet of Scripture that Oscar used to quote wove itself through his mind, slicing like a knife. "The heart is deceitful above all things and beyond cure. Who can understand it? I the Lord search the heart and examine the mind, to reward a man according to his conduct, according to what his deeds deserve."

John caught his breath. His own heart had deceived him mightily. The truth that had been veiled to him now lay stark and naked in front of him. He saw exactly what his conduct—his deeds—deserved, and it pierced his spirit to the quick.

John Brighton had once stood before a holy altar and spoken a solemn promise in front of God to *his* bride. Many years and much sorrow lay between; nevertheless, it was an eternal promise he had made. Even before that, before he'd ever met Ellen, the picture of that young college boy standing in a lonely dorm room, his father's crumpled obituary in hand, was vividly clear in John's mind. He had taken an oath to be the husband his father had never been.

A crystal recollection of that resolve came back to him now. John Brighton was a man of his word. Could he face his children, could he face Howard and MaryEllen or the memory of Oscar and Hattie; indeed, could he face himself, if he carried out what he'd sat in this church—this hallowed place—and planned to do? He knew now that the precipice he was about to plummet over was his very *honor.*

He had tried to justify his love for Julia, because, in a way, it *was* a pure love. There had been only one embrace, and they had both fled from that. Yet, the truth was, every time he saw Julia, every time he heard her husky voice, it stirred embers of passion that threatened to burst into flame.

Like all bridegrooms, he had made his promise to Ellen without knowing what the future held. Now it was time to redeem that promise.

Could he bear to give up Julia? She had been the only light in the dark nightmare he was living. Though he loved her with all his heart, he knew for certain he could not continue to see her without tarnishing his honor, without defiling the holy ground of his marriage.

He stood at a crossroad today, on the verge of trespass.

Deep sadness welled inside him. Yet stronger than the sadness was the peace that poured over him as he determined to do the thing he knew he must now do.

Oh, God. I've been so blind. Please forgive me, please! And give me the strength I need....

Cynthia was speaking her vows now. In the quiet of his heart, John echoed the words, renewing the promises he had made to Ellen at that altar so long ago. *I, John, take thee, Ellen...in sickness and in health, to love and to cherish from this day forward, and to thee only will I cleave as long as we both shall live...as long as it takes, El.*

The organ swelled and the soloist took the platform to sing a wedding prayer. What happened next, John could only call a miracle. Outside the chapel windows, the fog lifted almost instantaneously, and rays of sunlight flooded through the stained-glass windows. The sanctuary was bathed in a golden light that was almost tangible. He would have thought it an apparition that only he had seen, had he not heard the audible gasp of the congregation.

John felt he had received a holy blessing. What had begun as a willful decision to love Ellen anew, in an instant became a full-fledged emotion. A new, pure love for his wife rained down on him like a fountain, and he felt the cleansing the fountain offered as surely as though it were streams of living water.

Chapter Thirty-Two

In spite of John's sadness at knowing he must say goodbye to Julia, peace engulfed him, wrapping him in a blanket of assurance. He was doing the right thing.

It would be right for Julia, too. It had been unfair to tie her to himself as he had. Genuine love would let her go. It would free her to find someone to share her life completely, in a way he was unable to do.

He had been flirting dangerously with sin, and as the revelation unfolded, he was ashamed. He'd tried to fool himself into believing he was above temptation, but now he saw how close he had come to falling. He'd held God at arm's length, fearful of coming into the light, lest the true motives and intentions of his heart be exposed. They had been revealed after all—with glaring acuity.

His deepest guilt was that he had carried Julia along in the charade. Now he had to tell her of his transgression, and he knew it would hurt her deeply.

He was surprised to find that he spent no time worrying about what he would say to her. He trusted the words would be there when the time came.

* * *

He and his little family sent Brant and Cynthia off on their honeymoon in a shower of good wishes and love. John and Kyle stayed in Chicago with Mark and Jana Saturday night. Early Sunday afternoon Kyle caught a ride back to Urbana with a friend who lived in Chicago. John left for home a few hours later.

The ride back to Calypso was lonely compared to the revelry of the drive into Chicago with his sons. But he was glad for the time alone to think and to pray about the changes he needed to make in his life—and about how he would tell Julia.

He wanted to make a clean break. He didn't want to leave her hanging in any way. He had cheated her long enough of the chance to start a new life and make new friends and meet someone who could share her life.

In many ways she was still grieving Martin, even though it had been over two years since her husband's accident. It was partly John's fault that she still grieved, for he had put her in a limbo that had forbidden her to move forward in the process of letting Martin go. John knew Julia wouldn't see it that way, but he saw many things more clearly now. His decision had illuminated truths that he'd been completely blind to before.

In spite of the gnawing sadness, in spite of the aching emptiness he already felt at the thought of losing Julia, he felt like a man reborn. It amazed him. It was liberating to be doing the right thing, and to know without a doubt that it was right.

John turned onto Oaklawn just as the sun was sinking below the rooftops. His old house hadn't looked so warm and friendly in a long time. Even the stark gray branches of the January trees looked welcoming, ushering him home.

He wanted to call Julia…to warn her. It didn't seem right to spring this on her without preparing her. He wanted her to have time to see, as he did, that his decision was right.

He showered and dressed, then went to the phone on his nightstand and dialed her number. As the phone rang on the other end, and he realized he was about to hear her voice, his resolve weakened for the first time since Brant's wedding. But he steeled himself to go through with it.

"Hello?"

"Julia, it's John."

"John! Hi!" He didn't often call her at home. She sounded surprised. And pleased. "How did the wedding go?"

"It was beautiful. It was a nice weekend." Unexpectedly, sadness overwhelmed him. This was goodbye, and he knew she heard it in his voice.

"John? Is everything all right?"

"Oh, Julia. It is, and it isn't."

"John? What's wrong?"

The compassion in her voice drew him like a magnet. This wasn't going to be easy. "I have to talk to you, Julia. But…not on the phone." Impulsively he asked her, "Could you get away tonight for a while?"

"The boys are at Martin's folks. They won't be back till around ten. Do you want to come over here?"

He hesitated. He'd never been in her house before. "Yes, if you're okay with that. Ten minutes?"

"That'll be fine."

He felt as though he'd already blown it. He could hear the anxiety in her voice. Well, at least she wouldn't have to suffer long. In an hour it would all be over. *They* would be over.

He drove through the streets of Calypso, quiet on a wintry Sunday evening. Julia's porch light was on. John parked on the street and walked across the front lawn. She met him at the door and let him in without a word.

Her house looked much as he had imagined it. Earthy colors. Just cluttered enough to be warm and welcoming. One wall across from the fireplace lined with bookshelves. Original paintings on the wall. Classical music on the stereo.

She led him to the sofa in front of the fireplace where a huge log crackled and spat at the grate. She sat down across from him in Martin's recliner, pulling her stockinged feet up under her.

"Tell me."

Her words shocked John. They reverberated back through the years. The same two words Ellen had spoken that night forever ago when they'd found out about the Alzheimer's. How many times would he have to answer these words of a woman he loved?

"Julia, something happened to me at Brant's wedding. I'm not sure I can explain it clearly to you, but it… It's as if I've been blind for a long time, and suddenly, I can see. Oh, where do I start?" He sighed and fell quiet, thinking. He was glad Julia didn't try to fill the silence.

Finally he let himself meet her gaze. "Julia, I'm going to tell you some things tonight that I've never told you. But before I say anything else, I must tell you that I came here tonight to say goodbye. When I leave here, it will be for the last time. I don't want there to be any misunderstanding about that."

Julia's bottom lip began to tremble, and tears slid, unblotted, down her cheeks. John watched her, knowing his words had caused her pain. It tugged at his heart, but he knew he had to continue.

"Julia, I've been fooling myself. I think we've both been fooling ourselves. We thought we could be just friends, but for me, at least, that's been impossible. I'm pretty sure it's been impossible for you, too.

She looked at her lap, twisted a tissue between her fingers.

"I thought so," he said. "I'm sorry, Julia. As much as I didn't intend to, I've fallen in love with you." He held up his hand. "It may not be appropriate for me to tell you this now, but I want you to know that you're a woman a man can easily fall in love with."

"John…" She sniffed and wagged her head.

"No, hear me out. I know you'll find someone. You'll get married again. I've tied you down in the name of friendship, and that hasn't been fair to you. There's been a lot of unfairness all around on my part." He hung his head, struck anew with shame over what he had almost allowed to happen.

"But more than anyone, I haven't been fair to Ellen. At Brant's wedding, when he and Cynthia spoke their vows, I felt as though a bolt of lightning went straight through me. Julia, I stood at an altar nearly thirty years ago and promised Ellen that I would love her in sickness and in health, and I have. I've never stopped loving her—the real Ellen. But there's another phrase in the vows that says, 'and to thee only will I cleave.' I made that promise to Ellen also. I promised it for as long as we both should live."

She looked at him with watery, red-rimmed eyes.

"Julia, if I stay with you another day, I will break every one of those vows. I can't do that."

He told her then about his father and about the oath he'd taken when his father died. He realized now that the reason he had never told her the story before was that it would have required too much of him. He would have had to face the duplicity of his behavior and the compromise of his principles. He hadn't been willing for that.

"I know I will never have Ellen back the way she was, but I renewed my marriage vows to her this weekend, and God has renewed my love for her. I can't explain it, and I know it won't be easy, but I intend to keep every one of those vows if it kills me."

Julia got up and went for a box of tissues. When she sat down again, she blew her nose and wiped away the mascara that smudged her cheeks. "I—I'm okay," she reassured him. But her sobs came in racking heaves now.

It tore him apart. "Oh, Julia, if we'd met in another time, another place…" His voice trailed off. Hadn't he always told her it was no use thinking about what might have been? "You've been such a great joy to me, but in these past weeks you've also become a great temptation, and I don't think those two things can be allowed to exist in the same person."

She nodded understanding and drew in a ragged breath.

"Most importantly," he continued, "I've kept you from going on with your life. For that I need to ask your forgiveness. I recognize that I've been flirting with sin, and I'm so sorry I involved you. Please forgive me, Julia. I've been so wrong."

He went on to tell her all the thoughts he had pondered since Brant's wedding—how he had prevented her from grieving for Martin as she should, how unfair he had been to tie her to himself. And when all his words were finished, he waited for her to speak.

She took a deep breath and dabbed at her nose again. She looked so beautiful in the light of the dying embers, her eyelashes still spiked with tears. On the stereo, a violin concerto played softly, making the moment unbearably heartrending. John almost asked her to turn the stereo off, but somehow the music seemed fitting, and he let it go.

She looked at him and spoke in her soft, throaty voice. "John, it's probably no surprise when I say that I've fallen in love with you, too. And I love you all the more for what you've just told me. You see, I fell in love with you because of your trustworthiness, your integrity, your sense of honor. I've been in such turmoil since I first realized that I love you. I knew if I could get you to declare your love for me, then you weren't the man I thought you were. And if you were that man of integrity, then I knew I could never have you."

She smiled sadly. "Now I have the best of both worlds— I know you love me, and you still have your honor. I do forgive you, John. In the deepest part of my heart, I haven't felt right about us. I need your forgiveness, too, for not listening to God's gentle voice warning me. I was an accomplice, John, and I'm sorry." Again, she attempted a wavering smile. "Thank you, John. Though it doesn't feel like it right now, I know this decision is a gift. I know it's right. And, I know God will bless it."

They sat together and shared aloud how blind they each had been to think their friendship was right when they had felt the need to keep it secret. She'd neglected her boys at a time when they needed her desperately; he had given his time and energy to her, rather than to Ellen. Further, their growing love for each other had forced them to turn from God for fear of their relationship being exposed for what it really was.

In a new love of unblemished purity, they released each other forever. John rose to go, and Julia followed him to the door. He did not embrace her or even touch her. He didn't trust himself yet, and he knew Julia respected his weakness.

He turned out of her driveway—not toward Oaklawn, but toward his true home. Where Ellen was.

It was after nine when he walked through the front doors of Parkside. The nurses' aides were in Ellen's room, helping her get ready for bed.

"Thank you. I'll take it from here." He dismissed them politely.

Ellen stood statuelike in the middle of the room with her back to John. He went to her, and putting his hands gently on her shoulders, he turned her to face him, speaking her name softly.

Her eyes showed no recognition, but she gave him a wan smile. She wore a long flannel nightgown, and behind the vacant eyes, she was still beautiful. He led her to the chair by her window. He picked up her hairbrush from the bureau and began to brush her hair with gentle strokes, surprised at the familiar feel of the soft curls. It had been so long since he'd touched her in such an intimate way. She was quiet, alone in that faraway place of hers.

John smoothed her hair with his hands, moved by the tenderness his actions evoked. He poured her a glass of water and held the cup while she drank from it. He turned the bed down and helped her swing her legs over the side. He plumped her pillow and gently tucked the blankets around her. She closed her eyes peacefully. He pulled a chair beside her bed and watched her sleep, memories of their shared past floating in the semidarkness until the lights in the hallway were dimmed.

In a choked whisper, he repeated his wedding vows, promising to cherish her all the days of his life.

Then he went home and climbed into his own bed, at peace with himself and at peace with God.

He knew it wouldn't always be this easy. He knew there might be more babbling and tantrums, and uncontrollable weeping in their future together. More frustration and anguish.

He also knew that he had done the right thing. He could look in the mirror and, without shame, face the man he saw reflected there. Whatever he must bear in the days to come, he knew his faith and God's grace would bring him across to the other side, however wide the chasm might be.

His Bible was lying on the nightstand, and he noticed with chagrin that a fine layer of dust had gathered on its dark cover. Swinging his legs out to sit on the side of the bed, he opened the book in his lap and leafed through the pages, yearning for comfort and confirmation. Under his fingers the pages fell open to the book of Job. The words jumped off the page as though they were printed in boldface: "Though He slay me, yet will I hope in Him…. Indeed, this will turn out for my deliverance…."

John closed the book and slipped to his knees in gratitude.

Julia

Chapter Thirty-Three

The pungent scent of wood smoke hung in the crisp autumn air, and the yellow leaves clung tenaciously to their branches, rebelling against the inevitability of winter's arrival.

The small stadium—home of the Calypso Wildcats—was filled to capacity. Red coats and jackets predominated on the home side, while blue blazed across the field where the visiting Tannersville Tigers had assembled. Throughout the bleachers, steaming Thermos bottles filled with coffee and hot cocoa warded off the chill. Spectators clapped their gloved hands together, their breaths hovering in wispy clouds in front of their lips.

The football field was still lush and green. The chalk lines fresh and unmarred under the bright lights. Whooping at the top of their lungs, the Wildcats broke out of the dressing room under the stadium and ran onto the field. They held their helmets aloft, smelling another victory to add to a long string of wins.

Andrew Sinclair led the team onto the field and then crossed to the center to meet with the captain of the opposing team. The two players conferred with the referee, shook hands and turned to run in opposite directions back to the sidelines. Midway, Andy slowed, looked up into the stands and raised a clenched fist to the sky. Although his mother was seated high in the reserved section, he searched the crowd until he caught her eye, and she returned his salute of victory.

This pregame salute had become a talisman for Andy, and Wildcat fans had been quick to pick it up and make it a ritual of sorts. Now three hundred spectators followed suit to Julia's raised fist while the marching band blared out the school's fight song.

Julia still had a hard time grasping how quickly her boys had grown up. Andy was following in the footsteps of a big brother who had broken a bevy of Calypso's records. Sam was playing junior college football now. When he could, he came home to watch Andy's games, but his team was playing out of state this weekend.

Julia loved the energy that flowed through this stadium every Friday night. And she was unabashedly proud to sit here as the mother of the team's star running back.

The fight song ended in an uproar, and when the noise finally died down, a deep voice boomed over the loudspeaker. "Ladies and gentlemen…"

The voice belonged to John Brighton. Julia couldn't help turning to look up toward the press box. She saw him standing behind the statisticians, microphone in hand. A little chill went up her spine. She quickly shook off the unwanted feelings and turned her attention to the man beside her.

John's voice echoed again across the field. "Welcome to tonight's game between the Tannersville Tigers and the Calypso Wildcats." Again the crowd erupted into thunderous cheers. "Please rise for our national anthem."

Julia pushed the stadium blanket from her knees and stood up. Beside her, James Vincent put one hand over his heart, the other gently, but possessively, on Julia's back. She looked up at him and smiled.

Julia had met Jim at a church picnic six months ago. She and the boys had begun attending a small community church near their house, and one Sunday afternoon, Julia decided to attend a spring picnic the church was sponsoring. Feel-

ing uncomfortable and out of place at first, she found herself seated across from a soft-spoken, friendly man. Jim was
tall, balding and very attractive. She was drawn at once to
his kind spirit. Over fried chicken and potato salad, they
struck up a conversation. Julia learned that Jim's wife of six-
teen years had left him (and a teenage son and daughter) to
marry another man. Almost two years later, he was still reel-
ing from the rejection.

At the end of the evening, clumsily, he asked Julia for a
date—his first since his college days. Attracted to this man,
and feeling a kinship with his suffering, she'd accepted.

Jim was kind and intelligent and had a wonderful sense of
humor. He had been born and raised in Calypso and had
served as city administrator in the town for the past fifteen
years. Julia admired Jim's dedication to his career and his obvious devotion to his still heartbroken children.

She and Jim had found solace in their shared sorrows,
and Julia had grown comfortable with Jim. They'd become
somewhat of an "item" around town, and though the term
"going steady" seemed a bit juvenile to Julia, she supposed
that they were.

Now Jim cupped his hands and shouted across the stadium
as the game began. "Go Wildcats!"

She smiled at his enthusiasm for her son's team. She was
a lucky woman.

Calypso won the toss and the crowd stayed on its feet for
the kickoff. The Wildcats received and ran the ball back to
the forty-yard line. When the two teams squared off at the line
of scrimmage, Andy carried the ball all the way for a touchdown in the first play of the game.

Julia shot out of her seat and jumped up and down, cheering, her cheeks flushed from excitement and the cold. By the
end of the half, Calypso was ahead twenty to seven, and by
night's end, they had walked away with the win and a new
rushing record for Andy Sinclair.

Though the temperature had dropped below thirty, no one

seemed in a hurry to leave the stadium. Parents and students huddled together for warmth in clusters about the bleachers, rehashing each touchdown, play by play, waiting for the team to emerge from the locker room for another round of applause. Julia received enthusiastic congratulations for Andy's game, and she basked vicariously in his glory.

When the players went back to shower, and Julia and Jim finally made their way across the parking lot, it was almost ten-thirty. Jim had picked Julia up, and since he lived only six blocks from the high school, they'd driven back to his house to park the car. Now they walked briskly arm in arm with stadium blankets around their shoulders, trying to generate some warmth.

"Man, it is freezing!" Jim's words came out in little puffs of steam.

"I know, but we won! We won!" Julia did a little dance— a silly, girlish hopscotch that set them both laughing.

Suddenly Jim's expression changed, and he looked down at her with serious, unsmiling eyes. He took her by the shoulders and, turning her to face him, kissed her full on the lips. "I love you, Julia Sinclair." His usually calm voice was fierce with passion. "Do you know that, Julia? I love you."

Her heart began to hammer in her chest. It was the first time he'd ever spoken those words to her. She struggled to force John's long-ago declaration of love from her mind. *Oh, Jim, I'm not sure I'm ready for this.*

He kissed her again, gently this time, and stood back, forcing her to look into his eyes.

Not knowing how to respond, she just smiled, then impulsively planted another light kiss on his lips. But she couldn't will a declaration of love to form on her lips. She liked Jim— a lot. Maybe she did love him. But if that were true, why did she feel so confused right now?

Had she ever questioned her love for Martin this way? Even with John and all the obstacles of their friendship— when it came to a question of love, there had never been a doubt. Had there?

Since the night John had told her goodbye, Julia had prayed—prayed fervently, daily—that God would send her someone. Someone to share conversations the way John had. Someone to make her feel as cherished and special as he had. Someone she admired as much as she admired John Brighton.

Then Jim had come into her life. In many ways, he was all of those things. He was special, and Julia knew that she was the envy of many women because she "had" Jim. She couldn't have asked for anyone more solicitous toward her sons. She couldn't have asked for anyone with more integrity, or who was more respected in the community.

Except John Brighton.

Her mind churned with questions. Why couldn't she seem to give her heart fully to Jim the way he so obviously had lost his to her? Why couldn't she put the past behind her and embrace the gift of this man's friendship? Why couldn't she put the ghost of Martin, and the living specter of her relationship with John out of her mind? They were both dead to her. They were in her past, and she so desperately wanted to live for today. *Please, Lord, help me. I'm so confused. If this man is a gift from You…if this is Your will for me, I want to be in it. Show me, Lord. Please, show me. I need to hear from You.*

They walked along the sidewalk toward Jim's house, hand in hand, perfectly in step with each other. Only their boots, pounding out a soft rhythm on the pavement, broke the silence of the chill evening.

But Julia's thoughts spun out of control, a tumultuous irony against the steady rhythm of their footsteps. *He loves me,* she told herself over and over. What more do I want? Julia wondered if she could grow to love Jim with the deep love she remembered from her marriage. Maybe her memory deceived her, and it had taken time to grow into love with Martin—and with John. Maybe she just didn't remember.

Jim, in his sweet, quiet way, seemed to sense that she was troubled. "Julia, what's wrong? I'm sorry if I took things too fast back there." He motioned to the sidewalk behind them, as though it were the scene of a crime.

"No, Jim. It's not that." It was a lie, really, but she couldn't bear to hurt him for something of which he was innocent. "I'm just not myself tonight. I'm sorry."

They came to his driveway, and he invited her in for a cup of hot chocolate.

"I'm sorry, Jim. It's awfully late. Would you mind if I beg off tonight? I'd just like to get home."

"Sure." There was disappointment in his voice, but he opened her door for her and went around to start the car. They sat in silence waiting for the car to warm up, but after five minutes, instead of backing out of the driveway, Jim reached into his pocket and took out a small square box. Fumbling, he opened the lid and dropped the contents into his palm.

Before Julia quite realized what was happening, he reached across the console for her left hand, and pulling her glove off, he slid an exquisite diamond ring onto her finger. It fit perfectly.

"Julia, you have given me so much joy in these past months. I thank God every day for putting you in my life. You've given my life meaning again, and I love you with all my heart. Julia, I don't want to have to take you home ever again. I want our home to be together. I want you to be my wife."

His speech was clearly rehearsed, but Julia knew it came from his heart. His heart of gold.

Julia looked down at her hand. The ring's brilliance was magnified through the tears that spilled onto her cheeks.

"Oh, Jim…Jim…"

John

Chapter Thirty-Four

The morning Ellen died was the kind of day she would have declared perfect. The September sun was tempered by wisps of clouds, and the air was crisp with a foretaste of autumn.

The piercing jangle of the telephone roused John from a dreamless sleep. He looked at the clock—5:30 a.m. He knew even before he was fully awake that Ellen was gone. He had stayed with her until midnight the night before, listening to her rattled breathing, wishing he could take her next breath for her. Her skin was gray and clammy, and she gasped for air with a strength she hadn't possessed in years. John watched her, exhausted with the waiting, until finally the nurses had sent him home, promising to call him if anything changed.

Strange. Tomorrow would have been her birthday. He'd heard that people often held on until a birthday or anniversary. But, of course, Ellen had no awareness of time passing, and she had not been able to make it one more day. The fifty-sixth anniversary of her birth would have to pass without her.

More than three years had passed since John had made peace with himself and with God. While the sense of rightness he felt about his renewed commitment to Ellen pervaded everything, still, it had not been easy.

In the past year there had been one crisis after another. Ellen caught a virus that left her weak and susceptible to every bug that went around. She ended up with pneumonia, and though she finally pulled through, her lungs were scarred and weakened. In the end, it was pneumonia that came back—this time to claim her.

Mercifully, in the years since John had said goodbye to Julia, Ellen had taken on a new, quiet countenance. He felt almost as if he'd been given a gift—a reward for the sacrifices he had made. Yet he knew he had sacrificed nothing in letting Julia go. He couldn't sacrifice what wasn't his. Still, he was grateful for Ellen's peace. It was a thing they could share, a thing they had in common.

When she became bedfast—unable to walk, or feed herself, or even roll over in bed—John knew the end couldn't be far away. He felt a sort of panic at losing her. This solitary life of being Ellen's husband was all he knew. He wasn't sure he would know how to live any other way. What was normal, anyway? The normal he could remember from the past was full of teenagers, ball games, parties, and a pretty wife always at his side. He hadn't had a chance to learn how to live alone—even alone with Ellen. They had been running the treadmill that Alzheimer's forced them onto for so long. His family nest had been empty for such a long time, and today he would begin to learn how to live in its loneliness.

John arrived at the funeral home early the next morning. It had not occurred to him that walking through the doors of that building meant seeing Ellen. Recorded organ music drifted through the open doors of the sanctuary and drew John into the quiet room.

When he saw her lying in the front of the room amid a profusion of flowers, he caught his breath and reached for the back of the pew bench. He half stumbled down the aisle and stood trembling in front of the simple coffin.

She looked almost angelic. Gone were the lines that had

creased her forehead. The eyes that in her last years had reflected a haunting confusion, were now peacefully closed. It was freeing for him to see Ellen this way. His breathing evened out; his heart ceased its wild pounding.

Looking down at her, he was overcome with the sense that the ethereal form that lay before him was not his Ellen. People at funerals always said the deceased looked as if they were merely sleeping. And though Ellen looked beautiful and at peace, in no way did she look alive to John. Her beauty in death was fragile and pearlescent, like that of a seashell. It struck John that indeed, it was a shell that lay before him. The Ellen John Brighton cherished had broken the shard that for so long imprisoned her and had flown away home.

John slowly looked heavenward and whispered without guilt, "Thank you."

The funeral was a blur of familiar faces, warm with sympathy, but full of relief also. In the front row of the sanctuary Jana and Brant, along with their spouses, sat on either side of John. Howard and MaryEllen flanked Kyle, leaning on him for support. They were in their eighties now, stooped and frail, but mentally sharp as ever and so strong in spirit. The past years had aged them both. But, in a way, this day was almost a celebration for them. For all who had loved Ellen and beheld her suffering, this day gave cause for quiet rejoicing.

John held Jana's hand tightly, and his mind was flooded with memories of Ellen as she'd been before the ogre called Alzheimer's had come into their lives. For the first time in almost a decade, the memories came easily, and they comforted him.

He could see her sitting across from him at the China Garden, laughing and lovely. He saw the tiny apartment in Oscar and Hattie's attic as clearly as if he sat there now. He walked the fields of Ellen's childhood farm again as they said goodbye to their first baby. Perhaps Ellen was holding little Catherine in her arms at this very moment. The thought filled him with inexplicable joy.

He recalled not the milestones in their life together, but the little things. Impromptu picnics in the backyard when the children were small. Cheering the kids on together at ball games. And the too-brief time they'd had together after the children were grown. Quiet evenings by the fireplace, reading together on Saturday afternoons, unhurriedly making love.

John's reverie was broken by the clear, sweet voices of Ellen's nieces. They sang a hymn that Ellen had loved because of the poignant story behind it. The author had penned the lyrics in the nineteenth century after receiving the tragic news that his four beloved daughters had been lost at sea. The melody rose and soared through the rafters of the sanctuary like a living thing.

"When peace like a river attendeth my way,
When sorrows like sea billows roll;
Whatever my lot, Thou hast taught me to say,
It is well, it is well with my soul."

Unexpectedly, John's throat swelled and tears rolled unbidden down his cheeks. He thought he had shed all his tears, but the song moved him powerfully.

For so many months, so many endless years, he had been asked to travel a hard and bitter road. But this day he had come to the end of that path, and he could turn and look back from a new, high place. He saw each fork and each rocky incline with clarity, and he knew that his journey had been honorable and not without reason. He could say with conviction, "It is well with my soul."

Epilogue

John came in from the backyard to fix himself a glass of tea. It was July, and the air conditioning was on in the house, so he closed the door on the laughter behind him. The quiet of the empty house enveloped him, and he found himself reflective in the sudden silence.

He filled a tall glass with ice from the freezer and poured tea from a huge Mason jar that sat in a pool of sunshine on the floor in the conservatory. John smiled as he thought of his wife's insistence that her tea be brewed in the sun. The jar had sat in this spot all summer long—filled some days with raspberry tea, others with lemon—until a ring had formed on the dark oak floor. Once, the stain might have bothered him, marring the otherwise flawless wood. But now it was one of the things that marked this house as theirs, his and hers—the woman he loved. What joy she had brought back to this house on Oaklawn!

There were long months of bitter loneliness after Ellen's death—and yes, bitter years before that. Moments when John wasn't sure he could go on another day. When he sought God and felt utterly forsaken. When he screamed "Why?" to the heavens, but they were bereft of an answer, only echoing back his own tormented cries: *Why? Why? Why?*

In the years after he'd said goodbye to Julia, he had seen her a few times from a distance. But he made no attempt to contact her. It still sickened him when he thought how dangerously close he had come to pulling her into his trespass. In truth, though he knew he'd been forgiven, a trace of guilt still lingered for the sin that had almost entrapped him. Strange that temptation could be disguised in a package filled with such warmth and beauty.

And, too, the new purity of his love for Julia—a chaste love—had kept him from barging back into her life. He wanted in no way to be a source of confusion or a stumbling block to her as she made a new life for herself apart from him.

He had heard through the school grapevine that "Sam and Andy's mom" was dating the city administrator. It still hurt him to think of her happy with someone else. He had to keep reminding himself that Julia was a closed chapter in his life. He could not allow himself to think of reopening the wounds that his sin had inflicted on her—on both of them, really. He had overstepped sacred boundaries, and in doing so, he felt he'd lost the right to ever again be a source of happiness to Julia.

Through the years, his own wounds had healed over. But scars remained—deep scars that would always be a reminder of his mistakes. He considered himself whole, though, and forgiven; and on another level—a more selfless, honorable plane—he was glad for the news about Julia. He hoped she was finding happiness in her life.

Then, out of the ashes of his grief, when he least expected it, Julia came back into his life. A gift. He smiled at the memory.

He had been at the library, where he could escape the deafening silence of his house for a different sort of quiet. He was browsing the shelves of biographies, and suddenly she stood beside him.

"John. I thought it was you," she'd whispered.

"Julia." He'd barely been able to speak. He had forgotten how beautiful her voice was. He'd not heard that lovely voice for almost five years. Even in a whisper, it stirred him as it always had.

Boldly, he asked if she could go for coffee with him. Was she free? The meaning in his question clear.

They ordered cappuccino in a small café across the street from the library. The restaurant was empty, and as they lingered over warm cups, the years fell away.

"I'm so sorry about Ellen, John. I heard…"

"It seems such a long time ago, Julia. Over a year now, but of course, it was a long time coming. I'm sure you won't judge me if I say it was a blessing."

She nodded slowly. "No. Of course… I understand. Are you doing okay?"

"I've been lonely. But I'm all right." He'd forgotten how honest he could be with her; how comfortable she made him feel. "What about you?"

"Things are good. Different though," she sighed. "Time is going by way too fast. The boys are both in college now."

John shook his head and blew out a breath. "That doesn't seem possible."

"It was hard to send my baby off to school. I thought it was just something people said to make conversation—but kids really do grow up before you know it. I don't know where the time has gone." She shook her head, looking bewildered. Then she brightened. "How are your kids, John?"

"Good. Mark and Jana gave me my first grandchild two months ago." He smiled broadly, elated to be sharing this news with her. "She's the world's cutest baby, if I do say so myself."

Julia laughed, soft and low. "Oh, John. That's wonderful! Well, congratulations, Grandpa."

Her laughter brought the memories tumbling back into his mind. How he had missed her. She was as beautiful as ever—a few more lines creasing her forehead, a few strands of grey in her short dark hair. But as John watched her face, she became familiar to his eyes again, familiar to his heart— evoking the things that had made him cherish her so.

"I heard you might be getting married?" It was a bold question, asked tentatively. But John had to be certain of their freedom this time.

Julia smiled and shook her head. Her voice was teasing. "Boy, there are no secrets in a small town, are there?" But she quickly turned serious. "No, John. I was dating—" she rolled her eyes "—oh, how I hate that word. Anyway, I was dating Jim Vincent for, well, for quite a while. I guess the rumors got out. He did ask me to marry him, but we're not seeing each other anymore."

"Oh. I'm sorry." John couldn't tell if sympathy was in order.

She shrugged. "Don't be sorry. It was my decision. Jim is a wonderful man—salt of the earth. But…well, I wasn't in love—" she paused almost imperceptibly "—with him."

She dropped her head, obviously embarrassed by the implication of the pause. "It…it didn't seem fair to Jim. I'm afraid I made him wait far too long for an answer."

She looked up at him. A sadness had crept into her eyes, and John guessed that it had grieved her to hurt Jim by refusing his proposal and breaking off their relationship.

Impulsively, he reached across the table and put his hand over hers. A gesture of warmth, nothing more. But his voice was thick with emotion. "It's great to see you, Julia."

She smiled up at him, joy written on her face.

They talked late into the night, sharing the trials of the years gone by and the joys of the present. And as they spoke, he realized that the love they had once felt for each other had been rekindled—purified now in the fires of obedience and forgiveness.

When he drove her home, and they stood on the porch at her front door, he took her in his arms and pulled her to himself. And he knew it was right now.

With a full heart, he kissed her over and over. Gently on the forehead, the chin then more urgently on the lips. They stood together and wept in each other's arms, not needing to explain their tears. Each knowing they were shed for all the sadness gone before—and for all the joy yet to come.

The gift of liberty was now theirs for the taking. The seed of friendship, the kernel of passion that had been denied before, now unfolded and blossomed into a thing of beauty. At last they were free to declare their love, to celebrate their passion for each other.

They'd married in the spring. The ceremony was in the big backyard on Oaklawn with all their children gathered around them. And now Julia graced this home with her joyful spirit. He had known immeasurable blessings these past months.

John replaced the lid on the jar of tea and started back through the kitchen. He glanced out the tall window that looked out over the backyard. The lacy filigree of the curtains diffused the light, giving a surreal, dreamlike quality to the scene beyond. Spellbound, he gazed at the tableau before him.

Mark and Jana stood arm in arm at the edge of the lawn. Brant and a very pregnant Cynthia, and Kyle and Lisa, Kyle's bride of two weeks, were sprawled comfortably on the grass. Beside them, Sam and Andy—young men now—smiled as they watched their mother.

Julia stood in the middle of the lawn, barefoot and radiant in a pink summer dress. A squealing, sun-browned toddler romped at her feet as the lawn sprinkler sent a spray of glittering water high into the air above them. The icy droplets hit their target and fresh peals of happy laughter floated on the summer air into the kitchen where John stood.

Mark and Jana's little Ellen Marie was a tiny ray of hope, a budding promise of this family's blessing for the future. She had Ellen's auburn curls and blue-gray eyes. And when she smiled, John saw a reflection of Ellen's beautiful face. Such a sweet memorial to her namesake.

Everything that was precious to him was embodied in the scene before him. His family was bound together with an everlasting cord of love and commitment and faith.

An array of emotions flooded him—hope, joy, the most transcendent peace he had ever known. His throat swelled, and he sent a prayer of profound gratitude heavenward.

John opened the door and stepped out into the yard. Across the wide expanse of grass came the joyful cries of a curly-haired little girl. She ran toward him on pudgy legs, her silvery voice calling, "Grandpa! Grandpa!"

* * * * *

DISCUSSION QUESTIONS

1. Had John and Ellen's relationship and the dynamics of their marriage prepared them for the devastating blow of discovering that she had Alzheimer's? In what ways could they, or any couple, become better prepared for such a possibility?

2. When John and Ellen first discovered that Ellen had Alzheimer's, they were reluctant to share the news with their grown children. How fully should grown or older children be included in decision-making under such circumstances?

3. Was John justified in beginning a friendship with Julia Sinclair, a young widow? At what point, if any, do you feel that he overstepped the bounds of propriety?

4. Is it possible for a man and a woman to share a close but pure friendship when one (or both) of them is married? How and why might men and women answer this question differently?

5. What was Julia's responsibility in placing limits on her friendship with John? How did she succeed or fail?

6. It seems wholly unfair that John—still a relatively young and virile man—should have to forfeit his happiness and his future because of Ellen's affliction. Are there other possible solutions that would allow John to honor the essence of his commitment to Ellen without making such life-changing sacrifices?

7. How do you feel about John's decision to institutionalize Ellen? Discuss other possible options for someone faced with the same dilemma. What are the moral and spiritual aspects of each?

8. The main theme of this book is the value of commitment in marriage. In what ways do the marriage vows continue to have meaning and validity when one member of the partnership is unable to fulfill his or her end of the agreement, as Ellen was?

9. Are the vows taken at the wedding ceremony only between the man and woman who speak them, or do they perhaps extend beyond that? What might be the far-reaching effects of John's honoring his vows? What could be the far-reaching consequences of his choosing not to honor his vows to Ellen?

10. Discuss the epilogue of the book. Did John's ultimate decision dishonor Ellen or her memory? How might his decision affect his grown children? How might it affect other family members and friends who were close to Ellen? What challenges and emotions might he face as a result of his actions?

Trouble in Texas

LORI COPELAND

"Americana romance at its best."
—*Romantic Times BOOKreviews*

Bluebonnet
BELLE

LORI
COPELAND

A battle of wills ensued when Dr. Gray Fuller opposed
April Truitt's herbal alternative to surgery. But April was
determined to save other women from dying on the
operating table, like her mother did.

Gray couldn't help admiring April's spirit. Yet he couldn't
let this bluebonnet belle steal all his patients...even if she
was on her way to stealing his heart.

Bluebonnet
BELLE

Love Inspired®

Celebrate Love Inspired's 10th anniversary
with top authors and great stories all year long!

Look for

From This Day Forward
by Irene Hannon

❧ Heartland Homecoming ❧

Home is truly where the heart is.

Former workaholic Dr. Sam Martin was a changed man. Yet his kind invitation to his long-estranged wife surprised even him. Sure, she needed a place to recover from a traumatic attack. But in his small town? Perhaps it was time for both to overcome the hurts and betrayals of the past, in order to rediscover love and a future together.

Steeple
Hill®

www.SteepleHill.com

*Available November
wherever you buy books.*